- THE -

NEVER-ENDING ROAD

A Novel

PHILIP MAZZA

Also by Philip Mazza

From Under a Tree
Book One; The Harrow Saga

Shadow in the Flame
Book Two; The Harrow Saga

Children at the Gate
Book Three; The Harrow Saga

The Child of Fire
Book Four; The Harrow Saga
(Coming 2025)

The Neon Hive

The Quantum Gardener

At the End of it All

Beneath the Ashen Sky

The Road to Stillwater

I Know God is a Cat

The Cosmic Vending Machine

- THE -

NEVER-ENDING

ROAD

A Novel

PHILIP MAZZA

OMNI PUBLISHERS

www.philipmazza.com

Omni Publishers of New York
ISBN 978-0-9977109-4-6
Printed in the United States of America

First Printing: April 2025

For my mother. She never forgot a birthday, not even in her final year. Without fail, the call would come, her voice as lively as ever. "How old are you now?" she'd ask, and when I told her, she'd gasp in playful disbelief, "Oh my, that's old!" Now, each year, on the day of my birthday, I find myself waiting, hoping against reason that the phone might ring once more. It never does, of course. Yet her voice stays with me, clear and steady, a part of me I can still hear as clearly as if she were right beside me.

Mom, here's that love story you always wanted me to write.

For those who walk the never-ending road. May you find peace in your reflections, strength in your trials, and love in every step, even as the journey continues.

AUTHOR'S INTRODUCTION

Writing *The Never-Ending Road* has been one of the most personal and introspective journeys of my life. This story begins with a simple question: What happens to us after we leave this world? Over time, it evolved into something far more complex and profound - an exploration of the paths we take, the decisions we make, and the lingering connections that bind us to one another long after we are gone.

At its heart, this novel isn't merely about death or the afterlife, but about the lives we live and the impact we have on the people around us. The central character's journey into a realm that feels like heaven, only to discover it's a spiritual purgatory, mirrors a reality we all face: the need to confront our past, our regrets, and our buried pain. How many of us spend our lives moving forward without looking back, never realizing that to truly heal, we must first reckon with the parts of ourselves we try hardest to forget?

The relationships we hold with our loved ones are the threads that run throughout this novel. Through the central character's reunions with those who passed before him - people he loved, hurt, or misunderstood in life - he begins to see the ways his actions rippled through their experiences, often unknowingly. It's through these revelations that the story touches on something I think we all wrestle with: the desire for forgiveness and the struggle to forgive ourselves.

We live in a world where we're often taught to see things in black and white, but the truth is far more complicated. Life is not easily divided into good or bad, right or wrong. Like the central character, we are all navigating through shades of gray, carrying with us the weight of choices made and paths not taken. The road he walks is a metaphor for all of us, facing moments of reflection where we must confront the uncomfortable truth that our lives have been shaped not just by our intentions, but by our blind spots as well.

I should say this story is a mix of things - pieces of my own life, bits of emotion I've carried or borrowed, and fictional elements. Even though some of the events themselves may be imagined, there's something profoundly human in the way they would shape us, in the way we'd instinctively seek to mend wounds that time has merely scarred over. Perhaps there's quiet part of us that understands, on some level, that the measure of a life isn't found in what we accomplish, but in the love we leave behind.

The Never-Ending Road asks us to look at our own journeys with more compassion, both for ourselves and for those who have walked alongside us. At its core, it speaks to the enduring power of love - not the kind that fades with time or death, but a love that grows eternal, transforming everything it touches. I hope that this novel reminds us of something simple but true: no matter how far we wander, no matter how lost we think we are, there's always a way back. Even in the shadows of our past, where the hurts and regrets live, we can stumble across something unexpected - forgiveness, maybe, or understanding. And if we're lucky, peace.

Thank you for joining me on this journey. I hope it resonates with you, and that as you turn the pages, you might find reflections of your own life, your own struggles, and your own capacity for love and forgiveness.

A CHILD'S HOPE

Daddy, what's heaven like?

I don't know, son.

Why don't you know?

Because I've never been there.

Well, what do you think it's like?

I suppose it's a wonderful place where we can be with those we've loved.

That sounds like a pretty nice place to be.

It does.

I hope that one day I can find out for myself what heaven's like.

So do I. Until then, you'll just have to keep wondering.

TOO MANY NEVERS

Someone once said that writing is about putting things together. But my days of doing so are over. The words are gone. The stories fled. I sit at my desk, staring out the window at my gardens, and I can no longer summon the will to write.

I look at my hands. Wrinkled and spotted skin, veins like rivers. These hands created so many stories but now they're too weary to write.

How did I get here? Where did the time go?

I remember when writing burned in my belly. I'd sit for hours, writing and rewriting, chasing the perfect sentence. The need to create possessed me, to capture thoughts on paper. I didn't care if anyone read it. Writing was enough.

But that was yesterday. Today there's only emptiness. Words that once flowed easily are a struggle now. My fingers are stiff, my eyes dim, my thoughts slow.

I know that I'm not the only writer who has felt this way. All who create face the day when stories dry up and words won't come. It's a kind of death, losing what you love most.

A touch on my shoulder. Warm. Firm. My wife's hand. Her fingers press. Anchor me.

"You haven't packed much," she says. Soft voice.

My hand hovers. Rests on hers. "I've been avoiding it," I say.

She's quiet. Her fingers speak judgment. I look around. Boxes everywhere. Some empty. Some are full of books. Books on the floor. On shelves. Too many books.

"I've read them all," I say. "Some more than once. They're friends. Teachers. I'll miss them."

"We can't take it all," she said. "New life. New place. We let go."

It's not easy to say goodbye to old friends. I keep the thought to myself.

A cluttered desk stares back. A mountain of papers looms. Countless tales birthed here. Stories that brought joy to many. I remember first sitting here. Younger self. Ambition burning. Writer and professor. Stories penned. Drafts crafted. Books born.

But now I wonder. What good is a storyteller with no stories left?

I sigh. Close my eyes. Faces of characters crowd in. Like family. I've lived their lives. Felt their pain. Shared triumphs. Time to say goodbye.

"I'll miss writing," I whisper. "But I've said all I had to say."

She squeezes my hand.

My eyes find a small wooden box. Special contents. I touch it.

"Can we take her with us?" I ask.

I hear her smile. "Always room for Little Girl."

"Thank you."

"Did you finish? Your last story?" she asks.

"A few nights ago."

"Did you send it out?"

"No one will read it."

"Why say that?"

"Everyone's in the moment. No one cares about an old man's musings."

"I care."

I hold back tears. Look out at the gardens. Distant pear trees.

"I'll miss the birdsong. The smell of flowers. My grandfather would've loved our gardens."

"He would've. But we can't care for the gardens or the house anymore."

She's right. Too old to write. Too old for gardens. For the house. Too old for everything.

I meet her gaze. Bright eyes. Lined face. Years weigh heavy. She's been tired long.

"I know. Time for new beginnings," I say.

"Letting go is hard." She kisses my cheek. "I know."

Memories are treasures. Prized possessions. Life's stories. What makes us who we are. But they're a burden too. They weigh an old man down. Make moving on hard. They haunt him. Keep him awake. Torment him.

It's time.

I push up from the chair. Groan. Joints protest. Hands tremble on armrests. One step at a time. Deep breath. Balance found. Few steps to the shelf. Fingers reach. Arms strain for a book. It's heavy. Place it in the box. Reach for another.

"This was my sanctuary. Refuge from the world." My voice is hoarse with emotion.

"Let me help you." She smiles.

"No. I can do this."

She hugs me. Leaves.

I work slowly. Carefully. Packing up my life. I'll never return here. Never sit at that desk. Never gaze at those gardens. Never write another story. Never revisit the places that I enjoyed. Never see the faces that filled my day. Never will my mind conjure the thoughts that danced before.

Never feels like a chain. Too heavy. Too tight. Too final. Too many nevers to bend. Too many to break.

I reach for another book. My hand slips. The book falls. Pages fan out on the floor. I bend to pick it up . . .

BARELY A MOMENT

A drone, a tiresome mechanical sound that pulls me from the void.

Beep . . . . beep . . . . beep . . . . beep . . . . beep . . . .

My eyes open. All is white and bright.

I blink, squinting at the unfamiliar. The room is small and cramped. Low ceiling, white walls. A sterile scent hangs in the air. Machines click and whir, their tubes and wires connected to me. I'm a puppet, controlled by unseen hands.

Hospital.

Something is wrong, terribly wrong. I reach for the memory, but it pulls back, slippery as rain on stone, vanishing before I can grasp it. My thoughts scatter like leaves in the wind. Each time I try to hold onto one, it slips through my fingers, gone before I even know what it is.

My mind is failing me, a weak thing flickering at the edge of darkness, like a candle flame in a draft, bending and shrinking until it seems it might disappear entirely. There's a fog inside me, thick and cold, and I can't see through it, can't push it away. Everything's lost in that haze, everything that mattered, fading into some distant place I can't reach anymore.

I breathe deeply. Try to calm myself. It doesn't work.

I want to sit up. But my body won't obey. Every movement is a burden. I'm lead, heavy, and aching.

A touch on my hand.

"You're awake," a delicate voice says. "Rest now."

My wife. Her face has aged but in my mind, she's young, beautiful as the day we met.

I try to speak. My throat is sand, my voice weak.

"What's happening?" I finally manage.

"You're exhausted," she whispers, lips at my ear. "Shhh . . . save your strength."

Her eyes are scared, tearful.

The thought of her fear is an ache in my heart. I want to tell her I love her. Not to be afraid. But I can't find the strength.

A nurse enters, sweeping gaze. I want to ask her something but the shape of it escapes me. Her lips are moving, forming words I can't catch. I strain against the glare of the overhead lights, their harshness pressing against me. Her figure blurs at the edges, a silhouette of purpose that I can't quite hold in my mind.

A thought pierces the fog: they're keeping me alive, but I'm no longer living.

I try to remember my life but memories are hazy dreams. I'm peering into a shadowy chasm. Everything blurs. A chill seeps into my bones. A foul stench coats my tongue. Breathing is a struggle. I'm too tired to fight.

The nurse says something to my wife. Her face crumples and dissolves into tears. She kisses me, soft and gentle. It fills me with sorrow. I want to pull her close, feel her skin, hold her tight. Never let go. But I can't reach her. There's a wall between us.

Everything blurs like a fog creeping over the land. My vision softens, and the edges of the world dissolve. A warm breath whispers against my neck, and I hear sounds, faint and distant, like voices carried on the wind. Words, maybe, though I can't make sense of them. They slip through the cracks of my mind like water through a broken dam.

A hand, trembling and thin, presses something into my palm, fingers closing over mine, slow and deliberate. The weight of it rests there, heavier than it should be, and the warmth lingers. It holds me, this sensation, and wraps itself around me like something familiar, something I've known all my life but forgotten. There is love in it, more love than I've felt in years, and it pulls at me, drawing me into its quiet embrace.

Everything becomes still. There's no sound. It's as if the world itself has stopped to listen.

I am tired - tired in a way that doesn't ask for rest but for surrender.

I gather the strength for one last breath, and it comes, startling in its clarity, like stepping into cold water. It fills me, then spills out again, carrying with it a kind of relief. Sleep will follow, I think. Maybe dreams, too.

I close my eyes and feel myself drift away, a leaf on a stream. Darkness folds itself around me. I let it take me.

Barely the moment starts, and it's over before I can catch its meaning.

A HOUSE IN TIME

I wake, my eyes slowly pushing open. No annoying sounds. The white, the brightness, gone. I stand at the top of three concrete steps, bewildered at what I see.

Before me stands a house, a towering three-story presence that seems to rise effortlessly into the sky. I take in its rustic charm, the hand-split shaker shingles a deep forest green that speaks of age and care. It's the kind of place that feels both solid and inviting, like it's been here forever, waiting. A stained-glass window on the second floor catches the light, throwing little shards of color onto the lawn as if the house is offering up its secrets one piece at a time. Stretching across the front is a porch, its white trim gleaming beneath the shade of an overhang held up by delicate brackets - small touches that make all the difference.

The house is wrapped in gardens that seem to tumble outward, a quiet chaos of color and shape. White roses climb the trellises, their petals floating to the earth with a soft, unhurried grace, as if the air itself were their cushion. The hydrangeas, clustered in shades of blue, white, and pink, press close together, their heavy blooms swaying gently in the breeze, conspiratorial in their beauty. The whole scene has an untamed rhythm to it, as though nature has been left to its own devices, yet everything rests perfectly in place.

I know this house. It's my grandparents' home, where they lived for many years. A place alive with their presence, though that life is far behind us now. Still, here it stands, unchanged, as if time has miscalculated, allowing this one thing to remain untouched, a relic of a vanished world.

A memory comes to me. Sudden. Sharp.

I can see the day my grandparents moved out. They were fragile then, no longer able to manage on their own. My mother had agonized over the decision, but in the end, the house was sold, and they were moved into an assisted living facility. It felt like the end of something enormous, a kind of closing that left everything quieter, smaller, forever different.

A nice young family bought the house and made it their own. They covered the house in light brown vinyl siding, added a sunny room to the back, and replaced the gardens with a stretch of grass and a sturdy playset for their children. At first, I felt the pain of betrayal. This was my grandparents' home, after all. The place where I had grown up, laughed, cried, and made memories that would last a lifetime. But then I remembered my mother's quiet wisdom, her words offered long ago: "A house is a living thing. It changes and grows just like we do."

It's strange, though. The green paint, the front porch, the concrete steps - all are just as I remembered them. It's as if I had stepped back in time. I rub my chin. Am I dreaming of the past? Must be. There's no other explanation.

But this can't be a dream. Everything is so real. The sky is a brilliant blue, cloudless and vast, and the sun is warm and comforting. I raise my hands to the light. They're not the hands of an old man. No. They're the hands of a middle-aged man, strong and capable, with the faintest trace of age at the knuckles. I look down. I'm wearing white sneakers with blue jeans and a white shirt, clothes that I've not worn in years.

The air is sweet with the scent of flowers, but there's also a hint of something oily and tinny. I know where it's coming from -

the foundry down the street, where my grandfather worked. Through the trees, I can see the smokestacks, belching out thick black smoke.

This can't be a dream. Then a low-pitched, guttural sound.

Mrrr . . . Mrrr . . .

I know this sound. Looking down, there's a gray-striped cat with big green eyes. "Maggie Ellen, is that you?"

Mrrr . . . Mrrr . .

THE LITTLE GIRL

In our house, cats were not just pets; they were the silent architects of our shared life, weaving themselves into the fabric of our days with an effortless grace that left us in awe. My wife and I found ourselves drawn to their enigmatic nature, the way they could command a room with a flick of their tail or melt our hearts with a well-timed purr. Each feline that crossed our threshold brought its unique melody to the symphony of our home, yet they all shared a common refrain: the ability to fill our world with an inexplicable joy.

I can't begin to count the number of cats that have padded through our lives over the years. They blurred together in my memory like watercolors, each one distinct yet part of a larger, more beautiful whole. But for me, there was one who stood out from the rest. Her name was Magellan and her story began in the aftermath of a profound loss that had left my wife and I adrift in a sea of grief.

Before we adopted Magellan there was Lil' Man, a small bundle of fur with an oversized personality. He was barely more than a handful, yet he filled our home with a vibrancy that belied his size. Watching him navigate the world with boundless curiosity was like witnessing a tiny adventurer charting unknown territories. But life, in its cruel efficiency, had other plans for our little adventurer. Kidney disease crept in, an unseen enemy that slowly but surely began to claim him.

Even as his body failed him, Lil' Man's spirit remained undiminished. He continued to seek out sunbeams to bask in, to demand chin scratches with imperious meows, to curl up between us on the couch as if nothing had changed. We clung to these moments, storing them away like precious gems, knowing that each one might be the last.

When the end came, it was as gentle as a sigh. We found him one morning, curled up in his favorite blanket, having slipped away in his sleep. The sight was peaceful, yet it tore at our hearts with a ferocity that left us breathless. In that moment, it felt as if a vital piece of our world had been ripped away, leaving behind a void that echoed with memories.

The days that followed were a blur of muted colors and muffled sounds. We moved through our routines like sleepwalkers, acutely aware of the absence that seemed to follow us from room to room. The house, once alive with the pitter-patter of tiny paws and the jingle of a collar bell, now felt cavernous and empty.

Grief, we discovered, was not a linear journey but a winding path full of unexpected turns. Some days, we could almost convince ourselves that we were healing. Other days, the smallest reminder – a stray toy found under the couch, the phantom sensation of fur against our legs – would plunge us back into the depths of our sorrow.

One evening, as we sat in the living room surrounded by the artifacts of Lil' Man's life – framed photos, well-worn toys, the cat tree he had loved to scale – the weight of his absence pressed down on us with renewed force. The walls seemed to close in, the air becoming thick and heavy. I found myself gasping for breath, desperate to escape the suffocating grip of our shared pain.

"We should look at getting another cat," I blurted out, the words tumbling from my lips before I could stop them.

My wife's eyes met mine, a complex mix of emotions swirling in their depths. "I'm not sure I'm ready," she said softly, her voice barely above a whisper. "It feels . . . too soon."

I nodded, understanding the delicate balance we were trying to strike between honoring Lil' Man's memory and moving forward. "We can wait," I assured her. "We have all the time in the world."

But time, it turned out, had its own agenda. Days stretched into weeks, and still, the emptiness persisted. We went through the motions of our lives – work, chores, social obligations – but there was always something missing, a vital spark that had gone out when Lil' Man left us.

It was on a quiet Sunday afternoon when the subject came up again. I had been watching my wife, noting the sadness that still lingered in the corners of her eyes, when I found myself saying, "Don't you think we should -" I let the sentence trail off, unable to finish the thought.

She looked at me, a wistful smile playing at the corners of her mouth. "I miss him so much," she admitted. "But the thought of this house without any cats at all . . . it doesn't feel right."

"One . . . or two . . . or even three to love," I told her.

"It would be nice," she whispered.

"We can create new memories."

"Good memories," she smiled. "But only two kittens. I know you want more, but please, only two."

"Okay. The last time I was at the shelter I saw two kittens that were so cute –"

"What? You've already been to the shelter?" Her tone of disbelief nettled me.

"I'm sorry. I didn't want to upset you. But one of them is gray, just like Lil' Man."

"Alright, but only two," she reminded me with a smile.

The decision was made. I would visit the shelter, not to replace Lil' Man – for he was irreplaceable – but to open our hearts to new possibilities, new love. But only two.

The kittens were already waiting for me, a flurry of fur and paws in their cage. They chased each other and batted at each other's tails, their playful energy infectious. I couldn't help but smile. These tiny creatures would soon bring our home to life. One we'd name Drake and the other, the gray one, we'd name Livingston. They were our feline explorers and they were so adorable.

But fate, it seemed, had other plans. I was just about to leave, my coat half-buttoned, when a young woman approached. I recognized her immediately - she had been in one of my classes a few semesters back, her hand always raised, her face alive with questions. Now she was here, working part-time at the shelter. She held a kitten pressed to her chest, its tiny body nestled in the crook of her arm, careful and small, like it was something fragile.

"Oh, Professor," she said, her eyes sparkling with enthusiasm, "you have to take this one too. She's the gray kitten's sister."

I recognized the young woman but couldn't remember her name.

"Well, hi. How is your semester going?"

She smiled. "It's going fine. But I do miss your classes."

"I'm sorry but I've had so many classes and students over the years. You were in one of my classes a couple of semesters ago, I think."

"Yes. I was a sophomore in your creative writing class."

I smiled. "What author did we focus on that semester?"

"Vonnegut."

I smiled again. "So it goes."

Her smile came slow. Sharp. Knowing. She got the joke, even if it was subtle.

"What's your name again?" I asked.

"It's Sarah."

"Well, nice to see you again, Sarah. I'm glad you're doing well." I looked at the kitten. "And what's the name of this little one?"

"Her name is Liatris," she said.

Liatris – the blazing star flower.

"That's a beautiful name. But we can only adopt two."

Sarah wouldn't hear of it. She placed the kitten in my arms, and I carefully cradled her and stroked her soft fur. So delicate and fragile, I barely felt her close to my chest. She wriggled a bit, pressing up against me as if it were her rightful place, and I could feel her soft purr. She was so small and perfect, and I knew that I would love her forever.

"Okay, I think we can make an exception for her," I said looking into the kitten's large, green, round eyes – an irresistible look, both mischievous and innocent. "But we're going to have to do something about your name if you're going to become part of our feline explorer family. Let's see. We have Drake and Livingston. Hmmm." I thought for a moment, my mind rushing to find the perfect name, when it dawned on me. "That's it. How about Magellan? Yes. We'll call you Magellan, Maggie Ellen for short."

As I drove home with not two but three kittens, I rehearsed explanations in my head, preparing for my wife's disappointment. But when I walked through the door and she saw Maggie Ellen, all thoughts of explanations vanished. The smile that bloomed on her face was like the first ray of sunshine after a long, dark winter.

Drake, Livingston, and Maggie Ellen brought a renewed sense of purpose to our lives. They filled our home with chaos and laughter, with warmth and unconditional love. But it was Maggie Ellen who truly captured my heart.

She became my constant companion, meowing and pawing at me, whether I was grading papers or working on my most recent novel. At night, she cuddled at my side, and in the morning, she'd spring lightly onto my chest, her small body settling in with a practiced ease. One paw would press against my cheek, not insistent but steady, as her purring rose like a steady hum, filling the quiet with a sound that seemed to make the morning softer, more forgiving. It was her way of saying it was time to wake up. Over the years, my wife had a special name for Maggie Ellen. She called her Little Girl.

But as with everything in life, there's a beginning and sadly, an ending. We said goodbye to Drake after nine years, and to Livingston after thirteen. And then, sixteen years after she first came into our lives, we had to bid farewell to Little Girl. The grief was no less intense than it had been with Lil' Man. But this time the grief was tempered by the knowledge of the joy she had brought us, the healing she had facilitated.

Maggie Ellen, our Little Girl, would be our last cat.

It's something else

Seeing Maggie Ellen again fills me with warmth, a familiar joy that wraps around me like a favorite blanket. I scoop her up, cradling her close, and she nuzzles against my cheek, her purr a soft melody that echoes in my heart.

"You've always been part of me," I murmur as if speaking to a cherished memory rather than a living creature. "Always at my side. Life without you felt unimaginable."

Mrrr . . . Mrrr . . .

Settling on the top step, I place her in my lap, leaning forward to envelop her in a gentle embrace. Her warmth seeps into me, the silky texture of her fur both soothing and achingly familiar. As she gazes up at me, her purring grows louder - a rhythmic vibration that lulls my worries into quiet submission.

In this moment, there's happiness. It's simple and good. I run my hand along her back, slow and steady, and touch the soft place behind her ears. My heart feels full.

Yet, as I look around, at the house, at the familiar landscape, an unsettling feeling creeps in. There's a richness to it all - a tapestry woven with history and tradition. But something else lingers just beneath the surface, something elusive. Perhaps it's the way the breeze dances through the trees or how vibrantly blue the sky appears. Or maybe it's just that this all feels like a dream.

Dream?

Maggie Ellen?

How can Maggie Ellen and my grandparents' house be in the same dream? They belonged to different years and different places. I suppose in dreams, the lines don't hold. Anything can happen. The mind wanders where it wants, so I let it go for as long as I can. It's a good place to be.

But even the best dreams don't last forever. They always slip away and fade into memory.

"Oh, little girl," I whisper to her, "I don't understand why you're here or what this dream means. It's unlike anything I've ever felt before. The smell of foundry smoke mingling with the sun's warmth on my skin. Your soft fur against my fingers. Everything feels so . . . alive. But I'm not really here. I can't be. I'm somewhere else. I'm -"

The memory comes back. Hospital.

The word stops me cold. It chills me to the bone. I whisper it to myself. It tastes bitter on my tongue like iron. I can't dwell on that now. I need to ground myself in this moment - the earth beneath my feet, the air filling my lungs.

But there's Maggie Ellen's gaze, her eyes deep wells of understanding.

Mrrr . . . Mrrr . . .

The sound pulls me back, unspooling a thread of memories I'd rather leave untouched. It's her final chapter, and I see it so clearly.

The animal hospital became our second home, its fluorescent hum and antiseptic smell turning into the backdrop of our days. We waited, always waiting, suspended between what we wished for and what we feared.

I held her, her body impossibly light in my arms, her delicate bones beneath the soft veil of her fur. I whispered to her, promises of love and impossible bargains. Stay, I begged her silently. Stay. But I could feel her slipping, a current pulling her where I could not follow.

"I'm sorry for what happened," I murmur now, as her gaze meets mine from her place in my lap. Her head tilts, a familiar, almost playful gesture, and it strikes me as forgiveness. "For my choice to end your -" but the word refuses me, lodging deep in my throat, a thing too sharp to say aloud.

My throat tightens. A lump forms, hard and unyielding. I try to swallow but can't. The words come slow and painful.

"On our last morning together," I continue haltingly, "your paw reached for my face but lacked the strength to do more than barely brush against me. Your mouth opened as if to meow but no sound came. You fought so hard to cling to your familiar rituals, to your life. But it was too late."

A tear escapes. I feel it roll down my cheek. Hot and wet. "As we drove you to the vet that day, your beautiful eyes watched raindrops race down the windshield - innocent and trusting - unaware of what lay ahead. It tore at me because I knew our time together was slipping away."

The memories flood me. My chest tightens. "You were gone. And I was left with only memories and a deep sadness. I wanted to bring you back. But I couldn't. Now . . . now, you're here."

The words stop. I see her face. I feel her fur. I hear her purr. It's too much. More tears fall. Everything around me blurs. I can't speak. I can't breathe. I want to scream. To howl.

Her purring grow - a low thrum that resonates within me. I hear it. I feel it. She reaches out with a gentle paw against my cheek.

It's as if she senses my sorrow and is trying to comfort me in her own way.

"When you were gone," I begin, each word measured and slow, "I kept your ashes in a box. On my desk. For the longest time, I looked for you. Everywhere. Your favorite places. I knew them all. But you weren't there." I breathe out. It's heavy. "I'm sorry. For what I did. I thought you'd always be here. I thought you'd never die."

Her green eyes meet mine, steady and luminous, as if she's peering straight through the layers I've wrapped around myself. There's something there - something larger than me, larger than either of us. Her mouth opens, and for a moment, I expect a familiar sound, a meow to break the silence. But it's not a meow. It's a voice. Soft and low. Like wind at night.

"Nothing lives forever," she says, her tone gentle, the kind you'd use to explain something simple to a child. "Everything dies. Even you."

I gasp. She's talking. Really talking.

The pounding in my chest is so loud it drowns everything else. My skin chills as though I've been caught in a sudden draft. "It's only a dream," I tell myself, but even as I speak, the certainty wavers. Everything feels too real. Maybe I'm stuck between two worlds.

"Dreams and reality," she says, her voice calm and steady, "sometimes they're the same."

I'm unable to reconcile what's happening. "You can talk?" I ask, my voice unsteady, trembling with disbelief.

"Of course," she replies, her tone tinged with matter-of-fact humor as if I should've known all along. "I'm a cat."

I stare, my mind struggling to bridge the gap between what I know and what I see. "But . . . how?"

She blinks slowly, the gesture deliberate, a soothing lull that seems to say I'm overthinking. "It's simple," she says, her words light and effortless. "The same way you do." Her whiskers shift slightly, catching some invisible thread in the air, and she offers the faintest smile, one that feels like a balm. "Everything is fine. You have nothing to worry about."

My throat tightens, again. I'm scared. But her eyes. Her voice. They calm my fears.

"I know it was hard," she says. "At the end. I saw it in your eyes. The pain. Being brave. Being strong."

My breath hitches. Astonishment fills me as I ask breathlessly. "You remember?"

"Everyone remembers their last moments," she replies wisely. "Everyone does. You had to make a choice. A hard choice. The kind no one wants. But sometimes we must do what's right." She smiles. Her paw reaches out. "I saw you. You were there for me and I was glad for that. Glad you said goodbye.

Tears continue to blur my eyes. "I've never forgotten that day. It's burned into my memory forever. I still see it in my mind all these years later. The silent goodbye. All I had left were those images. And questions. So many questions."

"Questions?" she asks. Her voice is soft. It touches my raw feelings.

"So many," I admit. "Did you know what was happening? Were you scared? Angry? Would we meet again?"

"The answers were in you," she says. "In your heart. You just had to listen."

Her fur catches the light, soft and luminous. She grooms herself. It's intimate. Ancient. Each paw stroke on her face is like a prayer. Our histories mix. Grief and love blend. I pull her close. I kiss her head. It means more than words.

This dream is different. She's small. Perfect. A doll with bright eyes and soft fur. She knows everything about me.

I laugh. It bubbles up inside me. Unexpected.

"What's so funny?" she asks.

"Oh little girl," I say. "This dream. It's strange. Wonderful. I don't want it to end."

She looks at me knowingly and says calmly, "But it's not a dream."

"What do you mean?"

"Look at the backyard," she says gently.

I stand still cradling her and walk down the steps that lead to a screen door and the house's utility room. I take a few steps from the walkway and I'm on a freshly mowed lawn. The grass is soft beneath my feet. Smells fresh cut.

"What do you see?" she asks.

I look. My grandfather's backyard. I hear laughter. Talk. I follow the sounds. Down a gentle slope, by the gazebo my grandfather had built, under a large willow tree, I see them. Aunts, uncles, and cousins sitting in lawn chairs, laughing and talking. They notice me and greet me with warm smiles and waves.

I can't believe it. I hesitate. Smile back. Shy. Wave. Their voices carry. Whispers in the wind.

"They're all here," I murmur under my breath. "Like before. But . . ."

Maggie gives another slow blink. Her gaze lingers on mine. We're both thinking.

"Maggie, they've passed . . . they've passed . . ." I whisper.

The sun is bright and warm. It wraps around us like a blanket. The flowers are too bright. The birds sing too sweetly. It is all too perfect. Too vivid. Like it wants to lull me into believing it's real.

What's happening?

Maggie is right. This isn't merely a dream. It's beyond that. It's something else. But what?

I look at Maggie in my arms. She purrs. I feel it against my skin. She knows something. Something big. Something we both know but don't say.

"No matter where I look - everything feels familiar yet distorted somehow. I'm not quite sure where I'm meant to be." My voice shakes slightly as uncertainty creeps back into focus. "Where am I? What is this place?"

"You're exactly where you're meant to be," she tells me.

"But where?"

"It's not for me to tell you where you are."

My eyes search her face. "Who then?"

She doesn't answer but offers another slow blink. Silence stretches between us like an unbroken thread woven through time itself. It's a weighty pause filled only by breaths shared amidst uncertainty lingering thickly around us both now.

I'm confused. My breath is heavy in my chest. My thoughts swirl chaotically through my mind. Then it hits me. An unavoidable realization I know it now. It chills me to the bone.

"Is she here?"

"Who?"

"My wife," I say. My voice quivers. I'm scared but I want to know. "Is she here?"

Maggie looks at me hard. Her green eyes are sad but kind. She knows.

"She's not here," Maggie says. Her voice is soft but sure. "It's not her time yet. You have more to see. We should go in."

Maggie jumps down. She goes to the door that leads to the utility door. I follow close behind. Opening the screen door, it makes a stretching, springlike sound and she scampers inside. Then there's a loud snap behind us as it slams hard under the recoil of its hinge. The sound instantly takes me back to my childhood, to the anticipation of someone coming in. But now it feels different, somehow ominous.

The utility room is the same. Blue walls. Wood shelves stuffed with all sorts of things. An old washer and dryer. An even older washing tub with rollers. There's an old-fashioned ice box tucked to one side. Time-worn wooden steps that sag in the middle lead up to a large wooden door.

From behind that door, I hear the kitchen. Pots clang. Water runs. People talk. I know these sounds. They make me feel warm.

"You've heard this before," Maggie says. She knows more than she says.

"Yes," I say. It's just a word, but it means a lot.

She's soft. "You're almost there."

"But I don't know if I can . . ." I'm not sure.

"Just see what's behind the door," she says. Her voice helps me.

I kneel. I breathe deeply, gently stroking the top of her head.

"I'm scared," I say. My voice is small. "Will I like what's there?"

She purrs. It feels good. She says, "I think so."

A DOOR TO THE KITCHEN

The door creaks as I turn the knob and push it open. Maggie scurries away, disappearing into the kitchen. I stand at the threshold, another deep breath as if the air itself might prepare me for what lies beyond. With a tentative step forward, I catch Maggie's gaze, her eyes wide and expectant, a silent observer of the unfolding drama.

The kitchen swallows me whole, and suddenly I'm ten again, small and uncertain in a world of giants. The air is thick with memory, heavy with the scent of tomato sauce bubbling on the stove, garlic and basil dancing together, mingling with the yeasty promise of baking bread. There's my grandmother, silhouetted against the afternoon light, moving with a slow grace as she tends to her pots. She drops basil into the sauce and it hisses back at her, grateful for the attention.

My mother is at the sink, her hands plunged into water so cold I can almost feel the bite of it myself. She's washing lettuce, each leaf getting the full force of her attention. The vegetables shine under her touch, green as envy next to the silver band on her finger, that circle of promises that's weathered so many storms.

They're both wearing aprons, cinched tight at the waist, turning their housedresses into uniforms of domestic authority. These dresses, with their faded floral prints and practical cuts, belong to another era entirely, as if my grandmother's kitchen exists in a bubble of time, untouched by the world beyond its walls. Their hair is pinned up neat, cheeks flushed from heat or happiness, I can't tell which.

I study them, these two women who've made me who I am. My grandmother is all autumn, warm and rich, while my mother is the crisp clarity of spring. But there's a thread that binds them, stronger than blood or time, visible in the way they move around each other, a dance they've been perfecting all their lives.

It's a scene I know by heart, one that tugs at me something fierce. But there's a wrongness to it, a discord I can't quite place. Something's shifted in the landscape of my memory, and I'm holding my breath, waiting for the penny to drop.

At the table sits a woman I've never seen before, even though her movements are as familiar as my own heartbeat. She polishes silverware. Her hands move across the silverware, and I recognize every gesture as if they were my own. The way she polishes each utensil - methodical, precise - is my mother's rhythm, her dance. I see my mother's nose in her profile, the same determined set of her jaw that I've known my entire life.

These photographs I've carried in my memory suddenly feel alive. She is my aunt, my mother's sister, a ghost who existed before my first breath, who slipped away before I could truly know her.

Is this a Sunday?

The question drifts through my mind like a soft breath, carrying memories as fragile as spun sugar. Sundays in my childhood were not simply days, but entire universes crafted by my mother's and grandmother's hands. They were landscapes of ritual and love, painted with the most delicate brushstrokes of domesticity.

I remember Sundays with a warmth that settles inside me, quiet as rising bread. After church, we'd make our way to my grandparents' home, where the air itself seemed alive with generations of cooking. My mother and grandmother - always awake before dawn – would've already transformed simple ingredients into miracles: flour becoming pies, sugar spinning into cakes, fruits condensing into jewel-like jellies. Their magic was so ordinary, yet so profound, that it required no announcement.

The table would fill until it seemed to sag under the weight of it all, and we'd gather around, not just to eat but to talk, to laugh, to stitch together the little stories that made up our lives. The hours would stretch out, easy and unhurried, until the day turned soft and the last of us lingered with a deck of cards in hand, drinks nearby as if the laughter could hold off the night just a little longer. Those Sundays were more than tradition; they were the anchor that made us feel, no matter where we drifted, that we were always known and always loved.

But as time moved forward, and our family grew older, the Sundays of my childhood became fewer, slipping away unnoticed. Life got busier, schedules more crowded, and gatherings on Sundays became harder to hold on to. Little by little, the tradition faded, along with the memories we once took for granted.

Time is indeed a cruel thief. It robs us of the things we hold dear. It doesn't ask permission; it simply takes, leaving behind a hollowness, a space where something precious used to be. We're left to grieve not only what was but what could have been.

"I heard the door open. Who is it?" my grandmother calls, her voice thin and weathered with age. She peeks over her shoulder, her eyes crinkling at the edges when she sees me, a smile hiding in their lines.

My mother turns too, her face aglow, the same softness I remember from her sixties. There's a quiet wisdom about her now, the kind that settles in over the years. But beneath that, something deeper - a bond that feels both fragile and enduring, like a bird's nest woven from the thinnest of twigs. Love that persists, no matter what.

Her eyes are a haven. In their depths, I find the same calm and safety I once felt as a child, huddled in her arms. It's a warm embrace, a refuge from the harshness of the world. These are feelings I cling to, cherishing them as the most valuable of keepsakes.

Her smile is soft, her voice a melody I recognize instantly. "I was hoping it was you," she says. "Look at you, so handsome. We've been waiting for you, but now you're here. With us, again."

I smile back, feeling a quiet disbelief at the moment's tenderness.

"Welcome home," she says, her eyes shining with affection. "We've missed you more than you know. Where've you been all these years?"

My throat tightens, and tears brim as I shake my head, uncertain. "I don't know."

Her smile deepens, settling into the familiar curve I remember so well. "It doesn't matter, does it? What matters is you're here now, with us."

There's a comfort in seeing her again, in the warmth of her presence. It feels like something long wished for, finally real. But I can't help wondering - am I really here? Or will I wake up and find it was nothing more than a dream?

A MOTHER'S GIFTS

My mother's presence lingers, a soft whisper of memory as comforting as the well-worn patches of a cherished quilt. Though years have slipped away, her face has never faded from my thoughts. Her smile, ever-bright, held an ease of kindness, and her eyes gleamed with curiosity as if they could uncover a secret in every ordinary moment. I often marveled at how she looked at us - my two older brothers, the steady ones; me, caught in the middle; and my younger sister, always trailing behind with her hopeful questions. And what mattered most to her, above all else, was the future. She always spoke of our tomorrows with unwavering conviction, treating our aspirations like they were tangible treasures already nestled in our palms. Her pride in us was as natural and necessary as breathing, a constant companion in her every gesture and word.

In our childhood, my sister and I would follow her movements through the rhythm of the day - hands always busy, feet always in motion. Yet, amidst the whirlwind of domestic duties, she would stop, her tasks abandoned without hesitation, her work set aside without a second thought. I can still picture her, pausing mid-chore to gather us close or to weave a tale that transported us far from our kitchen table. These moments, brief interludes in her busy day, were like pearls on a string, precious and luminous in my memory.

Her past came alive in stories that flowed from her effortlessly, stories of her own childhood, simple and magical all at once. She told us about sunlit afternoons spent running barefoot through a garden, her hair braided with wildflowers, the air filled with the scent of blooming life. She would chase butterflies, listen to the songs of birds, and weave her own stories in her head as if the world itself whispered to her. These stories left us enchanted, wrapped in the warmth of her joy and wonder.

For my mother, there was magic in the smallest of things - a bird's song, a flower unfurling in the soil, the sound of children's laughter. She found adventure in the ordinary, each dawn holding the promise of something new, something beautiful, waiting to be revealed.

Then there was the story of how she met my father, how he asked her to marry him on a warm spring afternoon, and the joy that filled her in that moment. When my mother spoke of the past, it wasn't just remembering. It was as though she pulled those moments into the room with us, making them as vivid and full as the present, and we couldn't help but be caught up in the wonder of it.

But my mother was more than a storyteller. She was our compass when we needed direction, a steady voice in times of confusion. She listened as if nothing in the world mattered more than what you were saying. Her advice always came from a place of quiet thoughtfulness, shaped by years of living. And if words couldn't solve it, she would provide a helping hand, to fix what was broken. Most of all, she showed us that love was the truest thing we had and that kindness and care were what bound us together.

"Family is everything," she'd say. "You must tend to it, tend to it like it's a garden."

She was there for us in every difficult hour, an unwavering presence, and from her, we drew the strength to keep going. Her voice, so sure and so full of love, gave us comfort when we needed it most, reminding us that we were never alone and that there was always hope as long as we held on to each other.

There was a moment I would carry with me always. It was before I found my way into the hallowed halls of academia, back when I was just another suit in the great machine of corporate America. The economy was struggling, and the company I worked for was cutting back. I lost my job and the world seemed to tilt on its axis. Unemployment was an alien landscape, uncharted and daunting.

As the weeks slipped by, my confidence eroded, worn away by the relentless tide of rejection. Each unanswered application, each silent phone, chipped away at my sense of self. I became unmoored, a ship without a harbor, drifting aimlessly on a sea of uncertainty.

Then, came my mother's voice over the phone. "Come for dinner," she said, as if it were any ordinary day as if she hadn't sensed my despair from miles away. Her invitation was a lifeline, and I grasped it with both hands, my wife and I looking forward to the familiar comfort of my childhood home.

After dinner, we sat together, talking in the soft light of the kitchen. The conversation drifted from one topic to another, but inevitably, found its way to the anxieties that had taken up residence in my mind. My mother listened with that deep, attentive quiet that was so uniquely hers. It was a silence that seemed to absorb my words, to hold them with care. When at last I had emptied myself of concerns, her hand slipped into the soft folds of her housedress, retrieving a small, folded slip of paper. Without a word, she handed it to me. It was a poem she had clipped from a magazine.

"Here," she said simply, "I found this for you. When I read it I thought of you."

The poem was by John Greenleaf Whittier and titled *Don't Quit*. I read it to myself, and from that day on, it was always rooted in my memory.

> When things go wrong, as they sometimes will,
> When the road you're trudging seems all uphill,
> When the funds are low and the debts are high,
> And you want to smile, but you have to sigh,
> When care is pressing you down a bit –
> Rest if you must, but don't you quit.

At the bottom, she signed it with a simple, "Love you, Mom" and dated it.

"Thank you," I whispered as I hugged her.

"I never went to college," she said, her voice soft but steady. "I can't write like you do, with all those big, fancy words. But this says just what I want to tell you."

"It's perfect," I told her. "And so thoughtful."

She nodded, her expression growing serious. "Life's not always easy. There's disappointment, sadness, pain - more than you'll ever expect. But there's also beauty. Even when it's dark, you can find it. Whenever it gets dark for you, I want you to read this poem. Will you do that for me? Will you promise?"

"I promise," I said, meaning it.

That slip of paper remained a constant companion on my desk, always within reach. And as the seasons passed, its edges started to fray, the once-bright white paper surrendering to a soft yellow. But I could no more discard it than I could forget the moment of its origin. My fingers would trace its delicate surface, recalling her voice, the careful script of her handwriting, and the tender weight of her intention. Each time I looked at it, her words seemed to breathe again - fragile yet persistent, like a whisper that refused to be silenced. It was a small rectangle of memory that spoke volumes about love, about remembrance, about the way we keep those we cherish close even when they are no longer physically near.

Then one day, the darkness found me once more, an unwelcome visitor in the wake of my mother's passing. Grief engulfed me, threatening to pull me under. I reached for the clipping, holding it as if her words, immortalized on paper, could tether me to something solid. My fingers traced the delicate curve of her handwriting, familiar as if I'd touched it a thousand times before. That small scrap of paper offered a quiet comfort I had been desperately seeking since she left.

Though the ink had faded over time, her words remained steadfast on the page. "Love you, Mom."

I closed my eyes, trying to summon her voice - soft, soothing, the way it used to lull me to sleep. I could almost smell her, a scent drifting into my memory, warm and floral. It mingled with the embrace I would never feel again, but would never forget.

As the memories receded, I opened my eyes and looked at the clipping with her handwriting. It was all I had left of her. I clutched it to my chest and whispered, "I love you too, Mom. Always and forever."

Yet there was another clipping she would give me. Another gift. One without her handwriting. One that would evoke a different time and moment.

On our 30th wedding anniversary, my mother insisted on a family gathering, as if the occasion belonged to her as much as it did to us. She called it a celebration of marriage. Now, my wife and I had imagined something quieter, maybe dinner at the little Italian restaurant where we used to go when we were young and broke, a night to remember how far we'd come. Instead, we found ourselves in my parents' dining room, the smell of pot roast and floor polish heavy in the air, surrounded by my brothers and sister.

The house was full of warmth and laughter, the kind of evening where love wove itself through every conversation, every clink of glasses. We sat at the table, grateful for the feast she had prepared, for the chance to be together again. After dessert, we moved to the living room, drinks in hand, when she pulled out an envelope with a card inside and held it up with that familiar smile.

"There better not be money in the card," I said, eyeing her suspiciously.

She smiled, a quiet kind of smile that always seemed to hold more than she let on. "No," she said. "It's something more valuable."

As I went to open the card, a piece of paper fluttered into my lap. It was a clipping of a poem written by Emily Dickinson.

"Go on," she encouraged gently. "Read it aloud. It's so beautiful."

Clearing my throat, I began to read, the words filling the room like a melody we both knew by heart.

"My river runs to thee.
Blue sea, wilt thou welcome me?
My river awaits reply.
Oh! Sea, look graciously.

I'll fetch thee brooks
From spotted nooks.
Say, sea,
Take me!"

As I read the poem, emotions seeped through the paper at me. Joy, sadness, and hope danced together in a delicate interplay, each feeling resonating deeply within.

When the last word faded, a hush fell over us. My mother's eyes found mine, shimmering with unshed tears.

"Love is a river," she whispered, her voice rich with feeling. "It starts as a mere trickle, a faint spark between two souls. As it grows, it becomes a stream, a force of nature that carries us along its current."

"It's the most beautiful poem I've ever read," I said, leaning in to press my lips to her cheek. "Thank you for this wonderful gift."

She folded me into her arms. "Remember, life is a journey," she said softly. "And like all journeys, there are peaks and valleys, moments of joy and moments of sorrow. But there's always something to learn, something to appreciate and be grateful for."

At home, I placed the clipping on my desk, next to the one she'd given me years before. Each felt like a tiny portal into my mother's soul, a quiet reflection of her love, not just for us, her children, but for the world she held so carefully in her hands. I didn't know then, couldn't have known, how this particular scrap of paper - this poem from Emily Dickinson - would transform in meaning, that it would evolve into something else entirely when I needed it most. Something my mother might have known long before I did.

TIME IS ALL WE HAVE

"I can't believe it," I say to my mother. "You're standing right in front of me. This doesn't feel real."

The rush of emotions is almost too much - waves pounding, one after another, leaving me breathless. Love, disbelief, something close to fear - it all swells up inside me, tightening my chest. I want to reach out and touch her, to see if I can feel the softness and warmth of her skin. But something keeps me from moving and I stand there in tears.

She turns off the faucet and dries her hands with that old dishcloth, the same one I remember from when I was little. Then she smiles one of those smiles that's big and warm and wraps around me like a blanket. She draws me close, holding me with a steadiness that feels like it could anchor the world. I press into her, absorbing the warmth of her touch. For the first time in ages, I feel safe. I close my eyes and breathe in, catching her familiar scent of lavender and roses, and everything else just falls away. It's like I'm a child again.

"I've missed you so much," I whisper into her shoulder, my voice small. "Don't let go of me."

"I've missed you too," she says, kissing my cheek like she always used to, the touch of her lips soft and comforting. "I won't leave you. Ever again."

I feel her arms tighten around me. We are together, and that's all that matters.

But something isn't right. There's a tension here, a wrongness just beneath the surface. Questions rise, but I can't quite find the words to shape them.

"Mom –" I start, hesitating, not even sure what I want to ask.

She reads my face before I can say more. "What? What is it?"

"Where am I?"

She smiles, patient, as though I'm asking something simple. "Silly, you're at your grandparents' house. It's Sunday, your favorite day. Everyone's here, just like always. They've come to see you."

I shake my head. "None of this makes sense."

"Does it have to? Sometimes things don't make sense, and that's okay. You're home. Isn't that enough?"

I take a deep breath, trying to ground myself, to slow my racing thoughts. "Mom, but everything has to make sense. What's the point if it doesn't?"

She sighs and takes my hand. "I know. But sometimes things don't always work that way. Sometimes, you just have to be here, to feel it. Give it time."

I shake my head, frustrated. "But I have so many questions."

"And you'll get your answers, in time," she says. "But for now, just be here with us, in this moment. This is a new beginning, a safe place for you." Her hand tightens around mine. "Maybe ask your father. He's here too."

"Dad?" My heart catches. "He's here?"

She smiles gently, patting my hand. "Of course. Where else would he be on Sunday?"

Then, as if the moment has always been leading to this, she guides me across the room. "There's someone I want you to meet."

We walk over to where the other woman is sitting.

"This is my older sister," my mother says, her voice soft. "You never knew her. She left us before you were born."

My aunt stands. I smile, stepping forward to hug her. "I thought it was you."

"There's so much I missed out on," she says to me, a tinge of sadness to a smile. "I'm looking forward to getting to know you. My, how you look like your father."

"Everyone says that."

Suddenly, a voice barks. "What, you forget about your grandmother?"

The familiar voice of my grandmother, her accent, her tone, everything about her is like an echo of my childhood. Even in her eighties, her Italian heritage is unmistakable in her short but ample frame. Her round face is full of strength and kindness. Although her shoulders hunch over and she moves slowly, clearly showing the weight of her years, her brown eyes hold the sparkle of a much younger woman. Her presence is undeniable.

"Stop your talking and come hug your grandmother!" she calls out, her wooden spoon held high like a queen commanding her court.

I laugh, unable to resist the familiar warmth of her voice, and make my way across the room.

I put my arms around her and kiss her cheek.

"Careful now," she says, half-smiling, half-warning. "Can't you see I'm busy here?" She nods toward the bubbling pot, the spoon still poised, as if ready to defend her kitchen domain.

The rich smell of tomatoes, garlic, and herbs fills the kitchen. "Smells wonderful."

She beams, the wooden spoon moving in rhythmic circles. "Where've you been? Took you long enough to get here. Hope you're hungry."

My stomach growls. "I am."

"Before I forget," she adds, gesturing to the fridge. "There's something special for you in there. Your mother made it."

I open the refrigerator door and see the familiar glass dish, covered in foil. Lifting a corner, I peek inside.

"Icebox cake," I say, a flood of memories rushing back. "Thanks, Mom." Then I hesitate. "But how did you know I'd be here - today?"

My mother smiles. "A mother knows these things."

"We've work to do here," my grandmother tells me. "The men are in the parlor. Go now."

Parlor. It's a word that feels like it belongs to another era, one I haven't heard in years.

I turn to my mother. "Dad's there? And Gramps?" I ask.

She gives me that soft smile she reserves for moments like this and pats my cheek. "They'll be so happy to see you."

"Oh, and take that cat with you," my grandmother calls over her shoulder. "The kitchen's no place for an animal."

Maggie darts out from under the table, her small legs moving with a determined quickness that pulls me along in her wake. She leads me toward the dining room, the one that opens off the parlor. It's exactly as I remember: the mauve walls, their plaster cracked and unevenly patched, seem to hold the weight of years. The framed photographs of ancestors I never met hang just slightly askew, their solemn faces fixed on the wooden table below as if still waiting for someone to join them. The table is set with white linens and polished silverware catching the fading light. In the center, a vase of fresh flowers offers their sweet scent, a little too perfect, as though masking something else underneath.

Maggie slips under the table, her fur bristling, tail twitching. Her eyes narrow at me from the shadows, her little voice barely a murmur.

Mrrr . . . Mrrr . . .

"What's wrong, little girl?" I ask, bending down to meet her gaze.

She hesitates before speaking, her words soft, almost tentative. "Some of the people here don't like me."

I tap my leg, coaxing her out. "Come here. It's only because they don't know you like I do."

She slinks out slowly, brushing against my leg, the warmth of her fur grounding me.

"It's the older ones," she says. "They're mean to me."

"They're just set in their ways. Give them time. Time to know you."

Her tail flicks once, thoughtfully. "I suppose you're right. Time is all we have left."

Her words settle over me like a cloud, thick and impossible to see through. I wonder what she means, why those words sound so final, so heavy with something I can't quite grasp.

THE PARLOR

Mrrr ... Mrrr ... Mrrr ... Maggie's soft purr is a gentle rhythm that settles around me, a sound so familiar it's almost part of the air.

She guides me into the parlor, the most imposing room in the house, where the green walls hold a muted sheen, carrying the quiet imprint of lives once lived and tales long told. A fireplace commands attention on one side, its bricks arranged with a calm, deliberate precision. Across from it, wide windows face the porch, their view tempered by floral drapes that spill onto the floor in an unhurried cascade. Two slender, tapered columns rise gracefully opposite the hearth, framing the entrance to the home's front foyer with understated elegance.

In the corner, an old television murmurs faintly, its black-and-white flickers blending into the room's shadows like remnants of another time. The steady tick of a grandfather clock in the hallway echoes, the pendulum's swing marking time, but not rushing it. I close my eyes for a moment, allowing the space around me to envelop me - the hum of the TV, the rhythm of the clock, the faint creak of the floor - each sound pulling me back to a slower, more familiar world.

Someone clears their throat, and I open my eyes.

There's my grandfather, just as he always was, rooted in his easy chair, hidden behind the wide spread of the Sunday newspaper. Next to him, the old, wooden, standup General Electric radio, long silent but still there, as though waiting for a song to wake it. Across the room, my father sits at the end of the sofa, his eyes on the obituary section, as if he's already one step ahead, thinking of what comes next.

My grandfather clears his throat again, rustling the paper, and I see that smile - the one I remember when I was a kid when I'd done something to make him proud. He's exactly as he was then: an old man in his eighties, short, wiry but strong, the kind of strength that comes from a lifetime of work. His hands, large and knotted with arthritis, rest on the arm of his chair, but his eyes, bright and full of mischief, still shine with the same fire.

"Took your time getting here," he says in that deep voice of his, thick with the Italian accent that never left him. But he smiles, and I feel the warmth of it. "Thought you'd never make it."

I stand there, my heart full of the memories he's left me. Even though so many years have passed, the moments we shared feel close, like a favorite book you return to over and over, knowing exactly how it'll make you feel. These moments, tucked away in the corners of my heart, stay with me - unfaded, unforgotten, still alive.

Summers of wisdom

My grandfather was the kind of man who could work from sunup to sundown without stopping, tireless in his labors. Yet, beneath his tireless efforts lay a gentleness, a spark in his gaze that lit up whenever he spoke of my grandmother. Their love spanned almost seven decades, a steady thread running through every storm and season. As a young man, he arrived in America with little more than his faith in possibility, seeing this country as a place where his dreams could take root. He'd heard stories about people starting with nothing and building lives they could be proud of, and he was determined to be one of them.

His pursuit of the American Dream wasn't an easy one. The long hours in poorly paying jobs, the weariness that swept over him, the moments where it all felt impossible - he never let it break him. There was a kind of wild enthusiasm in him, a joy for life that never dimmed. He loved to laugh, play cards with friends late into the night, or sip wine in the backyard. Life, to him, was something to be embraced with both hands. I learned so much just by watching him live, by the way he savored the simplest things.

I remember one Sunday afternoon when I must've been four or five. My shoelaces had come undone after church, and I sat on the sofa, trying to tie them, my small fingers clumsy with the task. I glanced around, searching for my mother, but she was in the kitchen, too far to help. My grandfather, in his easy chair, noticed me.

"Come here," he said, patting a cushion on the ottoman. "I'm going to teach you how to tie your shoes. You'll need to know how to do that when you start school."

He made the loops carefully, explaining each step like it was a secret he was passing down. I watched, focused, trying to commit every subtle gesture of his hands to memory. Then he untied the laces, handing them back to me.

"Your turn."

I tried, my small fingers getting tangled in the laces, twisting them in knots. He sat there, offering no words, just watching with a quiet patience. After a few more tries that ended in frustration, I heard a soft sigh escape him. "Here, let me show you again."

This time, he moved through the steps more slowly, his hands steady as I focused intently on each movement. When I tried again, I got it right. I glanced down at my shoes, the laces neatly tied, a sense of quiet pride swelling in me.

"I did it!" I shouted.

He smiled. "I knew you would."

I felt a deep sense of pride. I had mastered something new, and I had done it with my grandfather by my side. It was a moment that would stay with me, one I knew I'd carry with me always.

Years passed, as they do, in a blur of seasons and milestones. The pride of that moment with my grandfather gave me a quiet strength I could draw upon. I grew taller, my voice deepened, and the world around me shifted in subtle ways. Yet some things remained constant - the smell of fresh-cut grass in summer, the creak of the old floors, the weight of his hand on my shoulder. It was against this backdrop of familiarity and change that my mother approached me one day, her voice soft with a request that would shape my summers to come. I was fifteen.

"Your grandfather's getting older, not as strong as he used to be," she said gently. "During the summers, would you help him around the house until . . ." She didn't finish her thought, but I understood. I agreed without hesitation, and I didn't mind. I looked forward to it. Three days a week, I helped him with gardening and odd jobs, but the truth was, I enjoyed the time with him more than the work.

There were so many moments, little memories that linger even now. Once, he showed me how to roll a cigarette, his fingers steady as they guided mine to sprinkle the tobacco evenly, to fold and lick the paper just so. I hesitated, clumsy and unsure, but he only laughed. "Nothing to be afraid of."

When I managed it, he took the cigarette, lit it with the ease of habit, and drew a slow, satisfied puff.

"Not bad," he said, smiling, as though I'd passed some secret test. Then he handed it back. "Your turn."

I took a puff, and the burn hit hard, rattling in my chest. I coughed until my eyes watered, and he laughed again, the sound rich with delight.

Another time, after a long morning in the garden, we sat outside having lunch. He always had a bottle of wine and a single glass. But this time, there was a second glass, waiting for me. He poured the wine, offering it to me with a quiet smile. "You're old enough now," he said, his eyes twinkling with a hint of mischief.

I took a sip. Then another. And another. It was sweeter than I expected, and it made my head feel light.

"You like it?" he asked, smiling at me. I nodded. "Don't tell your mother," he added with a conspiratorial wink.

I smiled. "I won't."

We clinked our glasses together, and I took another sip. We sat there for a while, sipping our wine and talking.

Those summer afternoons were filled with hard work and simple joys. We painted rooms, changed light bulbs, repaired shaker shingles, and one year, put a new roof on the gazebo. We also worked in all areas of the garden, from the vegetable patch to the flower beds, to the orchard. We planted rows of vegetables, tended to the flowers, picked the fruit when it was ripe, trimmed the hedges, and mowed the lawn. We worked hard, but we also found joy in our labor. There was something satisfying about seeing the plants grow and thrive under our care. We knew that our work would be enjoyed by others, and that made it all the more worthwhile.

"Hard work in life is important," he told me once. "It's the only way to achieve anything worthwhile. You can't just sit around and expect things to happen for you. You've got to go out and make your own luck."

I never forgot those words. I knew that if I worked hard, I could achieve anything I set my mind to.

As we worked, he would share stories about his childhood in a small Italian coastal village by the sea. The rhythm of the waves seemed to echo in his words as he spoke of fishing with his friends. He described how they would catch so many they gave it away to neighbors, or the bonfire they built big enough to cook it all. His stories pulled me into a world both distant and strangely familiar, a place that felt like it could have been home.

Despite the ways we were different, there was a connection between us that felt effortless. Now, looking back, those summers were a gift I hadn't realized I'd been given until they were gone.

THE SCAR

Over the years, I began to understand that my grandfather was not a simple man, but a puzzle. His warmth and generosity often came in waves, filling the room with a sense of ease, only to be replaced, without warning, by a sudden change. His face would tighten, the muscles in his jaw clenching, as though the tension of some invisible force was pushing against him. His shoulders would stiffen, his gaze sharpening into something I could not always place - something that made me cautious. In those moments of anger, I was careful not to press too hard, wondering what it was that made him this way. Was it his upbringing, the things he had lived through as a child? Or was it something else altogether, buried deeper within him, never to be fully understood?

I longed to understand the man behind the temper, to unravel the mystery of his choices and his way of life. But my grandfather was not a man who easily invited questions about his past. He was like an old house with rooms locked away, their contents a mystery to those who lived there. I could sense the weight of those hidden spaces, the way they pressed against the walls, shaping him in ways I couldn't quite grasp.

One Sunday after church, as the family gathered at my grandparents' house, I found myself walking with my father in the backyard. The air was thick with the scent of my grandfather's flowers, their blooms a riot of color against a weathered fence. It was there, among the nodding heads of flowers, that my father began to unveil the first layers of my grandfather's story.

"Can I ask you something?" I said, my fingers grazing the soft petal, the touch fleeting but grounding.

"Sure," my father replied, his voice steady but carrying an undercurrent of something hard to place.

"Why does Gramps get so angry?"

My father sighed, a sound as old and weary as the creaking porch steps. "Anger comes easy to him, like an old coat he pulls on without thinking. It doesn't fit him, I know. But you need to remember this – he's never been violent. That's important."

I thought about the times I'd seen my grandfather's face darken, his voice rising like a storm. "But it's hard on Gram when he gets like that."

"I know. It's hard on everyone. But your grandmother is strong. She's learned to weather his storms over the years." My father's eyes softened as he spoke of my grandmother, and I wondered at the strength it took to love someone so complicated.

We wandered through the garden, pausing to admire the flowers, their colors like splashes of paint, their scents sharp and sweet. At the edge of the yard, my father stopped and stared out at the fields beyond. The land stretched on, the patchwork of greens and golds undisturbed, as though it went on forever.

"Your grandfather's anger has deep roots," he said, his voice low as if he were sharing a secret. "Part of it's his nature. But much comes from his life as an immigrant in a country that didn't welcome him."

I frowned, trying to reconcile this image with the man I knew. "How does being an immigrant make him angry?"

My father was silent for a moment, his gaze distant. When he spoke, his words painted a picture of a world I'd never known.

"People don't like to feel foolish, and that's what happened to men like him," he said softly. "He came here as a young man, full of hope, ready to prove himself, only to find a country that wasn't always kind - a place where people were quick to take advantage. It left a mark on him, just as it did on many. Some managed to move on, while others - like your grandfather - never really did."

He paused. "Imagine being nineteen, leaving everything behind. You arrive alone, barely speaking the language, with little money to your name. Every day was a struggle. Even when he eventually found others like him, fellow Italian immigrants, he'd already suffered. People exploited him, cheated him, stole from him."

As my father spoke, a world I'd never fully seen before began to take shape. I knew my grandparents came from Italy, but I hadn't grasped the burden of that journey. It was like looking at a familiar landscape and suddenly seeing the layers of history beneath, the glaciers and earthquakes that had shaped the land long before I was born.

"They were outsiders, mocked for their accents and appearances," he continued. "It was isolating, a constant reminder of not belonging. But yet they persevered, working tirelessly, building lives for themselves and us. Your grandfather's strength sometimes hides behind his temper, but it's there. It's something to be proud of, to remember."

My father's words were a revelation, unlocking a history I'd never considered. He painted a picture of struggle and resilience, of sacrifices made and hardships endured. I tried to imagine my grandfather as a young man, facing a world that seemed determined to break him. It was like trying to see through a frosted window –

I could make out shapes and shadows, but the details remained frustratingly blurred.

"They faced a kind of hatred you can't imagine," he said, his voice heavy with the stories handed down through generations. "People said awful things, things that came from ignorance, things they couldn't have understood. Others preyed on them, assuming they were stupid. Making friends outside their small community was nearly impossible. They always felt isolated, always aware of how they didn't fit in. But they never let go of their dreams, always pushing for something better - for themselves and for the ones they loved."

He went on, describing their determination in the face of adversity. "They put in long hours for meager wages, fighting against poverty and injustice every day. But they never let go of hope, believing that their work would eventually bear fruit. It made them tough, made them strong, but it also kept them compassionate. You should be proud of their story. It deserves to be remembered."

I thought about my grandfather's hands, calloused and scarred, evidence of a lifetime of hard work. I'd always taken those hands for granted, never considering the stories they could tell. "But all that was so long ago," I protested, struggling to connect this history to the man I knew.

My father gave me a gentle look, the kind that made me feel both loved and slightly foolish. "The past is never truly gone," he said. "It shapes us, often without our realizing. It's like a deep wound. Even after healing, the scar remains, a reminder of the pain endured. The suffering may pass, but it becomes part of your story.

For many, like your grandfather, it never fully fades. It becomes an integral part of who they are."

I thought about the times I'd seen my grandfather lost in thought, his eyes focused on something far away. Had he been remembering those early days, reliving old hurts and triumphs? The idea that he carried such a rich, complex history within him was both fascinating and slightly overwhelming.

"Wouldn't it help if they talk about it?" I asked.

My father paused for a moment, his eyes drifting back to the house, where the soft murmur of conversation drifted toward us. "It's your grandparent's choice," he replied. "But they want to protect you from their pain. Their focus has always been on your life, your future. They don't want you dwelling on their struggles. That's in the past. And even though they don't want to forget the past, all they want for you is to focus on moving forward, always looking to the next day, the next step ahead."

I nodded, though the sense of it still felt distant. Wouldn't openness be better? Why keep such experiences bottled up? It seemed to me that sharing these stories could only bring us closer, and could help bridge the gap between generations.

"But it feels like they're hiding something," I said.

"They're not hiding anything," he assured me. "They're protecting you."

"But why shield me from the truth?" I persisted.

"Because they love you," he said simply. "They don't want to cause you pain. Sometimes, the truth hurts."

I'd never considered it from that angle before. The idea that love could manifest as silence, as a deliberate choice not to share, was a new and complex concept. It made me see my grandparents in a new light, their reticence, not a wall but a shield, carefully constructed to protect those they loved most.

"But his anger sometimes seems endless, like a storm that won't pass."

"When he's like that, forgiveness is key," my father advised. "It can free you from your own anger and hurt. It can help you understand him better. That's what I want you to do — to forgive and understand. Remember, he gave your mother life, and through her, you. It's up to you to make the most of that gift. Hold onto the love your grandfather has for you. Let it guide you through dark times. The world is full of so many temporary things."

"Temporary things?"

"Your grandparents won't be here forever," he explained gently. "Like everyone else, they age, grow frail, and eventually leave this world. Cherish the time you have with them. Make every moment count. Life is short. One day you see a young face in the mirror. The next, you notice gray hair and wrinkles. Then one day, you might not recognize yourself at all. Remember, son, each day is a gift. Treasure it."

His words hit me with unexpected force. I'd always seen my grandparents as constants, as immovable as mountains. The idea that they were mortal, that one day they would be gone, opened up a chasm of fear and sadness I'd never experienced before.

"What about you and mom? Is every day a gift for you?"

He smiled warmly, his eyes crinkling at the corners. "Your mother makes it easy."

At the time, I couldn't fully grasp his words. Their truth would only become clear years later when I understood the depth of love that could exist between two people, the way it could transform even the most ordinary days into something precious.

There was still so much I wanted to know about my grandfather - how he endured, how he found love after so much loss. Understanding his history felt crucial to understanding my own identity. I was a product of his journey, the choices he made, and the life he built.

I wished he would've shared his struggles and emotions with me. Hearing his story firsthand would've been invaluable. But I never asked about his past. I respected his choice to keep his stories private, and his desire not to burden us with old sorrows. Instead, I watched him more closely, noticing the way he'd sometimes pause in the middle of a task, lost in thought, or the gentleness with which he'd touch my grandmother's hand when he thought no one was looking.

In the end, I came to understand that my grandfather's story was written not just in words unspoken, but in the life he built, the family he raised, and the love he showed in his own gruff way. His anger was just one part of a complex whole, a reminder of the struggles he'd faced and overcome. And while I might never know all the details of his journey, I could honor it by living my own life with the same determination and resilience he'd shown.

As my father and I walked back to the house, the sun warm on our backs, I felt a new appreciation for the man waiting inside, grateful for every part of him, even the parts I couldn't fully understand. I never asked him about his past. I let it go, respecting his choice – to keep his stories to himself and his wish not to burden us.

THE ENVELOPE AND THE LAST MOMENT

As I grew older, the memories of my grandfather began to shift and scatter, much like autumn leaves carried by the wind. Time has a way of softening the edges of what once felt so vivid. But the sound of his laughter and his wide smile always seemed to be staring into my soul, never fading. They were pieces of him that refused to fade.

Among all the memories I held, two stood apart, clear and unchanging despite the passage of time. These moments felt anchored in my mind, untouched by the blurring that came with years gone by. They were the memories I returned to, again and again, as if they contained the essence of everything he had meant to me.

During those summer months when I worked alongside him, there was a rhythm to our days, punctuated by one ritual. On the last Friday of every month, come the afternoon, we'd stop what we were doing to collect my grandfather's monthly pension payment. We'd walk down the road, about a half mile or so, to the foundry where he had worked for many years. He knew his way around the many buildings, his pace brisk and purposeful. I followed him, trying to keep up.

We'd enter the office area still wearing our dirty work clothes. The tidy rows of desks with neatly dressed workers stood apart from us. Some of the office workers recognized him from his years on the job. They'd nod or offer a warm hello.

My first time there, one of the office workers asked my grandfather, "Who's that with you?"

"Ah, he's my grandson," my grandfather said with a smile. "He's been helping me with the garden all morning. A real hard worker, this one is."

"Just like you," the office worker replied. "Maybe when he gets older, he can work in the foundry too. Just like you did."

"No. No foundry work for him," my grandfather said with gentle authority and a smile. There was no mistaking his resolve. He meant what he said.

We kept walking past more rows of desks and office workers.

"One day, you'll be a big shot like everyone here," he told me. "You'll wear a shirt and tie and sit at a desk. No dirty foundry work for you. But you'll have to work hard." He stopped and looked at me. "You climb the ladder one step at a time. Nothing ever comes easy in this life. Remember that."

At the very back was the cashier's office where a woman sat behind a window. As soon as she spotted my grandfather approaching, she readied three things for him: an envelope containing $375 in cash, an empty envelope, and a pen. Sliding the window open, she handed them over with a smile, the kind that implied familiarity. They exchanged pleasantries, their words easy and unhurried. My grandfather, without fail, reached into the cash envelope and pulled out a crisp $5 bill, handing it to me with a quiet nod, as if this small ritual were as immutable as the seasons.

"Don't tell your mother or grandmother," he would say.

Then, he would take a crisp $100 bill, and slip it into the waiting empty envelope. Carefully, he would scrawl a name across

the front. After moistening the edge of the flap with a light touch
to his tongue, he pressed it closed, handing the envelope and the
pen back to the woman.

There was always warmth in his eyes and a smile on his lips
as he did this.

"You make sure he gets it," he'd tell her.

She'd return his smile. "Of course."

I stayed silent, watching, as he performed his familiar
routine with precision. Without fail, every last Friday of every
month, we'd replay the scene. Over and over. Again and again.

I knew every move he would make before he made it. I
knew the exact moment he would give me $5, the exact moment
he would place the $100 in the empty envelope, the exact moment
he would scribble the name and hand the envelope to the nice
woman. I knew it all by heart.

But there was one detail that eluded me: who was the money
for?

I never dared to ask. Whatever it was, it clearly mattered to
my grandfather, and I respected that. But I couldn't help but
wonder. Who was the person who, month after month, received
this quiet generosity? And why did my grandfather guard the
answer so closely?

That memory remained with me throughout my life, a
puzzle I carried through the years, yearning for resolution. Yet,
alongside it was another memory, one I carried not out of curiosity,
but with tenderness, its presence a steady reminder of something
deeply cherished.

It was many years later after the company I worked for
offered me a promotion. The opportunity felt like the culmination

of everything I'd worked toward, yet it came with the weight of change. My wife and I would be moving to the Midwest, leaving behind the familiar faces and places that had shaped our lives. Excitement hummed beneath the surface, but so did an undeniable sorrow.

Before we left, I knew I had to see my grandfather. He was ninety years old. His mind was still sharp, but his body was failing him. He could no longer walk without help, and he had trouble doing pretty much everything. For a few years, my grandmother and mother had done everything to keep him at home, to preserve the life he had known. But the time came when their care was no longer enough, and they made the decision none of us wanted, moving him to a nursing home where he could get the help he needed.

I knew this visit would be the final chapter in a story we had shared, one we had been writing together for as long as I could remember.

When I stepped into his room, I could see how frail he had become. He relied on the staff for every necessity, his independence was reduced to a memory. His eyelids, too weak to lift on their own, were held up with band-aids, a small, desperate gesture to keep his gaze on the world. An aide would appear quietly, administering drops to prevent his eyes from drying out. The sight of him, so diminished, was shattering. He reminded me of a wounded bird, fragile and grounded, waiting for a kindness it couldn't ask for.

Sitting with him, I told him about my promotion, and that my wife and I were leaving soon. As I spoke, his face lit up, his wrinkles deepening with a satisfied smile. It was a look I would never forget.

"Didn't I tell you you'd be a big shot?" he said. "You climb the ladder one step at a time. You work hard?"

"Yes, Gramps. Just like you taught me."

Lifting a finger on a shaking hand, he said, "Good. Nothing ever comes easy in this life. Always remember."

Those words always stayed with me. From the moment I heard them, I could never forget them. Through the years, they'd been a part of my life, a reminder of his presence.

"A couple of beers," he called out, then turned to me and said, "One last drink together."

He knew.

Sadness hit me.

I nodded wanting to say something, but my throat was too tight.

An aide brought us two cans of beer, and we smiled at each other as we raised them in a toast.

"Salute!"

I watched him carefully, the deliberate way he brought the can to his lips. His hand, though unsteady with the tremors of age, carried a precision born of habit. He sipped slowly, savoring the moment, his focus making the ordinary act seem almost ceremonial.

"Remember, never get old," he said with a sigh. "It's not worth it."

I smiled but I couldn't quite grasp what he meant. I was young and healthy, certain that time would always feel like it was on my side. But as the years passed, a quiet understanding began to settle in, and I came to understand exactly what he had meant.

We talked for some time. He asked me how everyone was and asked about his gardens. He had forgotten that the house had been sold. I told him everyone was fine and that his gardens were full of color and sweet scents. He smiled, pleased.

After a time, a peaceful quiet settled between us. I watched as his head started to droop, exhaustion creeping in after a long day. Carefully, I removed the band-aids from his eyes, allowing him to sleep, and pressed a soft kiss to his forehead. I whispered my goodbye and stepped away.

Leaving his room, I walked down the hall, feeling lost and alone. Outside the nursing home, I paused, standing there for a moment. All I could see was his face - his smile, his eyes. He had been such a constant in my life, and now I knew he wouldn't be for much longer. The emptiness stretched out before me, vast and unfamiliar. I knew those moments with him would be the last.

That night, I cried until there were no tears left.

About a year later, my mother called to deliver the news of his passing.

"I've some sad news," she started. "Your grandfather passed away."

The words hit me hard, leaving me breathless. My grandfather, who had been a constant in my life, was now gone. Accepting it felt impossible. I had always expected him to be there for me, and I could not imagine a time without him.

For days, I moved through the motions of my life, not quite understanding how to adjust to a world without him. Though I was so far from home, the absence of his presence left a silence in the world I couldn't fill, a constant ache that seemed to expand with each passing moment. In the quiet, as the weight of his loss pressed down, something else crept in - an unsettling understanding that life was fragile. The space he had filled was not merely an empty room; it was a void, a space that would never be fully restored, no matter how much time passed.

The reality of death was always there, lingering like a shadow we acknowledge but don't fully confront until we're forced to. Yet never before had it felt so near, so undeniable. For the first time, my father's words landed with brutal clarity.

The world is full of so many temporary things.

It was as if those words had always been true, but now they had an edge, a razor-sharp clarity that left me with nowhere to hide. I understood, in a way I hadn't before, that every moment, every conversation, every touch we shared with the people we loved, was part of something fleeting, something that would slip through our fingers like sand. The gift of time, as precious as it was, was always slipping away, leaving us with nothing but echoes, memories that would fade until even they were gone. The people we held close, the stories we told, the faces we would never see again - everything was temporary. All that remained was the void left in their place, a space that could never be filled.

"How's Gram doing?" I asked my mother.

"She's fine," she said. "Your grandfather hadn't been well for some time and the last couple of weeks became bedridden. I brought her to see him each day. She sat by his side and held his hand. She told him stories of their life together. Things like the time when they first met, how he courted her, about the happy times they had shared. She told him how much she loved him."

My mother started to cry.

"She told him stories about their past," she said, "and stories about their grandchildren and great-grandchildren, and how proud she was of all of them. She was there in his final moments. She held his hand tightly. It was almost as if she was trying to pull him back. But she didn't have the strength. He was gone."

After that call, I took out pictures I had of my grandfather and looked at them. Tears clouded my vision as I remembered the fond moments we shared. There were the lessons he taught me, the stories of his youth that shaped him, and the countless hours we spent just talking about life. I smiled through my tears, grateful for the moments of having known him. But it was hard to come to terms with the fact that I would never be able to again see his face, hear his voice, or share another moment with him again.

It was at that moment that a dark truth became clear to me. His experiences, the things he had seen and done – they were vanishing with him, like a tide receding from the shore. His journey, his identity, everything about him was being slowly erased. No amount of reminiscing or retelling could ever bring them back. Sure, there were pictures and memories, but these were only a fraction of who he was, and they too would fade with time.

The fleeting nature of life was an awakening. I had never given it much thought before, but now it was so obvious. One day, my time would end, and when those who remembered my grandfather were also gone, it would be as if he had never walked this earth. The thought was sobering in a way I couldn't quite put into words.

All we had were memories, and in the end, that was all we would be. But memories are delicate things. As time moves forward, they soften and blur, erasing parts of us along the way. It's a slow disappearance, unfolding in the quiet recesses of our minds.

What's the point of anything if it all just ends in nothingness? This question haunted me, a philosophical quandary that seemed to have no satisfactory answer.

But then I remembered my grandfather's words: "Nothing ever comes easy in this life."

Perhaps the point is not in the ending but in the journey. Perhaps it's in the connections we make, the love we share, and the impact we have on others.

My grandfather's life may have ended, but his influence continued. It lived on in me, in the choices I made, in the way I approached life. It lived on in the stories I would tell about him, and in the values I would pass down. In this way, he achieved a kind of immortality, not through eternal life, but through the ripples of his existence spreading outward through time.

And suddenly, I understood the importance of those monthly envelopes, of the secret generosity my grandfather had shown. It wasn't about the money. No. The point isn't in the ending but in the journey. It's in the hard work, the small gestures of kindness, the lessons learned along the way, and the love we give and receive. Even if time steals away the details and the faces we once held dear, there's meaning in the moments we share. My grandfather's legacy, much like the legacy of all those we lose, isn't in the things we can touch or the facts we can remember, but in the lives we shape and the hearts we touch, leaving behind a ripple that continues long after we're gone.

My father

Mrrr . . . Mrrr . . . Mrrr . . . The familiar sound of Maggie's purr pulls me back to the parlor.

"Didn't I tell you not to get old?" my grandfather says, his voice carrying both warmth and a playful reproach as if aging were a choice I had failed to avoid.

I shake my head, trying to clear the haze of memories clouding my thoughts. It feels strange to see him there, settled into his easy chair, newspaper in hand, the television murmuring in the background - a routine that has marked our Sundays for as long as I can recall. A wave of emotion surges within me, and I close my eyes tightly, fighting to hold back the tears, though I know they'll come no matter how hard I try.

"Took you long enough to get here," he quips, a hint of gentle sarcasm lacing his words. "I've been waiting. Heard you've become quite the big shot - a professor - writing books."

I stand there, caught in the surprise of him, the shape of someone I'd never let slip from memory.

He smiles. "What? Don't know what to start?"

"I'm just ... I didn't expect this. Seeing you again."

"It's been some time," he says. "But I'm glad you're here. I've missed you."

"And I've missed you - and Gram." I lean in and kiss his cheek.

He closes his eyes for a moment, rubbing his forehead as if the weight of the world rests there. "Ah, your grandmother. That old woman never changes. Always making things difficult for me.

It's never easy with her - always telling me what to do. But I don't know what I'd do without her."

With a smile, I take his frail hand in mine. He looks up at me, tears glistening in his eyes.

"There's someone else who's missed you," he says softly.

I feel it then - a familiar warmth enveloping me like a cherished blanket.

"Dad," I whisper, the word barely leaving my lips.

Turning slowly, I see my father standing there, newspaper in hand. His deep brown eyes shine with joy, and his full gray hair is as neat as ever - exactly as I remember him when he was in his sixties.

My heart swells with love.

A heavy silence falls between us. We both linger in this moment of reunion, uncertain of what words might bridge the years that have passed.

A VOICE TO EMOTIONS

I never thought I'd be able to write about my father. The task seemed as impossible as describing the taste of water or the feeling of air on your skin. How do you capture a life so rich, so complex, in mere words? My father, like many of his generation, carried history on his shoulders. At 19, he was thrust into the chaos of the Battle of the Bulge, a crucible that forged the men of his time. When he returned, he built homes with his brothers, their hammers and saws a counterpoint to the guns and tanks of war. Later, he traded his work boots for polished shoes, rose to the position of vice president at a bank, and ended his career with the ceremonial exchange of a gold watch and a handshake.

But these facts, these milestones, they're only the scaffolding. They leave out the sound of his laugh, the way his brow drew together in deep thought, or how he had this gift of making you feel singular, extraordinary, simply by listening. The love was vast, all-encompassing. I could try to shape it into words, but it would be like trying to hold sunlight in your hands, always slipping through, leaving only the warmth behind.

Then came the day I had dreaded - the day of his funeral service. The funeral home was packed, a sea of black-clad mourners with red-rimmed eyes. I sat there, surrounded by so many people, yet the emptiness inside me only seemed to grow. I couldn't find the words to explain what I was feeling, even though I knew I needed them.

But it was my mother who found them first. Her voice reached me through the noise, steady and familiar, like a breath I'd known all my life. When I turned to look at her, her face was a landscape of sorrow and gratitude, wet with tears yet carrying the faintest trace of a smile.

"I'm so grateful he was given to me," she said.

And there it was. The ocean in a teacup, the sunlight caught and held. Plain words that said everything I'd been trying to say for years. Sometimes, the simplest truths are the ones that echo the loudest.

I am so grateful he was given to me.

I WON'T LET YOU FALL

My father's life was a treasure, rich with memories that lingered like the scent of fresh pine. I remember one summer day from my childhood when I approached him with a question that brimmed with eagerness: could I help him and my uncles with their work? They were constructing small homes, and my heart swelled with the desire to learn their craft.

Without wasting a moment, my father smiled and said, "Of course you can help. But you'll have to get up early."

That night, anticipation kept me awake, the thrill of the morning ahead buzzing in my veins. As dawn broke, I leaped from bed, dressed in a flurry, and dashed to the kitchen. My father was already there, preparing breakfast, his smile greeting me like the sun breaking through clouds.

"Good morning," he said. "Are you ready to work?"

I nodded eagerly. "I can't wait!"

After breakfast, we set off with my uncles to the construction site - a sprawling landscape of homes in varying stages of completion. We pulled up to a work site of a nearly finished house, surrounded by stacks of lumber and piles of debris scattered everywhere.

My father showed me my tasks, and I threw myself into the work with boundless enthusiasm. The day was hot and filled with dust, but I welcomed it as part of the experience. I fetched tools, carried wood, and tidied the chaos around us. After lunch, he asked me to help him shingle the roof - an invitation that filled me with both excitement and trepidation. It would be an experience I would never forget.

"But I'm afraid of heights," I confessed, a whimper to my voice.

His smile was reassuring. "I know," he replied gently. "That's why I'm asking you to do it."

Though his words puzzled me, I sensed no room for argument. "Trust me," he urged as he climbed the ladder ahead of me. "You'll always give your best, I know. You can do this."

With each shaky step up the ladder, I dared not glance down.

"Keep both hands on the ladder," he instructed. "One rung at a time."

As I neared the roof's edge, I looked up to find him standing proudly above me, his strong arm extended in invitation. "Take my hand," he said warmly. "I won't let you fall."

Grasping his hand, he steadied me as I stepped onto the roof beside him. He handed me a shingle and showed me what to do. With careful attention, I followed his instructions - nailing each shingle into place as he passed them to me.

The wind tugged playfully at my clothes while the sun warmed my face, yet I remained focused on our task. With each shingle I placed, my confidence grew. We worked together, slowly but surely, until the roof was covered in shingles.

When we placed the last shingle, we stood together for a moment. He placed his hands on my shoulders and encouraged me gently, "Go ahead - take a look around."

I took a deep breath. We stood side by side, gazing toward the horizon. Scattered across the landscape were homes, each a chapter in its own story - some still under construction, their beams reaching skyward, while others thrummed with life, children darting through yards filled with the sounds of laughter.

"This is life," he said. "Isn't it beautiful? It has a way of revealing itself when you change your vantage point. All the things you can see. But don't forget. Life is for the living. So don't hold back." His voice carried the kind of warmth that made the words linger. "Take it in. It's not just what you see but how you see it. The small things you might've missed - they come forward, and suddenly everything feels new again. That sense of discovery, of finding wonder in the ordinary, is a gift. Go ahead. Let yourself really see it."

So I did.

At first, everything seemed the same, but then I began to notice what I'd always missed. The trees swayed like dancers in the breeze, sunlight lit the leaves in vivid green, and birds glided on invisible currents. Even the clouds moved with an easy grace, soft and unhurried. It was as if I'd been given new eyes, and the beauty of it was more than I could've imagined.

From that day forward, my view of the world shifted subtly but irrevocably. Life was filled with beautiful moments waiting to be cherished. All it took was a willingness to pause and appreciate them.

That day changed my life.

I LOVE YOU

But there was another memory of my father that stayed with me, vivid and unrelenting, further shaping the course of my life in ways I couldn't fully understand. It resurfaced as clearly as if it had unfolded only yesterday, a moment carved in time with the weight of its meaning still intact.

It was a cold winter day and the sky was a light gray. Snow was falling gently, and everything looked so peaceful and perfect, like a picture from a postcard. But it didn't lighten the heavy burden I was carrying. I was 52 years old, and I just received a call telling me my father was dying and I should go to the nursing home immediately.

Trudging through the snow, the wind whipped my hair around my face, and I could feel the cold seeping into my bones. I pulled my coat tighter around me and hurried towards the front door, under a frowning arch. I felt lost and alone, and all I could think of was how I couldn't be without him.

The nursing home had become an all-too-familiar part of my life in recent years. It stood as a haven of comfort, care, and genuine kindness, where the staff brought patience and dedication to their work. Yet beneath its reassuring façade lay an undeniable truth: time was ticking away.

Although the residents were well taken care of, and despite the best efforts of the staff to bring cheer to their days, there was always a tinge of sadness. There was an unspoken understanding among them that their days were finite, their paths narrowing toward an inevitable conclusion. Many had lived richly, their lives filled with moments that now felt distant, but some were afraid of the end. They held tightly to what was left, reluctant to release the threads of a world they knew, even though they knew that time was their enemy.

I pulled open the door where silence met me like an old companion. Pausing for a moment, I took a deep breath before heading toward my father's room. The door stood closed like a quiet sentinel.

With a gentle touch, I slowly pulled the door open. Inside, my father lay on the bed, his chest rising and falling in rhythm with the machine beside him, its steady beeps marking each heartbeat like a distant metronome.

Beep . . . . beep . . . . beep . . . . beep . . . . beep . . . .

The sound filled the room, persistent and unyielding, stretching across the stillness like a taut thread.

My mother was seated near the bed, her hands resting in her lap, her gaze fixed on my father. My siblings sat nearby, their presence a silent vigil.

A nurse greeted me, her expression calm but tired, as though she had borne witness to this scene countless times before.

"He's been slipping in and out of consciousness," she said.

My mother was there, as were my siblings.

My father looked weaker than usual; his skin was ashen. He saw me and gave a slight smile that spoke of the strength that had never truly gone away. No matter how much old age had taken from him, there was still a spark of the man he used to be. But that spark was fading.

"Is he in pain?" I asked the nurse.

"Hard to tell. He's refused to take any painkillers. So, I've been swabbing his lips with morphine."

"Does it help him? The pain?"

"I think so," she said with a nod.

My throat tightened with grief as I sat next to my mother.

"How are you doing?" I asked her.

She reached over and held my hand and smiled at me, not a tear in her eyes. "I'm doing fine. But why are you here? He wouldn't want to take you away from your work."

"This is where I have to be," I told her.

We were silent and I just sat there contemplating the inescapable truth I was about to face.

The end – death.

It's a part of life, a process of deterioration and decay. We are all born with a finite lifespan – our bodies slowly break down, and our minds gently recede. For some, the process of aging is gradual, while for others it's sudden and swift. But eventually, it happens to everyone, and when it does, it's not an easy thing to watch.

Yet, here I was, watching as death crept up on my father. I knew his pain had been relentless, his body weary from the long labor of living. I could only hope that death would come as a kindness, a gentle release from the hardship of his decline, a closing chapter that brought peace to a long, difficult journey.

I sat beside him, watching the gentle rise and fall of his chest, each breath as steady and familiar as waves meeting the shore. I could have stayed like that forever, anchored to the rhythm of his breathing, letting time slip by in those quiet, measured moments. And then, so gradually I almost missed it, the rhythm began to falter. His breaths became uneven, each rise smaller, each pause stretching longer. I held my own breath as if the stillness in my lungs could somehow coax his to continue. The machine that had marked his life in steady beeps suddenly flatlined into a single, unbroken tone. It was a sound that landed with a finality I couldn't prepare for, closing the space between hope and loss. Something deep within me gave way, expanding into a silence I could not name, filling every part of me until there was no room for anything else.

When I looked at my mother, a faint smile played on her lips, delicate and fleeting. My sister reached for her, steadying her as she rose from the chair. She bent down and pressed a soft kiss to my father's cheek, her movements filled with a quiet tenderness.

"Even in death, we're not truly gone," she said, drawing us closer as we guided her back to her seat.

What did she mean?

We spent some time in silence, cherishing the moment. It was our last with him, and my mother's words began to unfurl their meaning. She was right - our loved ones never entirely leave us. They remain in the recesses of our minds, in the stories that echo across years, and in the love we continue to carry forward, unbroken and enduring.

"Every moment is a gift, isn't it," I said to her.

She smiled, her eyes sparkling with emotion. "There were so many." She placed a hand over her heart. "And they're all kept here."

As a family, we gathered around my father and took time to hold his hand and say goodbye. We spent time with the nurse and other staff members and thanked them for everything they did for him. Then I walked my mother to her room which was in the assisted living section of the same facility.

The walk seemed endless, each step stretching further than the last. We moved through the still corridors, the sound of our footsteps soft against the floor. Now and then, we passed a nurse or an aide, focused on their work, their presence brief and unintrusive. They all seemed to understand what had happened - offering my mother their condolences, their voices gentle, eyes full of quiet sympathy. And then, at last, we reached her room.

"Are you going to be okay?" I asked.

"I'll be alright. I miss him already."

"Me too."

"We'll do our best to keep his memory alive."

I hugged her tight and felt a tear escape my eye. Everything had changed. I was no longer the same person I was before.

I drove home in the quiet of the early morning, the streets empty and unfeeling. The house, when I arrived, was still, and the silence seemed to deepen the grief I carried with me. Every step I took through the quiet rooms felt like an echo of something I couldn't escape. And though my body was drained, sleep didn't come. Instead, I found myself sitting in my recliner, tears spilling without restraint.

And then, it came. That thought. The one I had tried to suppress for days. It slipped into my mind, persistent, unyielding, and once it was there, it took hold of me, leaving me with a profound, crushing sense of despair.

I couldn't escape it. It was always there, lurking in the back of my mind. It was a thought that I knew would never go away.

There was something I had never said to my father, something important –

I love you.

Three simple words, so ordinary and yet so profound. But I never spoke them to him. I had whispered them to myself, countless times, in the quiet spaces of my mind. Still, they never made it past my lips. It wasn't that I couldn't say them. The words themselves were easy enough. It was just that, somehow, they never found their way out. Perhaps I was afraid. Maybe I felt it was something I wasn't supposed to do.

I love you.

The words played in my head over and over again. No matter how hard I tried to shift my focus, they remained, drifting in and out like a melody I couldn't shake. The more I tried to push them away, the more they lingered, settling into the corners of my thoughts.

I love you.

They held on tightly, refusing to let go. It was as if something deep inside me was still raw, a wound that refused to close, always tender, always aching.

I sat there, fists clenched, pounding the armrest in frustration. The urge to scream, to tear at my hair, to unleash the anger swirling inside me was overwhelming. But I knew it would accomplish nothing. The words were lodged inside, woven into me now, as if they'd always belonged there.

I would never be free of them.

My wife heard me, hurrying from the bedroom. When she saw me, she knew that my father had passed. "I'm sorry," she said. "What can I do to help?"

"There's nothing you can do," I growled through my tears. "You don't understand. I needed to tell him something. I just needed to tell him something."

"Tell him what?" my wife asked.

Sniffling, I wiped away my tears.

"Doesn't matter now. It's too late. He's gone, and I'll never have the chance."

My wife put her arm around me. "Come to bed and try to get some sleep," she said. "It's been a long day."

"I will. I will. Soon."

My heart ached with the empty feeling of where his presence used to be. I cried for a long time. I cried for my father, and I cried for my mother, I cried for my siblings, and I cried for myself. But I also cried for the words that I had never said. I cried for the many wasted moments in time.

When exhaustion finally overtook me and the tears had dried up, when I had emptied myself of everything, I made my way to bed. But sleep wouldn't come. I lay there, eyes fixed on the ceiling, and all I could see was his face - pale, unmoving, the stillness of death settling around him. Then, buried deep within my soul, the words emerged once again.

I love you.

As the first rays of the sun broke through the darkness, casting long shadows across the room, I heard the soft ticking of the alarm clock. I reached over and turned it off before it could start beeping and I wrenched myself from bed. Despite my exhaustion, I felt that I needed to watch the sunrise. I pulled on some clothes and a winter coat, ready to embrace a new day.

Stepping outside, I took a deep breath of the cold air. The sun was cresting over the horizon and I could feel the warmth of its rays on my skin. But it did little to warm the chill of the memory of having watched my father die. There was nothing I could do but watch helplessly as he slowly faded away into nothingness. The look in his eyes, the shallow breaths, and the gentle sigh of his last gasp of air would stay with me forever.

I closed my eyes, trying to push the memory back into the corners where it could no longer reach me. But it was still there, vivid and unrelenting. I breathed again, slower this time, trying to ground myself in the present - the sound of the wind brushing through the trees, the sharpness of the air against my face. A shiver ran through me, and I pulled my coat tighter as if that might shield me from the past I couldn't escape.

But then, I felt something else. A warmth, like a gentle hand on my cheek. I opened my eyes and looked up. The morning sky was ablaze with color. And the snow sparkled like diamonds.

I stood there for a long time, just watching as the sun rose higher in the sky. The shadows grew shorter and the air began to warm. It was such a beautiful sight, and it filled me with hope. It reminded me that even in the darkest of times, there's always light.

Another deep breath and I turned away from the sunrise and went back inside, determined to start a new day. But the words were always there.

I love you.

ANSWERS

Mrrr . . . Mrrr . . . Mrrr . . . Maggie leans against my leg, a quiet insistence that almost feels like a delicate nudge. I glance down, surprised by the depth of her presence, as though she's not merely seeking attention, but something more, something quiet and unspoken.

I raise my eyes again, standing before my father. Time feels strange, elastic, surreal, stretching out in a way that almost doesn't make sense. It has been so many years since I last saw him, yet here he is, solid and real in front of me. A deep sadness fills me, like looking at a ghost from a life I no longer recognize. The oddness of it all leaves me unsteady, adrift in a whirl of emotions.

I don't know how to react. I'm caught between the urge to embrace him and the fear that he'll vanish if I dare to reach out. So, I just stand there, frozen, looking at him.

He extends his hand, a formal gesture that feels woefully inadequate. Without thinking, I rush to him, throwing my arms around his shoulders. For a moment, his body remains tense, unfamiliar with the weight of my presence. Then, slowly, his arms shift, pulling me closer. I bury my face against his shoulder, taking in the scent of him, as time and distance seem to melt away in the quiet space we share.

As we hold each other, the words that have lived in my heart for so long bubble to the surface. I pull back slowly, my pulse thundering in my ears.

"There's something I've been meaning to say," I begin, my voice soft, as if the words might shatter the stillness. "Something

I've carried with me for years, something I thought I'd never get the chance to say."

His gaze holds mine, his expression filled with concern as he looks at me, as though trying to understand. "What is it?" he asks, his voice tender.

"I love you."

The words come out, almost unbidden, but once they're spoken, they feel like they've been waiting their whole lives to be released. It's a subtle miracle to hear them spoken aloud as if they belong to a world I'm only just beginning to understand.

He's silent for a moment, his face unreadable, giving me nothing to hold onto.

"I'm sorry I never told you before," I say, the words rushing out as if they'd been waiting all this time. "I don't know why I couldn't."

His face softens, worry lines melting away as he smiles with understanding. "Thank you, son," he says, his voice steady, calm, and warm. "I love you, too. But you didn't need to say it."

I meet his gaze, momentarily taken aback. "Why not?"

There's a calm certainty in his eyes. "Because I already knew. From the first time I held you as a baby, I could see it then." He gestures to the sofa, as though inviting me to settle into this newfound ease. "How about we sit for a while?"

We sit down on the sofa, side by side, the familiar presence of him beside me both comforting and surreal. "I'm sorry that was something you had to deal with," he says. "Regret is like a fire inside us, something we can never put out. It consumes us from the inside, a reminder of what could have been. I'm glad that you've finally let it go."

"I'm glad too," I reply, feeling lighter than I have in years.

"It's been a long time," he says. "But you're here now."

I open my mouth to ask where "here" is, but I'm interrupted by Maggie leaping into my lap. Her purrs rumble through me as she settles in.

"My, she's a pretty one," my father says, admiring her.

"Do you remember her?" I ask.

"A little. I was very old at the time. My memories of those days are sometimes cloudy."

"I understand," I say, then hesitate. "Dad, I need to ask you -" but the words die on my lips as a new scene unfolds before us.

My mother enters the dining room, placing a plate of meatballs on the table. The smell of tomato sauce, herbs, and something warm and familiar fills the air. From the kitchen, the scent of garlic bread toasting drifts in.

My stomach growls a deep sound that feels out of place. How can I be hungry in what could be a dream?

Just as she turns to head back to the kitchen, my mother catches our gaze on the meatballs. "Don't you two start eating before everyone else," she says with a smile, then returns to the kitchen. "They're for everyone."

I can't help but smirk. "She knows us all too well."

My father's eyes gleam with mischief as he rubs his hands together. "Why don't we get a head start on the others?"

"But mom said —"

He presses a finger to his lips, eyes twinkling. "Shhh . . . We'll have a couple, then rearrange what's left on the plate. She'll never know."

I smile, though doubt pulls at me. I want to ask him what this all means, but I'm afraid of the answer.

He gets up from the sofa and takes a few steps toward the dining room, but I stop him. "Dad, wait."

He notices the fear in my eyes and sits back down. "What is it?" he asks gently. "If something's on your mind, you know you can talk to me."

My heart races, and I take a shaky breath. "I'm so confused," I say.

"Confused about what?"

"Everything. None of this makes sense. I can't figure out what's happening to me."

His smile is warm and comforting. "I know it's a lot. You're safe now, with your family. Where you belong."

But the unease still won't leave. "I don't get it," I say. "One minute, I'm living my life, and the next, I'm here, in this crazy dream, where everything feels so real."

"I know. It's a lot to take in."

"Can you explain it to me? What is all this? It's a dream, right? Please tell me it's just a dream."

He looks at me, thinking for a moment, then reaches over to pet Maggie, who purrs softly.

"It's not a dream," he tells me in a low, calming voice. "You've entered a new phase of life."

I look at him, confusion swirling inside me. What does he mean, a new phase of life? Doesn't he realize he is -

"But Dad, you're –" I stop, the word caught in my throat, refusing to leave my lips.

Maggie raises her head, her eyes fixed on me with an unwavering intensity, as if she can see through me.

He smiles softly. "Dead? Was that what you were going to say? Dead?"

I nod, cautious.

"I am," he says simply, "and so are you."

THE NEVER-ENDING ROAD

Dead . . . The word echoes in my head, a hollow, cold sound. I can't believe what my father's telling me.

I am dead. How can that be?

The thought circles in my mind, disjointed and impossible, as though the words themselves are a language I was never meant to understand. I want to cry out, to shatter the stillness with some defiant act, but my body refuses to obey. I am fixed in place, a spectator to my confusion.

The parlor stretches around me, familiar yet devoid of meaning. I scan its corners and surfaces for some kind of explanation - something hidden in the folds of the drapes, or reflected in the glass of the grandfather clock - but everything holds its place, unchanged. There's no revelation, no sign that the truth might be anything other than what my father has said. It feels like standing in the shadow of something I cannot see.

Questions come not in a rush but with the slow insistence of water rising past my ankles. A quiet, steady dread trickles in from the corners of the room, pooling somewhere deep inside me. Could he be right? Am I truly gone? Is this what it feels like to have reached the end?

The idea is strange, even impossible to grasp. It drifts toward me like a chill carried on an open wind, seeping into my bones. A sharper thought follows close behind, unbidden, unkind.

I have no memories of death.

I close my eyes and reach backward, trying to find something solid, some tether to anchor me to the life I am sure I've lived. But there's nothing. Just darkness.

I take a breath and speak before the silence crushes me. "I don't remember dying," I say to my father. My voice feels smaller than I intended as if the words were swallowed the moment they left my mouth.

"It's not easy to understand," he says. "Think back. What's your last memory?"

Taking a deep breath, I close my eyes again, trying desperately to find the last moment I can remember. But everything is a blur until it comes to me. I see it. White walls, sterile smell, beeping machines.

I open my eyes and find him watching me. "I remember a hospital room," I say, the words feeling distant.

He smiles, the kind of smile that carries a lifetime within it, and though neither of us speaks again, something passes between us - something beyond language. I can almost feel his thoughts on that first day, the moment I drew my first breath, and now, here we are, together at what feels like the edge of everything.

It's strange, this thread that connects us. To know he has been there, weaving himself into every moment of my life, from its fragile start to now. The thought fills me with a quiet ache, one part sorrow and one part comfort - a reminder that I was never truly alone.

He pulls me closer, his arm a steady presence, his warmth reaching me in a way that feels like more than just heat. It anchors me and brings the world into focus. Whatever comes next, he'll be beside me. That much, I can hold onto.

And then, like a door opening in my mind, everything that was blurred sharpens. The understanding I couldn't grasp when Maggie greeted me outside suddenly reveals itself, staring back at me with a ferocity that feels like both a promise and a reckoning. It's not gentle, but it's clear,

My breath catches in my throat. "I just feel different," I whisper. "Like I'm not really here."

"Death isn't an end," he says softly. "It's a beginning."

I look at him, my eyes wide. My voice trembles with uncertainty. "What do you mean?"

"It's the beginning of the journey down the never-ending road."

"Journey? Never-ending road?" my voice hardly a whisper.

"Just as your past life was a journey, so too is this - your next life. It's a journey where horizons remain just out of reach, filled with beauty in its unfolding landscapes and unexpected encounters. There will always be something more to discover." He pauses for a moment before looking at me closely. "Are you okay?"

"Why didn't I think of it?" I say aloud, feeling a mix of shock and acceptance. "That I was dead,"

"Not the kind of thought that comes easily, is it now?"

I sigh deeply. "We're ghosts."

"We've always been ghosts," he says. "We live on in the memories of those who love us," he explains gently. "We're never truly gone. But then comes the time when there's no one left to remember us - just ghosts waiting to fade away."

The words land with a quiet inevitability. I've thought this before, but hearing it aloud makes it sharper, like a thought I was too afraid to own.

He studies my face, catching the shift in my expression. "It's a lot," he says, his voice dipping into something gentler. "I know. But don't worry. It's not something you need to understand all at once. It comes, little by little."

I nod, though my chest feels tight. He's right - he has to be - but the knowing doesn't stop the fear from creeping in, the hollow ache of what it means to fade, piece by piece, until there's nothing left at all.

Looking around the parlor, I take in its familiarity. The fireplace, the old television and radio, the round wood columns, the heavy floral drapes. It's all so familiar, but it feels different now. Like I'm seeing and hearing everything through a cracked lens.

It's all so overwhelming.

I try to gather my thoughts, to quiet the racing uncertainty inside me. I need clarity, a thread to follow through the haze. Closing my eyes, I attempt to summon images of my past - my wife, the stories I wrote, the friends I thought I'd never lose. But the memories refuse to come together. They splinter into fragments, flashes of sound and color slipping away before I can hold on to them. The harder I reach, the further they slip from my grasp, leaving me untethered. The world around me grows dim, as though I'm drifting into some dark expanse where nothing familiar remains.

"Are you with me?" My father's voice rises, pulling me from that abyss.

"I'm here," I answer, my voice stronger than I feel. "I'm here."

A deep breath follows, and with it comes an unexpected lightness, as though the air itself has shifted, carrying something more certain. It isn't clarity that finds me, but something softer - an understanding, a sense of belonging I hadn't realized I was missing. It feels like stepping into a warm room after being lost in the cold.

And now, I know. I understand, with an unsettling clarity – I am dead.

The truth arrives not with shock but with a strange relief, as if this is what I'd been searching for all along. I don't fight it. Instead, I let the realization spread through me, quieting every lingering fear. Death isn't the absence of life but the presence of something else entirely - something freeing, something whole.

"Life became too small," I confess to him. "I was weary of it. The things I loved slipped out of reach, and I found myself circling the same path every day. I didn't know how to escape it, how to change direction. I craved something unknown, something to shake me awake. I wanted to feel alive again. And now – here - everything feels unfamiliar but in the best possible way. The air carries a clarity I'd forgotten. The sky stretches endlessly, blue rich and vast, a color that seems to outlast even the farthest memory. Even the simplest things seem charged with meaning. It's like I'm seeing the world for the very first time. Life has returned, though not in the way I ever expected."

Strange that I use the word life when I know I'm dead.

My father squeezes my hand gently - a silent gesture of understanding - and his warmth reassures me further.

"I'm here for you," he says. "This place is yours now. You don't need to worry about anything anymore. All those troubles are gone - there's no pain or fear here. Death is merely a new beginning. You're free."

"Is that what mom meant when she told me this was a new beginning, a safe place?"

His smile broadens slightly. "That's exactly what she meant."

"What happens now?" I ask.

"That's up to you," he says, his voice carrying the kind of measured thoughtfulness that makes you want to lean closer. "There's so much to discover."

The words unfold before me like petals opening in sunlight. My thoughts spiral outward, but still, questions press close.

"Is this heaven?" I ask, the words coming quietly as if they might shatter something delicate.

"This is your new life," he says, simply but firmly. "It's yours to shape into whatever you need it to be. Maybe that will feel like heaven."

"And God?" I press. "Is there a God?"

He hesitates, his head tipping slightly to the side, as though the answer rests somewhere just out of reach. "Even here, like in the past life, answers don't come easily."

He pauses again before continuing. "That doesn't mean we can't believe. In something bigger than ourselves. Something that ties us together. But what that is . . . well, it's still a mystery."

I sit with this, the thought unfurling in slow, uneven waves. "Maybe it's part of the journey," I say at last, half to myself. "The never-ending road."

He nods knowingly. "You're starting to understand."

"And time? Does time exist here?"

"It's not the same," he says, his tone almost gentle, as though he knows how the answer will land. "Everything happens all at once."

The idea unmoors me and leaves my mind grasping for some point of stability. Time had always been a structure, a scaffolding for my life, the thing that gave every moment its place. Now, it slips through my fingers, unknowable and vast.

"I don't understand," I say, the words carrying a trace of frustration.

"That's alright." He glances around the parlor again before continuing: "Understanding isn't always the point. But right now - it's Sunday afternoon - the family is here, at your grandfather's house after church, just like always."

The memories flood back, vivid and bittersweet. Sunday afternoons, warm with the aroma of marinara, fresh basil, and baked bread, laughter mingling with the clink of dishes. Plates piled high with pasta smothered in tomato sauce and hearty meatballs. The sauce clinging to each strand is rich and fragrant. Deep red wine in large glasses catching the light like liquid rubies. Freshly baked bread, its crust crackling as it gave way to soft warmth. And a bowl of crisp romaine, cherry tomatoes, and cucumbers, glistening under homemade vinaigrette.

"I miss those days," I admit quietly.

"Time has a funny way of reshaping things, little by little," he says staring off into the dining room. "Traditions come and go. The laughter softens, becoming less frequent. One chair is left empty, then another. Eventually, the table becomes too big for the number of plates set upon it. We grow into different people, fractured in ways we can't describe until those Sundays are no longer possible. The afternoons that once bound us are gone, as if they had been packed away with the good dishes, waiting for some future that would never come."

"I saw it happen so many times. Too many times. But I always had the memories, something I was thankful for."

"In life, we try to hold on to what we have," he reflects thoughtfully. "But everything slips away, little by little, no matter how tightly we cling to it. We slowly close our eyes as the world moves on without us, as our loved ones forget us. We become the unseen, nothing but memories until the day there's no one left who remembers us. Strange thing, to be forgotten. It's like being erased from existence. But I suppose it's the natural order of things. We all come into the past life and we all leave it."

His words stay with me. We close our eyes, and life moves on, leaving us behind, until we become little more than shadows - barely seen, until even the shadows are gone, and no one remains to remember.

"But here, in this next life, we're remembered, right?" I ask.

"There are no lost moments here," he assures me gently. "Everything is preserved - every thought, every feeling."

The idea fills me with wonder - a world where nothing is ever forgotten.

"Can we —"

He cuts me off gently knowing where my thoughts are taking me.

"We'll talk more about this place. I'll help you to understand how things work. There are some things you can do and other things you can't. Think of it like wandering through a library, browsing the shelves, and picking out memories to visit. But it's best to go about things slowly."

I look over to my grandfather sitting in his easy chair, reading the newspaper. He holds it close to his face, squinting to make out the words, his lips moving silently as he reads. A sliver of light glints off the rim of his glasses.

"What about Gramps? Does he understand all this?" I ask in a whisper.

"Never asked him," comes my father's hushed response. "He's happy as long as he has his wine and cigarettes."

We share a quiet laugh, the kind that feels like a memory itself, small and comfortable.

I picture my grandfather wandering in the familiar library of his mind, choosing this memory over and over again, the way he might choose a favorite book from a shelf to read again.

"How many times do you think he's read that same newspaper?" I ask.

"Hundreds I suppose. Maybe thousands and thousands. But do numbers matter here?"

I don't know the answer.

And then my grandmother, too, is in my mind's eye, always busy in the kitchen, making meals. Here, it seems, the past is never fully gone.

"And Gram? What does she think about all this?"

"Never asked her, either. I don't think your grandparents understand what's happening, and I don't mean that in a bad way. Remember, they're from a different time when the world was a simpler place. Back then, the times, the people, were more innocent. They didn't have all the technology and distractions, the complexity that you had."

"Life was slower, more meaningful," I add.

"Exactly. No complicated thoughts because such thoughts didn't put food on the table. All that ever mattered was living the day and surviving for the next one. Here, they wake up each morning and go about their day as they always did. If I had to guess, I think they believe they're still alive – living their lives, even in death."

"What about Mom?" I ask.

"You know your mother. Doesn't like to talk about things she doesn't fully understand. She's a person of great faith and it's that faith that sustains her. For her, this is heaven."

"Why does she think that?"

"Because she's forever with me."

His words make me smile. "She picks those memories with you in them."

"She remembers all those times we were together," he says, "and she holds on to them."

My mind wanders, skimming the surface of ideas, each one fluttering away before I can grasp it. Is this an eternal dream, where we're suspended in time with no way forward? Or is there something more, something beyond my reach, pushing us into this unyielding repetition? A gnawing feeling settles in my chest as if we are all trapped in a cycle, condemned to replay the same moments without ever breaking free.

"Are we," I stop, searching for the right words, "stuck, then? Stuck in time? Tied to what we lived, to our memories?"

My father chuckles softly. "There's that complexity I was talking about," he says. "Not sure exactly what you mean by all that. But what I do know is, over time, you'll pick up things here. Some of them will surprise you."

The idea whirls in my mind. "What things?"

He sighs, the kind of sigh that carries more than just air. "I wanted to give you space, to let you take your time here, to let you grow into it. I wanted to teach you everything I know about this place. But now . . . I don't know if that's still possible. You were always so curious."

"I'm sorry."

"Don't be," he smiles. "I should've known better. Where to start? Hmmm . . . let me see. Well, you'll be able to visit some of your favorite places, either as they are currently or as you remember them. You'll be able to move through your memories and relive them, or move through other people's memories, those you were part of when they relive them. And others will share their memories with you if they want to. When that happens, you'll see and feel whatever they feel, their thoughts and emotions too."

My thoughts churn, each one trying to latch onto the fragments of what he's saying. I can't seem to catch hold of it all at once.

"How do I do all that?"

"Usually, it begins when you think of a memory. Before you know it, you're there, right in it. But controlling where you go takes practice. Be patient."

"How can you control your thoughts and emotions? It seems like an impossible task to me."

"Just be patient," he reminds me.

"What if you think of a hurtful memory?"

His hand is warm and heavy on my shoulder. "There's no wrong memory," he tells me. "The important thing is not to be afraid. Recognize and acknowledge the emotions each memory brings up. Do this, even if it's painful. But you don't have to stay stuck in those emotions. With awareness and practice, you'll learn how to observe them, how to accept your feelings without letting them overwhelm you."

"You said . . . relive. Can you change your memories? Change what happened?"

He shakes his head. "Can't rewrite the past. Can't make memories go away. No matter how hard you try. They stay with you."

"And you can see the memories of others?"

"Even though I'm here with you, I'm also in other places, with other people and their memories, as they relive them. It's a strange sensation. You're with them, feeling their emotions as your own. You see the world through their eyes and feel their joy, sorrow, laughter, and tears. They become a part of you."

"Several places all at the same time?"

He nods. "Like I told you before - everything happens all at once. What was that term you young folks used? To describe doing many things at one time."

"Multi-tasking?"

"That's it. It's kind of like that, I guess. But sometimes the connection to the past, being in so many places all at once, can be too much. It stretches you. You feel like a leaf blown from a tree. No roots, no moorings. You're at the mercy of the wind."

My father didn't realize it, but his words mirrored my own.

I whisper. "We're lost in time, Our memories are all we have to hold on to."

He hesitates briefly. "After a while, you get used to it, to all the movement. Sort of like slipping into an old pair of shoes."

"We've always been ghosts," I say. "The unseen."

He nods with a smile.

Even though everything he tells me is hard to comprehend, it somehow is beginning to make sense — in a way that only the next life can.

"If I'm here in this moment, on a Sunday afternoon, one of my favorite memories, where are you? What other places?"

He closes his eyes, and I can see the memories flitting across his face. "I'm everywhere. With your mother on our wedding day. With your grandparents playing cards on a Saturday evening. With your mother as she holds your brother in her arms just after he was born. With my father working the fields of the farm. With a friend in a meeting at the bank. And I'm at some of my favorite memories."

His eyes open, and his gaze meets mine, steady and clear.

"What's your favorite memory?" I ask, feeling the words rise out of my own curiosity, hoping to catch a glimpse of something treasured from his past.

His smile deepens, an expression so soft it fills the quiet between us. "This one," he replies. "Right here, with you."

The simplicity of his answer stirs something in me, a warmth spreading with undeniable certainty. And suddenly, I know he's right. This moment is exactly where I want to be - right here, with him.

"I'm sure there are other memories you cherish," I say. "Memories you often visit."

"There are many," he says softly. "A few that came one after another, a long time ago."

"Was I there with you?"

"No. You weren't born yet."

I feel a question forming, the urge to ask him to show me, to invite me into those moments. But I hesitate, unsure if he would rather keep them to himself. The words don't come, so I just sit there, watching him, waiting.

He looks at me and smiles, already understanding. "You want to see them, don't you?"

"Only if you want me to," I say, my voice barely a whisper.

He smiles. "I want you to," he says. "I want you to know me. Now remember - you'll see and feel everything I experienced. You'll feel my thoughts and feel my emotions. You'll remember what I experienced. Do you understand?"

"I understand," I say, steeling myself for what is to come.

Maggie gives a soft growl that startles me. She stands just ahead, her fur fluffed out, ears pulled back with a wary look in her eyes. It's as if she's trying to tell me something only she can sense.

"Be careful," she says. "Sometimes the past can show us things we'd rather not see."

"It's all right, girl," I reassure her, reaching down as if to calm her. "I'll be fine." Then I turn to my father. "Will I?"

He smiles, extending his hand. "Take my hand," he says, his voice carrying the quiet assurance I've leaned on all my life.

I look down at his hand, age-worn yet steady, and a rush of memories comes back - how many times that hand has guided me through dark places, and taught me to trust the steps ahead. For a moment, I pause, and then I reach out, feeling the warmth of his grasp.

We stay like that, connected, his hand in mine, our eyes meeting in a silent exchange.

"I won't let you fall," he tells me.

I smile, giving his hand a gentle squeeze. "I know you won't," I say closing my eyes.

THE WAR

It's October 1945. The Atlantic Ocean spreads wide and endless before me, its surface alive with vessels moving in steady purpose. Tankers, ore carriers, cargo ships, and massive battleships make their way toward the United States. Amid this procession, my attention narrows to one - a steam-powered troop transport, the USNS Aiken Victory, making its way to New York City.

There, on the deck, I find him: my father. He looks impossibly young, barely in his twenties, one of countless soldiers being ferried home from the front lines of a war that has consumed the world for years. As the ship rolls with the waves, he leans against the railing, his gaze fixed on the distant horizon. I call out to him, but my voice is lost in the wind and swallowed by the rhythms of the sea.

I watch as a soldier sidles up next to my father, leaning against the railing. He lights a cigarette. "Whatcha goin' to do when you get home?" he asks, his voice carrying a hint of a Southern drawl.

My father takes one last drag from his own cigarette, holding the smoke a moment before exhaling into the salt-laden breeze. He flicks the stub into the waves below. "Haven't given it much thought," he replies, his voice low and steady. "Been too busy trying to stay alive."

The soldier beside him gives a small nod, his gaze drifting momentarily to the ocean before shifting upward to the towering steam stacks of the ship. "That's all any of us were doing," he says, turning away from the railing to look up at the tall steam stacks of the ship. "Me, I'm goin' back to my family's farm. Just outside a lil' village in Georgia called Zebulon."

"What crops do you grow?" my father asks, his interest piqued.

"Corn," the soldier replies simply.

A faint smile appears on my father's face, the kind that barely lifts the lines around his mouth. "Same with us," he says. "We grow corn, some lettuce, other greens, too. Up in New York. Upstate. Near a town called Liverpool."

The soldier lets out a slow whistle, dragging the sound as though savoring its simplicity. "New York? Well, you're gonna have a much shorter trip home than me once we dock in the big city."

"Yeah," my father agrees, his voice softening. "I'm ready to see my family again."

"Me too," the soldier says, a wistful look crossing his face. He turns around, looking out over the ocean. "It's been too long." He pauses, then grins at my father. "Look at us. Just a couple of ol' farm boys."

My father nods with a hint of amusement in his eyes. "Guess so."

They stand there for a moment, watching the waves lap against the side of the ship. The sun warms their faces, and the wind tousles their hair. Despite the horrors they've witnessed, there's a sense of hope and excitement in the air – they're going home.

"Got a gal?" the soldier asks, breaking the companionable silence.

My father slides his hand into his pocket, the gesture careful and unhurried, as though he's reaching for something more than a simple keepsake. When he pulls out the photograph, he holds it carefully between his fingers with a reverence that makes the moment feel larger. "We just started dating. Then the war started," he explains, showing the picture to his newfound friend.

I lean over his shoulder to catch a glimpse of the image. It's my mother, decades younger. Her face radiates a calm confidence, her eyes bright and full of a life not yet shaped by the years ahead. The picture captures her beauty in a way I hadn't fully appreciated before, and for a moment, it feels as if she's right there with us.

The soldier studies the picture and nods, a small, easy smile crossing his face. "She's real pretty."

"What about you?" my father asks, his thumb grazing the edge of the photograph. "You got someone waiting for you?"

The soldier shakes his head, a small, amused smile tugging at the corners of his mouth. "Never had much time for them. But there's this one girl - she's a friend of my sister's. Red hair, green eyes, and a smile that could light up the whole place. She's sharp, funny, always knows how to get me to laugh. Been thinking about her a lot lately. I'm gonna ask her out, I think." He takes a slow drag of his cigarette, the smoke curling into the air. "So, where'd you fight?"

"The Ardennes, Battle of the Bulge. 9th infantry. The old reliables," my father says, a hint of pride in his voice. "You?"

"Normandy. Germany. 3rd army. 9th armored."

"Patton," my father says, recognition dawning.

"Yessir, old blood and guts himself."

There's a moment of silence as they both contemplate the weight of their experiences. "Heard you guys were at one of those camps," my father says quietly.

The soldier's expression changes, a shadow passing over him. "Yeah," he says, his voice uneven. "We were. Worse than anything I could've imagined. Never seen anything like it. The things that those poor folks went through." He looks away, as though searching for something in the distance. "I still dream about it, and not in the way you'd want to remember anything."

My father shakes his head. "I can't imagine. I've seen some things in my time, too. Things that I wish I could forget."

"Do you think we'll ever forget them?" the soldier asks, his eyes haunted by memories. "Forget the terrible things we've seen?"

My father doesn't answer right away. He stares out at the ocean, searching for the answer in the endless blue. Finally, he says, "I sure hope so. But I'm afraid there are some things too terrible to forget. They stay with us, always."

A heavy silence falls between them. They've seen things no man should ever have to see, done things no man should ever have to do. But they survived.

"At least we can talk about it," my father says. "I guess we're the lucky ones."

The soldier smiles sadly. "Yeah, we're the lucky ones alright." He pats my father on the back. "Well, good luck to you. And say hi to that girl of yours for me."

My father returns the smile. "I will." His eyes follow the soldier as he walks away, swallowed up by the mass of troops on deck.

I watch my father's face shift, his expression smoothing into something unreadable, a careful distance settling over him. He closes his eyes, and I find myself wondering what's in his mind. Is it the smell of smoke and blood? The sound of gunfire and screams? The faces of friends, dead and dying?

When he opens his eyes again, they're filled with a determination I've never seen before. I know, in that moment, that he's made a decision. He'll never speak about the war again. He can't bear to relive it, can't make it a burden on others.

But as he turns his gaze back to the vast ocean, I see the truth written in the set of his shoulders, the clench of his jaw. The war is part of him now, etched into his soul. Time may silence the sounds of gunfire and explosions, and may fade the images of death and destruction, but it'll never erase them completely

As the USNS Aiken Victory pushes through the waves toward home, my father stands alone on the deck, a young man shaped by war. The salt air stings his face, and the steady thrum of the engines vibrates through his boots, but his mind is somewhere far off, lost in the haze of what has been and what might come. He tries to picture a life beyond the battlefield, beyond the suffocating grind of four years of hell. Yet the future feels uncertain as if it exists just beyond the edge of what he can see, hazy and unformed.

Did we build a better future? he asks himself.

The question lingers in his mind, unanswered, as the vast ocean stretches endlessly before him. My father grips the railing, the cool metal grounding him in this moment, even as his thoughts drift. The waves rise and fall in an unbroken rhythm, indifferent to his doubts, to his hopes.

Did we build a better future? The words repeat themselves, not as an accusation but as a plea, a desperate hope that everything endured had been for something more than survival.

He closes his eyes, the roar of the sea filling the silence left by his uncertainty. Faces flash in his memory - friends who will never stand on a ship like this, their laughter now a ghostly echo in his mind. The sacrifice feels impossibly large, almost beyond understanding.

Could a better future ever be enough to balance what was lost?

But then he opens his eyes, and there, on the horizon, a faint smudge of land appears. It's still distant, indistinct, but it's there - a promise taking shape. He doesn't know what awaits him when he gets home: the joyful faces of his parents; the nervous, hopeful smile of the girlfriend he left behind, my mom, waiting to see if time and distance have changed him beyond recognition.

A gull wheels overhead, its cry sharp against the steady hum of the engines. My father exhales slowly, releasing some of the tension knotted in his chest. He thinks of my mom - of the letters he kept folded in his pocket, worn thin from handling. Her words were a thread that pulled him through the worst of it, promising a future he could almost believe in.

The horizon grows clearer now, the smudge resolving into skyscrapers, the faint outline of the big city. The first step to getting home. He doesn't know if the future is better, doesn't know if peace will feel anything like it should. But for the first time in years, hope feels real - not a distant idea, but a tangible thing, just as close as the shoreline drawing near.

THE STATUE

After a long journey at sea, my father's ship edges toward New York City. The skyline, unfamiliar and electrifying, begins to take shape in the hazy morning light. He's heard the stories, of course, but no words could prepare him for the scale of it all. The towering buildings rise like monuments to a world he's yet to know, their silhouettes cutting sharply against the pale sky. The ship inches closer, and the noise of the city begins to spill over the harbor - the hum of voices, the thrum of engines, the clamor of lives intersecting.

He leans against the rail, squinting to catch every detail. People swarm the docks and streets, moving with a purpose that seems both exhilarating and impossible to match. After the slow monotony of the voyage, with nothing but the endless horizon to mark the passing of time, the frenetic energy of the city feels overwhelming. Still, beneath his anticipation lies an undeniable pull - a yearning to stand among them, to anchor himself to this unfamiliar earth and feel its vitality coursing through him. The air is different here, heavy with salt and industry, and it fills him with the quiet certainty that his life is about to change irrevocably.

The ship nudges forward, tracing its path toward the upper bay. In the distance, the Statue of Liberty emerges, steady and luminous against the backdrop of water and sky. It grips him - not just for its beauty but for the ideals it seems to embody: the belief in possibility, the call to freedom. He remembers his father's voice, steady and firm, and I hear it in his mind.

"Never forget – you're an American first."

My father smiles as he thinks of his father's words. They always resonated with him, and now they feel more important than ever. He's an American, and he's proud of it.

All the people who struggled to come here to make a living, and all those who fought and died for this country Their sacrifices, their hopes, are what have shaped this country. He feels small before their collective effort, humbled by the vastness of it all.

The ship draws closer to the Brooklyn Navy Yard, and he closes his eyes, letting out a deep breath, the kind that seems to carry years of strain and longing. From the docks, cheers swell, hands rise and wave - an embrace made of sound and motion. His throat tightens. Pressing his lips together, he absorbs the enormity of the moment: four years of war, of watching life stripped bare, and somehow he has made it through. He is here. Home again.

When the ship finally docks, he sees the families waiting on the shore, their faces lit with an eager brightness. Wives clutch children to their sides, their hands restless in nervous excitement. Then, at the first glimpse of a beloved face, they surge forward, an unstoppable tide of joy and relief. Husbands and fathers are swept into tight embraces, laughter spilling into sobs, the salty air carrying the sharp, unmistakable notes of homecoming.

My father doesn't step forward immediately. He surveys the scene before him - the hum of joy that ripples through the crowd, electric with reunion. Yet, beneath the celebration, an unspoken sorrow threads its way through his thoughts, thoughts of the men who once stood shoulder to shoulder with him, now absent. Their faces surface in his memory, etched with the life they once shared, their voices murmuring fragments of jokes, dreams, and futures they would never live to see.

Finally, he steps off the gangplank, the cheers and embraces surrounding him filling the air with a strange, unfamiliar warmth. It's a moment of joy, but one that feels oddly distant as if it belongs to someone else. His heart, heavy with the remnants of what he's left behind, can't quite catch up to the celebration. There is a hollowness within him, a quiet ache that no amount of welcome can erase.

Too many have returned in caskets. Too many families have lost precious souls.

Will they ever find a way to heal? To let go?

So much has been lost.

Still, he moves forward, one step after another, toward whatever waits. The air hums with possibility, but beneath it lies a truth he cannot shake: the war may be over, but its shadows remain.

HOME

My father is sitting on a bus, his eyes fixed on the passing landscape as if trying to memorize every detail. The fields and forests blur together, a patchwork quilt of greens and golds that seems both achingly familiar and strangely foreign. Just that morning, at the Brooklyn Navy Yard, he had been processed out, the crisp creases of his discharge papers still pressed into the pocket of his coat. Now, he's on his way north to Albany, where another bus will take him home, a place that feels both distant and near.

The journey stretches out before him, eight hours of highway and loneliness. But my father doesn't mind. He's content to simply sit and watch the world go by, each mile bringing him closer to the place he's dreamed of for four years. He makes the transfer at Albany. Another bus, the familiar hum of a new set of wheels beneath him. He's heading home now, and that, he thinks, is enough.

As the farm fields roll past the window, my father is silent, a kind of quiet settling in that I can't quite place. The joy he'd expected, the relief of finally being back stateside, seems to have slipped from his grasp, replaced by something more elusive and unsettling. Memories of war rise in him, sharp and uninvited. The acrid smell of gunpowder, the raw taste of fear, the faces of comrades lost in battle - his mind holds them all, as clear and close as if they were standing beside him. Each image tugs at him with a familiarity that feels like a wound, one that hasn't fully healed.

I can hear his thoughts in my mind, though they aren't spoken aloud. Will time heal these scars? Should it? Is there something wrong with letting it all fade, with forgetting the faces of those who didn't make it home?

The bus hits a pothole, jolting my father from his thoughts. He blinks, realizing they're nearing his stop. As he gathers his meager belongings - a duffel bag that seems to weigh as much as his memories - he catches sight of his reflection in the window. The face that looks back at him is older, harder than the one that had left home four years ago.

Will they recognize me?

Three quick steps down, and suddenly he's standing on solid ground again. The morning air is crisp and sweet, carrying the mingled scents of earth and growing things. He takes a deep breath, letting it fill his lungs, chasing away the phantom smells of war that have haunted him for so long. Down the dusty dirt road, he can make out the familiar silhouette of the family farm - neat rows of apple trees standing in quiet order, waves of corn stalks swaying gently in the breeze. It's a scene straight out of his dreams, one he'd clung to during the darkest nights overseas.

Though his mind is still a battlefield of memories, being home makes them feel a bit more distant, like thunder rumbling on the horizon rather than explosions at his feet. The familiar sights, smells, and sounds of home bring him a sense of peace, easing the burdens of the past. As he starts down the road, his steps growing lighter with each familiar landmark, he looks forward to seeing everyone.

As he nears the old farmhouse, its weathered clapboards glowing in the morning light, he sees his parents standing at the door. They've been waiting for him. His mother's apron is dusted with flour, evidence of the welcome-home pie she's no doubt been baking since dawn. His father stands beside her, his hands, worn from years of labor, reach for him first, steady and sure.

"We've missed you, son. More than you can ever know," my grandfather says, his voice gruff with emotion.

My grandmother wraps her arms around him, her tears dampening the shoulder of my father's uniform. "Every minute of every day," she whispers, "we worried about you and your brothers. Everyone is back home and safe now."

The scene unfolds before me like a photograph come to life, blurring the lines between memory and reality. My grandmother, a woman I had only known through stories and old photographs, moves with a life I never expected to see. She died shortly after I was born, leaving behind a legacy that always felt just out of reach. Now, watching her with my father and grandfather, I feel as though I've stepped through the looking glass into a world both familiar and utterly foreign.

My father stands quietly, overcome by a swell of emotions too powerful to put into words. He inhales the scents of his childhood - the lavender soap his mother used, the earthy richness of his father's tobacco - and something inside him shifts, loosening, as though a long-held tension is finally being released.

"I'm home," he finally manages, the words barely a sound.

"Yes, you are," my grandmother smiles through her tears. "And we're never letting you go again."

They hug once more, a tangle of arms and emotions that seems to stretch on forever. My father doesn't want to let go, afraid that if he does, this fragile moment might slip away, like the dreams of home he had clung to during all those years apart.

I'll never take both of you for granted ever again, his thought wanders to me. I'm blessed to have you in my life.

They make their way inside the farmhouse, my father's footsteps heavy on the worn floorboards that creak a familiar welcome. The kitchen is warm and bright, suffused with the aroma of cinnamon and apples. My grandmother pours him a glass of fresh milk, cool and creamy, and settles beside him at the table, its surface scarred with the marks of a thousand family meals.

"So," she says, her eyes bright with curiosity and concern, "tell us everything."

He shakes his head, suddenly weary beyond measure. "No, Ma," he says softly. "I'm home for good now. I want to try to leave those memories behind, all of them."

She understands and reaches across the table, her hand, rough from years of labor, gently covering his. They sit together in a comfortable silence, the steady ticking of the old mantel clock marking the passage of time.

Finally, my father takes a deep breath. "Ma, there's someplace I need to go," he says, his words carrying a sense of finality. "I don't expect you to understand, but –"

"I know," she says softly, her eyes filling with a deep sadness, born of a mother's intuition. "I understand. You do what you need to do."

The air in the kitchen seems to thicken, laden with unspoken grief and understanding. My father stands, the chair scraping against the floorboards, a sound that seems to echo the scraping in his heart. He knows where he needs to go, and his mother knows it too.

THE BOY AND THE OLD MAN

But as the memory of my father's return gradually softens and slips away, another one begins to emerge. It's a memory of war, one my father could never shake, a place he would always return to, and he showed it to me.

It's November 1944. The Allies are closing in on Nazi Germany from all sides. The Russians are pushing from the east, the British and Americans from the west, and the Canadians and French from the north. It's the last days of the war and the Nazis are in retreat. Hitler and his inner circle are holed up in a bunker beneath the Chancellery in Berlin. Defeat is inevitable, but they're not going down without a fight. In one last, desperate attempt, they begin to conscript children as young as eight, arming them with rifles. The children are told to hunt down Allied soldiers and to kill without hesitation.

I can see my father among the other soldiers, standing at attention, listening to their commander.

"It's tough!" the commander barks, his voice hard and demanding. "I know it's tough! But if a kid comes at you with a gun -" He pauses, his face pinched with some sorrow that I can't name. "You know what you've got to do. This isn't just a fight! It's more than that! This is war! Don't forget that. You've got to be ready to do whatever it takes to protect yourself and your fellow soldiers."

The battalion starts its march through a small German town, a slow and steady advance through the narrow streets. The air hangs heavy with smoke and the sharp scent of gunpowder Tanks roll down the middle of the street, their massive treads shaking the earth beneath them, flanked by infantry on either side. The town is eerily quiet, and the only sound is the soft crunch of the ground beneath the tanks' weight. In the doorway of a collapsed house, a woman stands, her figure outlined against the ruin. Her face is pale, drawn with exhaustion, and her eyes are pools of sorrow, the kind that only time can carve deep.

I see my father, his face grim and determined. His gaze sweeps over the town, sharp and searching. Something bad is about to happen. He mutters under his breath, trying to convince himself it's just nerves, that his instincts are overreacting. Still, he can't quiet the gnawing sensation that something is wrong.

He keeps scanning the surrounding area, looking for anything that can be a threat, but there's no movement, nothing.

That's until a boy steps out from the shadows of an alley. The boy's face is dirty and smudged, his eyes wide with fear, and his body tense.

Slowly, he raises his hand, and I see that he's holding a pistol. His hands are shaking, and the gun wobbles in his grip.

My father's movements are quick, automatic - his rifle raised before he even fully processes the threat. His finger rests lightly on the trigger, the sensation familiar, but he pauses. The boy, no older than ten, stands frozen in front of him.

The thought of squeezing the trigger tightens something inside my father, a relentless tension. His heart beats faster, each pulse harder than the last. Sweat gathers on his forehead, cold against his skin, but he still can't bring himself to move. He watches the boy, the stakes clear in his mind, and waits for something he cannot name.

There's a panic in the boy's eyes, a frantic search for a way out that isn't there. But my father stands steady, rifle aimed with an unsettling stillness. He knows the power he holds, the ease of ending it with a single motion, but he hesitates. The tension in the air seems to thicken, and my father feels a sharp, sour taste of fear rising in the back of his throat.

They stand there for what seems like forever, frozen in time.

Then, from the distance, a voice breaks the silence - a shout, piercing the stillness.

"Nim die waffe runter! Nim die waffe runter!"

The voice cuts through the air, catching my father off guard, but he doesn't flinch. His gaze remains locked on the boy, rifle steady in his hands, his finger poised on the trigger. The boy doesn't look away either, his eyes fixed on my father, sharp and unwavering, as if neither of them would break the standoff.

Again, the shout comes, more cutting this time. "Nim die waffe runter! Nim die waffe runter!"

My father doesn't flinch. He remains fixed, his gaze steady, locked on the boy. His face offers nothing - no sign of fear, no sign of pity. Just silence. The boy meets his stare, but there's a tremor in his eyes now, a sheen that gathers, threatening to spill over.

"Bitte, töte mich nicht!" the boy cries, his voice rising, desperate. "Bitte, töte mich nicht!"

My father doesn't understand. He doesn't even blink. His eyes stay trained on the boy, still, waiting for something, a twitch perhaps, anything that might tell him what comes next.

The shout comes again from the distance. "Nim die waffe runter! Nim die waffe runter!"

With a trembling hand, the boy slowly, ever so slowly, lowers the pistol, allowing it to slip from his fingers. It tumbles to the ground, landing with a dull thud. Without a second glance, he turns and runs, his footsteps quickening as he disappears into the shadows of the alley.

My father watches as the boy slips into the shadows, his figure swallowed by the dark. He lowers his rifle, a long, slow exhale escaping him. The tension lifts, just enough. Turning toward the voice, he sees an old man standing off to the side, leaning heavily on a wooden stick. The man's clothes hang in tatters, threadbare and frayed. His face is a map of time, every wrinkle telling a story, his eyes reflecting a deep, quiet sorrow that feels too large for him to carry alone.

"Geh nach hause zu deiner familie," he says to my father with a tired voice. "Lass uns in ruhe."

My father doesn't understand the old man but there's something in his eyes that makes him listen.

"Geh nach hause zu deiner familie," the old man repeats with a wave of his hand, his words falling out in a rush. "Geh nach hause zu deiner familie. Lass uns in ruhe."

The old man shakes his head, his lips pressed into a thin line, a quiet disapproval settling over his features. With a careful step, he turns and begins to walk away with a slight limp. His shoulders are stooped and his head hangs low, as though the weight of years has pulled him into himself.

As my father watches the old man go, he turns to the other soldiers. "Does anyone know what he said?" he asks.

"He told the kid to drop the pistol," a soldier says.

"What about what he said to me?"

"Told you to go home to your family. That it's all over. To leave them in peace."

My father has seen men like him before, men broken by the things they've seen. He thinks of the boy, wondering about the life he once knew, about the home he once had, and what it must look like now. He images ruin - a roof that has collapsed, floors scattered with broken remnants, furniture upended, and windows boarded up against the world outside.

His parents . . . are they alive?

He wants to believe they are, but he can't shake the fear that they may have been killed in the fighting.

What has the war done to him?

My father imagines the boy before it all - laughing, running with friends through sunlit fields, his eyes full of hope for a future he couldn't have known would slip away.

But the boy is not that boy anymore. The lightness of youth, the freedom of those days, is gone, consumed by the brutality of war.

The boy - he's something else, now. But what?

"You okay, soldier?" the commander startles my father.

My father gives a quick nod. "Yessir."

The commander places a hand on my father's shoulder. "War changes everything and takes so much. Things that are lost can't be replaced and will never return. It's a hard truth, but one that we all gotta learn to accept."

My father looks down into the shadows of the alley one last time. The boy is gone, lost within the heaps of stone, wood, and broken glass. He knows that the war is close to being over, but he also knows that the scars it leaves will never fully heal.

A LESSON

My father's memory slips away, becoming distant in a haze. I blink and find my focus caught on a slice of icebox cake, sitting on a fork I'm holding. It glistens - layers of chocolate pudding, whipped cream, and softened vanilla wafers, each one poised to melt and dissolve in an instant. Without thinking, I take a bite. The pudding is rich, the wafers just soft enough, and the cream lightens it all. It tastes like a memory that comes back to life.

My mother and grandmother are gathering plates and wiping the table, but they both stop to watch me.

"How is it?" my mother asks with a knowing smile at the corner of her mouth.

I mumble through another bite, "Just like I remember. So wonderful. It's been so long."

They exchange a glance, a quiet understanding in their eyes, something rooted in years of shared experience. My father sits across from me, his hands wrapped around a cup of coffee, his gaze steady, offering the comfort of his presence without needing to say much.

"You didn't fall," he says with a hint of pride, nodding as if he's more certain of it now.

"No, sir," I reply, swallowing the last bite. "I didn't."

He takes a slow sip of his coffee, his gaze distant, as if his thoughts are caught somewhere just beyond reach. "So, what do you think?" he asks.

The question catches me off guard. I look down at my empty plate, letting his words settle between us, their impact quiet but undeniable. "War . . ." I begin, the word feeling foreign in my mouth. I pause, searching for the right way to frame something so vast. "I can't pretend to understand it - the pain, the loss, everything you endured. It feels too big, too far from anything I've known. But you kept going. I don't know how you did it."

My father's gaze drifts past me, his eyes fixed on something invisible but immense. The silence between us thickens. It's the kind that demands more patience than words. When he finally speaks, his voice is low, careful, as if the truth he's about to share might splinter under its own gravity.

"What choice did any of us have?" he says, his tone carrying a trace of bitterness that doesn't quite land, softened instead by something like resignation. "You look for something in yourself, even if it's buried so deep you're not sure it's even there anymore. You tell yourself a better day's coming. Not for you, no," he adds, his mouth pulling into a faint, humorless curve. "Maybe not even for the people you know, or for anyone you'll ever meet. But for someone - someone further ahead, someone who has yet to exist. And you keep moving forward because . . . well . . . because believing in that is better than the alternative."

He pauses, the words heavy but not unwelcome. I shift slightly, unsure whether to respond. But before I can, he exhales a faint, weary laugh. "It's a cruel kind of hope, isn't it? The sort that doesn't belong to you but still demands everything from you." His eyes finally meet mine, and there's something in them - not quite despair, not quite resolve, but a mixture of the two that feels uncomfortably real. "It's all that we had," he says simply. "And it was enough."

I look at him, studying his face as if seeing it for the first time, and his words take root in a way nothing he's ever said has before. Growing up, he seldom talked about the war. When I'd press him, he'd wave the questions away, saying it was in the past and that life was about moving forward. Now, hearing him, the meaning comes through at last, whole and unbroken. All those years, he had been trying to teach me something simple and unshakable: that sometimes, continuing is all there is, and that is enough.

"The now that passes produces time, the now that remains produces eternity," I murmur.

He gives me a curious look. "I don't understand?"

"It's about the future," I explain. "Always moving forward, never turning back."

He smiles, taking another sip of coffee, his gaze soft.

"Can I ask you something?" I venture.

"Of course."

"Why did you show me that memory of the German boy? How could it be one of your favorites?"

He lets out a quiet breath. "Because it taught me something invaluable. Something I'm grateful for, even now."

"And what's that?"

He pauses as if choosing his words carefully. "That you don't have to die to be a casualty of war."

He reaches his hand across the table, and when I take it, he holds on, closing his eyes as if finding strength in the quiet gesture.

A LIFE OF SECRETS

Daddy, why do people keep secrets?

Sometimes people keep secrets because they don't want to hurt someone's feelings.

So . . . it's okay to keep secrets if it's for a good reason?

As long as it's for the right reason.

Right reason? What's the right reason?

That keeping the secret doesn't hurt anyone.

I think I understand, Daddy.

Good. But always remember - when you know a secret, it's important to think carefully about whether it's something you should share.

Daddy, do you have secrets?

Everyone has secrets, son. Everyone.

THE FEEBLE MAN

I find myself in my grandfather's backyard. A memory that drifts around me quietly like a mist, hardly noticeable until it's there. My eyes are drawn to the gazebo. In my later years, I remembered it as run-down, the paint peeling away in strips, the wood sagging and tired. But now, it stands proud, almost unfamiliar in its transformation. Made of cedar, it glows softly, gleaming a gentle blue and crisp white trim. The shingles on the black roof are perfectly aligned, each one reflecting the meticulous effort of the gazebo's builder. It's a place that invites you to step inside, nestled under the willow tree that seems smaller than I remember, though its branches stretch outward with the same grace.

I can see my parents sitting together in the gazebo, their heads angled toward each other, drawn close by some invisible force. They're young, their faces lit with an ease that feels almost unfamiliar to me, their laughter rising and falling in a rhythm as natural as the breeze. The air around them seems lighter, and softer, as if this moment belongs to a world untouched by everything that would come after.

Their eyes meet, and in that quiet exchange, there's something more profound than words could ever convey. It's a kind of knowing, an understanding so deep it doesn't need to be spoken aloud. Watching them, I realize that this must be a time before they were married, before the responsibilities that would later shape their lives, when they were simply two young souls reveling in each other's presence, unburdened by anything but this gentle moment.

Watching them from a distance, it's clear they're just themselves, two young people wholly focused on each other, their happiness untouched by anything outside this moment. It's a snapshot of possibility, a version of them that feels both softly out of reach and so near it almost hurts.

My heart fills with envy. I remember my younger days with my wife, when the world felt wide open and we moved through it without a map, certain only of each other. But those days are past, and now I'm only a ghost, watching from the shadows of my father's memory, catching fragments of a memory that isn't even my own.

I take a step closer. My father is tall, his presence commanding yet familiar. His dark, thick hair sweeps back, drawing attention to the sharp line of his jaw and the quiet kindness that lingers in his eyes. He's dressed in a light brown suit, perfectly fitted, paired with a slim black tie that seems chosen more for simplicity than effect. Everything about him speaks of a calm assurance as if ease were something he carried with him, effortlessly.

And my mother - she's radiant. I've only seen her this young in photographs, but nothing quite captures it. Her skin is fair, with a softness like the petal of a rose, her cheeks tinged with a blush that seems fresh from the morning light. Her hair, dark as a raven's feather, falls in loose waves past her shoulders. She wears a simple white dress that flows just below her knees, and around her neck rests a delicate silver necklace with a heart that catches the light. She's the essence of beauty, untouched by time.

I move closer still, just enough to feel the warmth of her breath brushing against my cheek. I gaze into her eyes. They're dark and fathomless, like two soft glowing embers, warm yet distant. There's something in them, something I can't quite reach, and I find myself drawn in. They hold so much, so many unspoken things, and I can't help but want to know them all.

She glances up and smiles at me, and my heart falters in response. A breath catches in my throat, too quick, too loud.

Can she see me?

I hold perfectly still, not even daring to breathe, my senses sharp, straining for any hint that she might notice.

Does she know I'm here?

It's impossible. This is my father's memory, not mine. I'm nothing more than a silent observer, a presence without form. And yet, there's this nagging sensation, a prickling at the back of my mind, that somehow, she knows I'm here.

She turns away from me and snuggles up to my father. I take a breath, relieved. But even as I watch them, something lingers - an image of her gaze, direct and unblinking, as if she knew I was there, watching.

Seeing my parents so genuinely content makes me smile. The depth of their love for one another is deeply felt. It's a strong and special bond that'll last a lifetime.

When I was young, I would remember waking in the quiet of the night, my room a shadowed place, the world outside dimmed and distant. Somewhere in the house, my parents' voices would rise and fall, their words indistinct, but their tone a familiar comfort. It was a rhythm that didn't need to be understood - it simply was. I would lie there, the sheets pulled tight around me, listening as their voices filtered through the walls, becoming something like music.

A lullaby, not in melody but in the gentle reassurance of its cadence, offering a peace no rhyme could match.

I would close my eyes and picture them, not as they appeared during the day - my father with his steady gaze, my mother with her easy smile - but as they were in those moments when the world grew quiet. Their faces seemed changed then, gentler, as though the night had softened the sharp edges. The light from the moon would fall over them, transforming my everyday parents into something otherworldly, figures from a story, both familiar and strange.

In those moments, suspended between wakefulness and dreams, I'd make a silent vow to myself. Someday, I too would find a love like theirs. I'd discover what it meant to be so entwined with another person that their heartbeat became a second pulse in my own chest. It seemed like a fairy tale then, but it was one I desperately wanted to believe in.

Years later, I found that love with my wife. It wasn't a carbon copy of my parents' relationship - how could it be? We were different, our lives unfolding in their own ways, shaped by our individual histories, our peculiarities, and the things that made us whole. But at the heart of it, there was something undeniable, something enduring, that mirrored what I had witnessed. We'd lie awake, side by side, in the quiet hours, sharing thoughts too intimate to speak aloud in the light of day. Our fears, our desires, and all the vulnerabilities we rarely dared to name floated between us, examined and held gently. And through it all, there was one thing we knew for certain: no matter what came, we'd face it, together.

I smile.

Looking around, the backyard is awash in sunlight, as the flowers in the beds burst forth in a vibrant kaleidoscope of color. The sound of voices floats in the breeze and my attention is drawn to the group of people gathered just beyond the gazebo and willow. They are strangers to me. Well-dressed, they laugh and talk, carefree and happy. They seem like they belong to a world I can't quite reach, a world where I've never been.

I stare at them, mesmerized, caught up in their effortless harmony, trying to understand. What's the occasion? What brings them together?

Then, it comes to me. It's a Sunday afternoon, and these must be family and friends, gathered after church to share a meal.

I glance back to my parents, just in time to see my father lean in to kiss my mother. It's a brief kiss, a soft touch of his lips to her cheek, yet it makes her laugh, a smile spreading across her face that seems to brighten everything around us.

But then I notice something about my father. He shifts, his eyes darting, like maybe he's forgotten something. There's a slight stiffness in his posture and a restlessness in the way he moves. He's been planning something, and he's going through a mental checklist.

He wonders if he has it.

Has what?

He presses his hand against his suit pocket, fingers brushing the fabric, feeling for something.

Yes, it's there.

My mother notices that he's preoccupied with something. "It made me smile when Dad told me you were going to church with us today," she says to him, her voice soft, almost teasing. "It was a nice surprise."

"I wanted to be here," he replies, the words coming slowly. "Make up for the time lost . . . with everything that's happened. The war and all."

She reaches out, her hand resting lightly on his arm. "Those days are behind us. You're here now, safe, back with us."

He looks at her for a moment, his expression shifting as he asks, "Do you remember when we first met?" His eyes, steady and warm, stay fixed on hers.

"How can I forget," she says with a smile. "It was on a Saturday. Mom and me went to the market for some vegetables and chicken. I'd seen your family stand before, with your younger brother and sisters there, but never you. And then I saw you, in the back, taking bushel baskets of lettuce off the truck. I knew I had to talk to you. But I wasn't sure who you were. I thought maybe you were a farmhand. So, I asked your brother. He laughed and told me you might as well be a farmhand, before calling you over. Do you remember our first conversation, what you said to me?"

My father laughs. "Of course. I said, 'How can I help you?'"

"What did you think when you first saw me?" she asks with a precocious smile.

There's no hesitation.

"You were the most beautiful thing I'd ever seen," he says, feeling a bit embarrassed by his frankness. "I felt like I was standing in a dream where everything around me stopped. I couldn't take my eyes off you. Every part of you was a masterpiece, from your hair to your eyes. Your skin was like porcelain, and your lips were the perfect shade of pink." He takes a deep breath and lets it out slowly. "I wanted to touch you, to stay in that moment and never leave."

He's surprised at how emotional he is.

They hold hands in a moment of silence, listening to the gentle breeze through the willow.

"Do you hear it?" my father asks.

"Hear what?"

"The music. It's all around us. If you listen closely you can hear it too."

They sit, lost in the sound, something like a thousand harps playing in unison, their strings woven together in a soft, wonderful harmony.

"Beautiful, isn't it?" my mother says, her voice drifting. "So peaceful. When you're in love, nothing else matters. There's no need for words, just the melody of the wind to fill your ears."

My father's gaze softens. "You know, I kept a picture of you with me," he says, his voice quiet, almost a confession. "Whenever things got rough, I'd take it out and think of you, of us, of us together. It was my reminder that there was still good in the world, even when I couldn't see it. It was the only thing that kept me going."

She snuggles into my father's shoulder, her head resting against his chest. "There's a picture of you on my dresser." Her voice is a thread of sound, barely there. "While you were gone, I looked at it every day, just thinking about you, hoping and praying you were safe. But sometimes my mind would wander to dark places. I'd worry that something had happened to you. If I had lost you, I don't know what I would've done. You mean everything to me. I'm so glad that that horrible war is over."

My father's arm tightens around her. "I'm here now," he says. "I'm not going anywhere."

A thought from him comes to me, quiet, but clear: Now is a good time.

He clears his throat.

"You know, we're different in more ways than one," he says, his voice low, almost reflective. "You're always so full of life. You meet each day with this bright-eyed excitement like there's something new to discover around every corner. You dive into experiences, headfirst, without hesitation. Me? I'm more careful. I think things through too much, always weighing the risks."

She nods, absorbing his words. "That's true. We don't always see things the same way. But I think it works for us. It gives us a chance to grow by learning from each other."

"You really think that?" he asks, a note of surprise in his voice.

She grins, her smile wide and confident. "Of course. If we were alike in every way, we'd get bored so fast. But with our differences, there's always something new to discover about each other. We're never at a loss for conversation, for something to do. It makes things feel new every time."

He exhales, the tension in his body easing slightly. "I never thought of it like that," he admits, his breath a little shallow. He pauses, as though testing the weight of his next words. "There's something I've been meaning to ask you."

"What?"

"I'm going to get some money for being in the war."

"Really?"

"Yes. All the GIs are. My brothers too."

"That's great."

His eyes brighten, the excitement in his voice barely contained. "We're going to take the money and open a hardware store. We already found a spot, close to where they'll be building houses. We're going to have everything the other stores have, but we'll have a bigger selection of tools, and our prices will be better. We're even going to buy a truck, so we can make deliveries."

"That all sounds fantastic. So exciting. But . . . who's going to help your father with the farm?"

"He's going to sell most of the land and maybe work in the foundry."

"Foundry? The one where my father works?"

My father nods. "Yeah."

"That's a lot of change," she says, her eyes full of wonder.

"There's one more thing," he says, his voice lowering.

"What is it?"

"My father's going to give me a couple of acres of his land to build a house."

"A house? What for?"

I can feel my father's heart pounding in his chest. He hesitates, a rush of things filling him up. He's rehearsed this moment for weeks, but now that it's here, his thoughts are tangled.

Taking a deep breath, he reaches into his suit pocket, his fingers fumbling with the fabric. He pulls out a ring, a simple gold band with a small diamond. It sparkles with all the promise of the future. He takes her hand, his heart still pounding.

My mother immediately gasps, covering her mouth with her hand. Her eyes widen and her face flushes.

He lowers his voice, the words coming out slower than he intended. "I know it's not much," he says. "I wish it was more." His throat tightens, and he takes a breath, trying to steady himself. "But I need to ask you . . . will you marry me?" He hesitates for a moment, then continues, his words almost tumbling over one another. "Before you say anything, I want you to know that I spoke with your father first. I asked for his permission, and he gave it."

She looks at the ring, then back at him.

For a moment, everything else disappears. There's no noise, no movement - just the two of them. My mother, aware of the depth of his love, feels it rush through her, clear and undeniable. It's a love she's always known, but never so openly, so fully given before. In this moment, she understands - he is the one. The one she has always imagined beside her, the one with whom she will share her future. There's no hesitation, no doubt.

Her arms move before she can think about it, wrapping around his neck, and pulling him close.

"Yes," she says, the word catching in her throat. She blinks back tears, the happiness welling up inside her like a fountain, almost too much to contain. "I will marry you."

They embrace, their bodies fitting together like pieces of a puzzle, a perfect union. She can feel the steady rhythm of his heart against her own, a sound that resonates deep within her - a melody unlike any she has ever known. In that fleeting moment, time itself seems to pause, erasing all distractions. Nothing else exists but him and the two of them entwined in this shared space.

With her eyes closed, she inhales the essence of him: the familiar scent of his skin mingling with the warmth radiating from his body. This is where she feels most at home, cradled in his arms, anchored in the simplicity and beauty of this moment.

"I'll give you the life you deserve," he says.

Wiping her tears, she gives him a gentle kiss on the cheek. "I know you will. And you'll keep me safe and secure, while I go about my adventures, experiencing new and exciting things."

He laughs. "Never change. Promise?"

"I promise," she whispers in his ear.

They leave the gazebo hand-in-hand, my mother's face turned up to my father's with a smile that was both tender and wistful. As they walk toward the house, my mother announces to the others that they are to be married. The response is immediate - a chorus of congratulations and well-wishes. Glasses are lifted in a toast, and the sound of them clinking fills the air, followed by the joyful cry of "Salute! Salute!" Everyone begins to sing and dance in merriment.

But something catches my attention. There's a man in a lawn chair, his head drooping forward, his body shuddering with each movement. I come closer to him. His hair is gray and thinning, suggesting he is old, but his eyes don't match his appearance. They are bright, and full of life, as though they belong to someone far younger, someone still untouched by time's heavy hand. Beside him, a woman, much younger, sits close, her face inches from his. She speaks softly, her words a whisper meant only for him. He stirs, his head jerking slightly in response, and a faint smile on his lips.

My parents seem to follow me toward them, and the man, hunched and frail, struggles to rise from the chair. His hands grip the armrests so tightly his knuckles go pale. The woman places a hand on his arm and helps him to his feet, her touch gentle but firm. She stands close, her body leaning into him, her fingers curled around a belt loop at the back of his pants, offering him the support he needs to stay upright.

My father's hand closes around the man's hand in a firm handshake, his grip strong and steady. My mother leans in to kiss the man's cheek, her lips brushing his skin with a tenderness that lingers just a moment longer than necessary. Her breath, warm and fragrant, fills the space between them. She speaks slowly to him in Italian, her words like a caress, her voice a soft murmur that only he can hear. He appears to be listening attentively, his gaze never leaving her face. But as my mother speaks, the woman is also speaking to him, her words a soft breath in his ears. His eyes widened in recognition at her words, and he grins and twitches a nod.

The woman smiles and kisses my parents on the cheek. They talk briefly, and then she and my father help the man back to his chair. I watch as the man takes a deep breath of relief, his shoulders slumping in exhaustion. His eyes flutter shut for a moment, the marks of discomfort still lingering on his face.

My parents wave goodbye to the man and woman with smiles, but I can see sorrow lurking beneath, like shadows in still water. As they walk back to the house, my father's voice echoes in my mind, unbidden and insistent.

"I can't imagine what it must've been like for him. The instant when everything familiar crumbled away? One moment, you're standing in the center of your life, and the next, you're adrift in a sea of uncertainty. I wonder what he felt first. The shock of it all? Or maybe anger at the unfairness? Or was it just an overwhelming sadness for all that was lost?"

TIME IS FICKLE

The memory fades and I'm back in my grandfather's backyard alone with my father beside me. We've stepped into a moment that feels neither here nor there, where time seems to slow, the last gasps of our family's history before it vanished completely.

The garden, once my grandfather's pride, now tells a story of neglect. Weeds, opportunistic and brazen, have claimed dominion over the flowerbeds. They twist around the remnants of roses and choke the life from forgotten perennials, a tangled reflection of the passage of time and the frailty of human intention.

I find myself staring at the gazebo, a faded reminder of those golden days I'd just left behind. The once-bright white paint has given way to peeling strips, each curl like an old photograph, the edges worn and discolored with time. The wood beneath is scarred by seasons, weathered to a gray so deep it feels as though it is slowly crumbling back into the earth. I can almost hear the groans of the building, the creaks and protests of a structure worn down by time. The roof, once firm and secure, now sags under the burden of years, its strength giving way to the slow, unrelenting force of gravity. It seems a shadow of its former self, tired and diminished.

As I stand there with my father, I realize we're bearing witness to the inevitable march of time. This place, so woven into the fabric of our family's history, is slipping away, piece by piece, with each passing moment. I understand now that it's not just the gazebo or house or the garden we're losing, but a link to the past -

something real that connects us to who we were, to the people we had been, and to the dreams we once shared here.

"Like everything in life," I say softly, my voice barely audible above the rustling of overgrown grass, "time isn't kind."

My father's gaze drifts to the weathered gazebo, its once-bright paint faded and peeling. "Time is fickle," he muses, a hint of melancholy in his voice. "Cruel and kind in equal measure. But the gazebo, well, it held its own. At least to my eyes."

"It didn't last much longer," I say.

"It lasted as long as it needed to," he tells me. "It saw a lot of memories in its time, and even now it'll see a lot more."

I look at him, his face etched with memories. "More memories? How?" I ask. "It's eventually going to be torn down by the new owners."

He doesn't answer.

We stand in silence for a moment, listening to the wind in the willow, a thousand harps playing. Then my father says, "Let's sit down for a bit."

We sit on a bench inside the gazebo, the old wood creaking beneath us. Bees have built a hive in the corner, and the air is filled with their low, thrumming sound.

Mrrr . . . Mrrr . . .

Maggie is here. She jumps into my lap and I cuddle with her.

She begins to purr, but the rumbling quickly ends as her ears perk up at the sound of the bees. She freezes, her fur bristling, as she watches them. Their wings are a blur as they buzz around the hive in the corner of the gazebo. With wide eyes, she bares her teeth in a hiss, but they're unfazed by her warning.

"Annoying creatures," she growls.

My father and I laugh.

"They won't bother you," he tells her. "They're just going about their business. You have to marvel at their efficiency and how they work together."

I stare at the beehive, struck by the intricacy of its structure and the care that went into its creation. Each hexagonal cell is perfectly formed, nestled neatly into the one beside it, creating a pattern that seems almost intentional. It's hard to fathom that such an elaborate design could come from creatures so small. The symmetry, so clear and intentional, feels almost removed from the usual randomness of nature.

"Still, annoying creatures," Maggie tells my father.

Her tail twitches and her ears flatten. I tickle her under the chin. She squirms in protest, and I ruffle her fur which bothers her. But I only laugh harder.

"What? You don't like that?" I ask.

My father reaches over and gently strokes the top of her head. She relaxes and starts to purr under his touch.

"That memory. It was wonderful," I say to my father. "Thank you for taking me there. Mom was so beautiful."

"The most beautiful woman ever. It's funny. No matter what memory I visit, when she's there, I see her as a young woman."

"Really?"

"It's what happens here. Time loses all meaning. Probably has happened to you."

"It has?"

"When was the last time you remember seeing your wife?"

I pause to think. I sigh.

The memory unfurls like a delicate flower, its petals soft and fragile against the harsh backdrop of the present. I close my eyes, letting the scene wash over me, as vivid and immediate as if it were happening now.

"The hospital," I say. "She was there, holding my hand."

My father's eyes meet mine. "And how did she appear to you?"

The realization startles me, a pebble dropped into the still pond of recollection. "Young," I say, wonder coloring my voice. "As fresh and vibrant as the day we met. But that can't be right, can it?"

He didn't answer directly, instead gently nudging me back in time. "Think of the first time you saw her. What was she like?"

I turned my gaze to the overgrown garden, its wild beauty a fitting canvas for my memories. "She was . . . radiant. A vision that outshined everything around her. Even now, that image burns bright in my mind, untouched by the years that followed."

As I spoke, I now understood the truth that had been there all along, waiting to be discovered. "It's the same look I saw in the hospital. That same light in her eyes, that same warmth."

My father's smile was soft, and understanding. "Some things are eternal. They exist outside of time, unchanging and perfect."

"Love, true and deep, isn't bound by the linear march of days and years," I say. "It's a constant, a light that shines just as brightly at the end as it did at the beginning."

He smiles. "That image of her will live with you forever."

Then I remembered something. "But your memory. The most recent one I visited. There was something strange in it."

"What?"

"A man. He looked old. But there was something about him that made me think he was younger than he looked. He was feeble and there was a woman who helped him. Who was he?"

My father thinks for a moment.

"Ah, you're talking of Nicolo."

"Who is he?"

"A friend of your grandfather."

"There was something about him. Something different."

My father hesitates.

"I think it's best that you speak to your grandfather about him."

"Why?"

"Just talk to your grandfather," he says, his voice burdened with something unsaid.

A PROMISE

The backyard stutters then disappears as the parlor comes to life before me. I'm standing by my grandfather in his easy chair watching his chest rise and fall with each gentle breath. A soft snore escapes his lips, and I smile fondly. I reach out and take his hand, my fingers curling around his. He stirs at my touch, and his eyes flutter open.

"You're back." He leans forward clearing his throat. "Where'd you go?"

"Dad shared some memories with me. One was when he proposed to Mom."

His face lights up with a warm smile. "I remember that day," he says. "Your mother was so happy. Whenever she looked at your father her eyes sparkled with love. She was so beautiful."

I nod. "She sure was." But I want to find out about the strange man. "Gramps. There was someone who was there that day. Dad said his name was Nicolo. Do you remember him?"

He stares at me, his eyes steady and piercing, never wavering. I fight the instinct to turn away, feeling a coldness seep through me. I can tell his mind is elsewhere, drifting far beyond my reach, caught in a space I cannot follow.

His stare holds me firm. His eyes are like two dark pools, and I feel myself sinking into them. The past reflects in his eyes, the memories of a life that I know little about.

Finally, he says, "Of course, I remember him. He's a good friend."

A mixture of love and sorrow threatens to overwhelm me. Does he realize where he is now, in this place beyond the veil of life? I choose my words carefully, like selecting delicate china from a high shelf, afraid that the wrong move might shatter this fragile moment.

"What's he like?" I ask, my curiosity a gentle tide lapping at the shores of his recollection.

My grandfather's eyes grow distant as if peering through the mists of time. "A good man," he says, his voice rough with emotion. He clears his throat, a sound like gravel shifting. "A fisherman in the old country. Strong hands, but gentle with the nets. We worked together at the foundry." He pauses with a faint smile. "He taught me to curse in English. Said it was more satisfying than Italian. We'd grab a beer after our shift, talk about things."

"Sounds like he's a good friend."

"A good friend for many years," he replies, his voice quiet, thoughtful.

I study him, looking for something in his expression. "Gramps, when I saw him, he looked old, but I wasn't sure. Is he old? Or is he sick?"

"Don't want to talk about it," he says gruffly, the words rough-edged as river stones. But beneath the brusqueness, I sense a deep well of emotion, carefully dammed and hidden from view. Whatever secret he's keeping, it's precious and painful in equal measure. I let the silence stretch between us, filled with all the things we can't or won't say.

"Gramps, what's wrong?" My voice is gentle, trying to get him to open up. "Please, you can tell me."

He gives a heavy sigh. "Some things are better left alone," he mutters. "Don't want to talk about it."

My heart sinks as I look at him. There's something in his eyes, a darkness of worry or pain, that tells me he's keeping something from me. Something difficult, something he doesn't want to burden me with.

"You don't have to talk about it if you don't want to," I say softly. "But if it's easier for you, you can take me there instead."

He slowly withdraws his hand from mine, his eyes now have a weary look.

"Been there too many times," he says. "It's not a place I like to visit. I can still see it, the shadows, the pain. I can still hear the screams."

I feel memories lingering in his gaze, pulling him toward a time and place he wishes he could erase. He tries to push them away, to forget, to lock them in a corner of his mind where they can't reach him. Yet they remain - quiet, patient, always on the edge of his thoughts. But he's strong, refusing to let them consume him.

"Take me there," I whisper. "Please. For me. There's so much I don't know about you, about your life. This is a chance for me to get to know you better."

I hold my breath, waiting for his answer. Will he do it?

His eyes meet mine, and there's a flicker of something in their depths. Is it hope? Or is it fear?

I realize then - he knows. He knows that he's wandering in the next life, and he's frightened.

"If I do this, you must first promise me something."

I lean forward, my heart quickening. "Anything Gramps. What is it?" I ask, not knowing what to expect.

He takes a deep breath, and I can see the effort it takes for him to gather his thoughts. "You must promise that you won't leave me again." He pauses. "And that we'll only speak of Nicolo just this once."

I hold back the sting of tears.

"I'll never leave you, Gramps," I tell him, swallowing hard. "I'm here to stay. And Nicolo . . . we'll only speak of him just this one time."

A ghost of a smile touches his lips as he leans back, sinking deeper into the chair. He extends his hand, and I take it, surprised by the enduring strength in his grip. His eyes flutter shut, and I feel myself swept into a memory, carried back to a time that feels worlds apart.

THE FOUNDRY

The parlor falls away dissolving, and I'm lifted into a strange, searing expanse. A foundry stretches around me, alive with unbearable heat. It presses from all sides, almost alive in its intensity, making my skin tingle and my hair curl. The air carries the sharp odor of molten metal, sharp enough to taste, and every breath feels weighted with smoke and grit. The noise is relentless - metal clashing against metal, the roar of the furnace swallowing even the sharp hiss of escaping steam. The space feels foreign and primal, a realm forged of fire and noise where familiar rules no longer apply.

I look down in wonder.

The foundry stretches beyond comprehension, a maze of metal and fire. Overhead, catwalks and machinery crisscross the ceiling, while massive furnaces along the walls blaze with relentless heat. The light from their mouths spills outward, painting the space with shifting orange shadows.

Every corner reveals something new: whirring machines, a floor scattered with slag, and workers moving with purpose. The place is beautiful and terrifying, and I feel small amidst its vastness.

Below me, hundreds of workers disappear into the haze of sparks and clanging metal. Their faces are streaked with soot, but their eyes burn with determination. They move with the fluidity of necessity, bodies aching from the endless work. The noise and heat merge into something that drives them forward.

Yet there's a heaviness in the air, a darkness clinging to the edges of the factory. The work presses on them, relentless as the machines themselves. Fatigue ripples through the workers, frustration etched on their faces. Some falter, their bodies struggling to keep up. I inhale, the sharp scent of sweat mixing with something darker - fear.

The foundry looms large, its walls pressing in, a constant reminder of the danger within. The workers move swiftly, with purpose in every step. A misstep isn't just an accident; it's a descent into a world where jobs are scarce and hunger waits. Their lives depend on this place, a fragile arrangement of labor and survival they make with gritted teeth.

Endurance is their only currency here, a grim music that drowns out complaint or rebellion. To stop, even for a moment, risks everything they've managed to hold onto. For them, the foundry isn't just work; it's the line between what little stability they have and the chaos waiting beyond its doors.

I imagine what it must be like - this unrelenting monotony, no space for escape. Life, it seems, is reduced to a series of tasks dictated by forces beyond their control, a trap with no release. A waking nightmare.

My thoughts leave me hollow as I try to understand. Below, the workers are tiny against the vast machine. They remind me of ants - relentless, each convinced of its role in a task too large to comprehend. The machine hums around them, indifferent to the lives it consumes.

I search for my grandfather, but instead, I spot a man. There's no reason for him to stand out, yet he does. His movements are purposeful, and unyielding, as if fatigue has no claim on him.

I watch as he unloads raw materials from railway wagons, muscles straining, sweat glistening in the heat. He trundles handcarts up ramps to the furnaces, his breath ragged. Once there, he uses a hoist to tip the materials into the fiery depths. Over and over, he performs the task with quiet confidence.

His movements are fluid, with a calm efficiency in how he handles the materials. It's natural, almost effortless, like a dance only he knows. His body moves with purpose, unobserved, lost in the task at hand.

The hoist creaks. For a moment, I think it will hold, but then the sharp crack of breaking metal splits the air. The handcart crashes into the furnace with a deafening boom, sending the man tumbling from a great height. I watch, frozen, as his body strikes the side of the furnace with a sickening thud. The fall is inevitable.

The impact reverberates in my chest, twisting something deep inside.

The silence that follows is suffocating. I remain still, lost in a dark place in my mind. He's gone. I know it.

Dizziness takes over. My pulse quickens, panic rising in my throat. I lower myself to the ground, legs unsteady, and lean against a cold pillar for support. I focus on my breath - slow and steady - trying to calm the tremor in my chest. Gradually, my heart slows, my body loosens.

A horn blares, its shrill cry snapping me back. Workers rush toward the man, sprawled near the furnace.

The stench of charred flesh claws at my throat. The air thickens with it, sour and suffocating. The metal, once so useful in shaping and crafting, now serves only to harm, its heat eating through his clothes and skin, leaving behind patches of ruined flesh. Blood pools, dark and slick, beneath the harsh light. Blood pools in the harsh light, slick and dark, and my stomach churns. I gag, the sour taste of it rising in my throat.

The man lies on his back, breathing in shallow, uneven gasps. Each exhale brings up gray phlegm that splatters across his chest. His eyes are open, vacant, distant, fixed on something beyond reach. There's a hollowness there, as if he's already left the place, but still bound to it, searching for something that no longer exists.

He's alive, but barely - a thread holding him here.

A high-pitched moan fills the air, piercing my ears like needles. He writhes in pain, terror in his eyes, a strangled cry escaping his lips. I want to look away, but I can't. The blood, the screams - it's overwhelming, yet I can't tear my eyes from him.

"Nicolo!" someone shouts.

More voices join in, panic rising. A group of men surrounds him, lifting him from the foundry floor. One of the men is short and thin. It's my grandfather.

A BREAKFAST RITUAL

The foundry shifts, its walls blurring, almost liquid in their motion. Without warning, the familiar scent of breakfast wafts through the air, pulling me back. I blink my eyes open, finding myself in my grandparents' kitchen. My grandfather is sitting at the kitchen table, his usual breakfast laid out before him: three soft-boiled eggs, three slices of toast, and a steaming cup of strong coffee. To the side, a bottle of whiskey rests, a steady companion to the morning ritual.

He reaches for the whiskey, the glass catching the pale light of morning. He pours a generous measure into his coffee, the smoky flavor warming his tongue and throat. He sighs, content. Cracking an egg at the small end, he peels away the shell and removes a bit of the white. He lifts it to his lips, sucking out the yolk and savoring the taste, then scoops out the rest with a spoon. After a bite of toast and another sip of coffee, he moves on to the second egg.

This ritual shapes his mornings, a constant amid the changes in his life. There's comfort in the sequence, in the small act of peeling an egg cleanly or the whiskey softening the bitterness of his coffee. In this moment, the world feels far away, and he finds a brief, reliable peace in doing things the same way he always has.

I remember one time when he said it to me, his voice low and urgent as if he were imparting a secret of great importance. "There's no order to the world," he said. "Nothing certain. No way to know what'll happen next. There aren't many things you can rely on. But breakfast - that's constant. A little piece of the day you can hold onto, steady and familiar amidst all the rest."

As I watch him, he takes his time, enjoying each bite and each sip. There's no hurry, no rush. He takes another bite of toast.

"Now you know," he says, the faint click of his dentures cutting through the silence. The sound of age, of things breaking down. "Now you know why I don't go there."

"It was Nicolo who was hurt in the foundry, wasn't it?" I ask.

My grandfather nods slowly, his eyes clouded with distant memories. "Never came back to work," he says, each word deliberate. "Can't work, can't provide for his family." His hands, worn with age, rest on the table between us. "His wife . . ." His voice softens. "She has to take care of the children, pay the bills. They just keep coming." He pauses. I feel the story surrounding us. "His life," he says, meeting my eyes with a sharp, quiet understanding, "changes forever that day." The clock ticks steadily on the wall, marking time even as we sit outside of it.

Suddenly, my mind connects invisible threads to another memory.

"The $100. Each month. It was for Nicolo, wasn't it?"

His voice is gentle. "Since I've been retired. Before that, I gave his wife money from my weekly pay. Others did too."

"For how long?"

"As long as I can remember," he says, his gaze distant. "His wife struggled to make ends meet. They have no family here. None of us do. We become his family."

I almost see the memories moving behind his eyes. "A few of us pitched in. A dollar here, a dollar there. It added up. We never told anyone. It was our secret. But the doctor's bills kept coming."

"But didn't insurance cover them?"

He shakes his head, dismissing the idea with a wave. "Insurance? There's no insurance in the foundry. No sick time. No time off. No nothing. Not like what you have. We worked six days a week. Sometimes seven if the boss tells us. All we had was the pay they gave us." He takes another sip of coffee. "His family would've never survived without our help. We always helped those who needed it. We looked out for each other. That's what we did."

A question pushes against my chest, urgent. I hesitate. It's a question whose answer could change everything, and I'm not sure if I'm ready for that. But I have to know.

"Gramps, do you still give him $100 from your pension?"

He pauses, eyes holding mine. Something unreadable crosses his face before he answers. "Of course," he says as if it's the most natural thing. "The last Friday of every month. Why wouldn't I?"

"But Gramps, you're –"

The words catch in my throat. I can't bring myself to speak the truth that hangs between us. It's too sharp, too final.

Dead. He's dead. We're all dead.

I watch him, noting the tilt of his head, and the way his fingers grip the coffee cup. He knows this isn't his past life because he took me to a memory. Still, something doesn't add up. Why does he cling to this monthly ritual? The question drifts unanswered, suspended in the air.

He continues his breakfast, unaware of my gaze, his mind still in the office. I see him pass the workers bent over their desks, their attention fixed. He stops at the cashier's window and leans in to speak to the woman behind the glass. The $100 bill rests in his hand only briefly before he returns it with a smile.

I hear his voice. "You make sure he gets it," he tells her.

She smiles back. "Of course."

This memory replays in his mind, a loop he can't escape. Why does he force himself to relive it? Is it fear of forgetting, or a desperate need to understand? Maybe he hopes that by reliving it, he can somehow change the outcome.

I try to picture being trapped in an endless cycle, this constant replay of a single moment. There's no escape, no respite, no hope of change. It's a prison of the mind, as confining as the foundry ever was.

I want to reach out, to show him I care, to help him break free. But how do you free someone from a prison they've built within themselves?

We sit in silence, and I can't shake the memory from the foundry. It's dark and harsh, but beneath it - there's something fragile. Even in the worst moments, when the world feels stripped bare, some still reach out, those who believe in kindness for its own sake. And that act, however small, finds a way through.

Though our past life is gone, the basic goodness of people remains, here in this new existence. It's a thought I embrace.

I stand and wrap my arms around him, feeling the frailty of his body against mine.

"What you did all those years was remarkable," I say to him. "Most people wouldn't have the strength or the will. I'm so proud to call you my grandfather, and I'm grateful to be here with you now. I love you more than I can say."

He smiles and his eyes shine.

He touches my face, his hand gentle against my skin. "I love you too. Remember your promise."

My eyes mist over, the world blurring at the edges. "I will."

Leaving the kitchen, I glance back at him. He sips his coffee, steam rising softly, and reaches for a slice of toast. There's a quiet ease in his movements, a simple moment borrowed from a simpler time, untouched by the shifting world outside.

As I turn away and head down the stairs to the utility room, that calmness stays with me for a moment, but soon, a quiet stir begins to grow. It's subtle, not fully formed, yet persistent. It doesn't stop me, but it's there, pulling gently at the edges of my mind.

Closing the kitchen door behind me with its familiar sound, a flash of memory strikes - of the foundry, sharp and unsettling, like a sudden lightning strike bringing with it a frightening realization that stings at me.

My grandfather, in his past life, was a small part of that vast, relentless machine. He knew every inch of the foundry, every creak and groan, his body worn from the endless work. It was his world, his identity. Now, in this strange new life, he can't shake the remnants of that past. He remains a small cog, but in a different, incomprehensible machine, one that's unfamiliar to him and to everyone else, its workings as mysterious as the passage of time itself.

Outside, the sun shines bright against a clear blue sky. I close my eyes, letting the noise of the foundry wash over me - the clanging metal, the workers shouting, steam hissing. The heat from the furnaces presses in, and I see the workers moving quickly, small and insignificant.

A feeling of unease stirs within me. It's not fear, but a quiet awareness of our place in the universe. We're tiny, and our lives are but brief moments in an endless stretch of time.

When I open my eyes, the foundry disappears, replaced by a burst of color - flowers scenting the air, my relatives' voices weaving across the lawn. I smile. Time has shifted.

The universe, vast and unknowable, looms over us. Our lives are brief flashes, fading unnoticed in the machinery of existence. It's easy to feel lost, but in that vastness, there's a spark - an understanding of freedom.

We can live like ants, unnoticed, or we can burn brightly, cutting a path through the dark. What we leave behind may be fleeting, but the choice to make it matters. The decision is ours.

Noise and distraction

Sitting on the concrete steps, I bask in the warmth of the sun. The air is still, save for the distant sound of my relatives' voices, sifting through. Closing my eyes yet again, I let the moment sweep over me. Memories of my many visits here push into my mind – relatives and friends, the laughter, the good food, and the love of being surrounded by family.

Maggie leaps into my lap, catching me off guard. She has a way of appearing out of nowhere like she's walked through some invisible door. It's a trick she's mastered over the years. I feel her warmth, the gentle press of her paws, and for a moment, everything around us fades.

I hug her tightly, comforted by her soft purring.

Mrrr . . . Mrrr . . .

"Still sneaking up on me, little one?" I ask.

"It brings me joy," she replies in her sweet voice. "Where did you go?"

"I went back in time. Not just a little, but far - back to when my father and grandfather were young men."

Her eyes widen. "You went back in time?"

"It was strange - being there but not really there. Everything was clear, sharp, like watching a movie, but the emotions weren't mine. They were foreign, intense, but distant. I was a shadow, present yet detached."

There's a soft growl. "Well, you are a ghost. Did you like what you saw?"

"I can't say. It was interesting. Not sure I'd want to live there, though."

"Why not?"

"The world was different then, a different place altogether. And the people were different. Not like the ones in my time. It was like stepping into another world, a simpler world, but also a harder one. No technology. No conveniences to make life easier. So much poverty and hardship. And then there was the war."

"Maybe it was a time when people were more connected. Less noise, less distraction," she says.

"Maybe. People had to rely on each other more. They knew their neighbors, helped when needed. It was simpler, but also more meaningful." I pause, then met her gaze. "Even then, there was noise. The world always offered plenty to keep them awake at night. As I think about it, it's clear that while things change, we don't. We keep reaching for each other, trying to make sense of everything around us. That's what time really carries."

"Funny thing about time," Maggie muses. "It never stops. Just keeps going. It's all we have."

I nod. "Always moving forward, even when we don't."

The screen door creaks open, then slams shut. My mother appears, framed by the light. "There you are," she says, sitting beside me. "Want breakfast?"

"Oh no. But thanks."

"Okay," she says, gently rubbing Maggie behind her ears. "I remember this one. She was just a kitten."

"She had a tough time of it . . ." I say, then stumble over my words. ". . . before she came here."

"Poor little honey," my mother says. Maggie begins a deep rumbling purr content in the warmth of the present moment. "I've been meaning to ask you something."

"What?" I ask.

She has a big smile on her face. "Did you ever write that love story I asked for?"

I laugh. "Oh, I remember. I remember the day I gave you a copy of my first novel. You looked it over. Flipped through a few pages. Then read the back jacket. All you could say was, 'Why can't you write a love story?'"

"That's right," she says. "I was disappointed. I thought you had it in you. But you just kept writing those strange stories about dragons and wizards. I wanted you to write a love story."

I shake my head. "Me. Write a love story?"

"Why not? You're a talented writer. So, did you?"

I smile. "I did. You'll see."

"Well, I can't wait to read it," she says, smiling back.

I take a deep breath and look around, my eyes lingering on the familiar sights and sounds. The colorful flowers, the soft grass, and the laughter of relatives in the air. It's all so familiar, and yet it feels different now.

"Mom," I say, my voice barely above a whisper. "I want to ask you something. Promise you won't get mad."

"Of course not," she replies. "What is it?"

"Where do you think we are?"

She looks at me, her eyes catching the light. A slow recognition spreads across her face, and a smile forms - gentle and tender, like something both familiar and new. The silence between us feels heavy, waiting for her answer.

"We're in a place," she says, her voice soft with wonder, "where all love stories are held." She pauses, letting the thought settle. "Heaven," she adds.

Maybe she's right. Maybe this is heaven, a place where every love story ever written lives on forever. But as I look into her eyes, a small part of me wonders if everything is as it seems.

"Oh," she says, her voice catching for a moment, a fleeting thought pulling loose. Her expression softens, the lines around her eyes easing. "It just hit me. How quickly it's all gone." She stretches her hand out, a slight tremor in her fingers. "All these years, and yet here you are." A wistful smile pulls at her lips, holding both warmth and sorrow. "I still see that little boy running through the yard, pockets full of rocks and leaves, knees always scraped."

She pauses, her gaze distant. "It feels so close, doesn't it? And yet, look at you now."

I watch her, moved by the quiet ache in her voice. "Time flies, Mom," I say, trying to lighten the moment. "Are you okay?"

She nods, her hand resting briefly on Maggie's back. "I'm fine. Time does fly. One day, you're chasing your children, and then you turn around, and they're grown. Off on their own. It feels distant sometimes."

"It was a lifetime ago," I reply with a small smile. "And it's been far too long since we've all been together."

Her eyes glisten, but she blinks quickly to clear the tears. I pull her into a hug. She feels small in my arms, and I wish I could protect her from everything that's hurt her.

"Much too long," she agrees.

"It's okay," I say. "But we're here now. And that's what matters."

She nods, her lips pressed tightly together, her breathing uneven.

I lean closer, lowering my voice so that only she can hear. "I love you," I whisper.

Her eyes close for a moment, and she exhales, a sound so soft it barely reaches me. "I love you too," she says.

We sit in silence, side by side, letting the moment unfold. After a while, she reaches for my hand, her touch warm and familiar. We stay that way, connected, letting the simplicity of being together fill the quiet of the day.

"You know," she says, "you were my miracle baby."

Her words bring back a story she often tells - the time she almost lost me when she was pregnant. I wonder if she'll share that memory now, but I hesitate to ask.

A smile tugs at her lips, knowing and playful. "I can see it in your eyes," she says, her voice soft. "You want to know about the time when you were just a promise inside me."

"I would," I reply. "I'd very much like that."

She looks away as if searching for something in the distance, and I sense hesitation - some quiet fear. After a deep breath, she turns back to me, her eyes warm and loving.

"The past is a story we tell ourselves," she says. "But it's a story we can never rewrite." She pauses, a small smile touching her lips, acknowledging some private truth. "I think it's time," she adds, squeezing my hand gently. Her touch is reassuring, a bridge between the past and the uncertain future.

The once vibrant scene begins to blur, replaced by a dreamlike haze.

A MIRACLE BABY

As the haze begins to clear, I spot a bus crawling down the road beneath me. Its engine hums with a deep, relentless growl, the vibrations running through the metal frame, rattling the windows. The tires kick up a fine cloud of brown dust that hangs in the air, swirling and catching the light.

Peeking over the horizon, the sun casts a golden glow over the cornfields that stretch out on either side, rows, and rows as neat as the teeth in a comb. But the beauty of the scene is lost on me, for inside the bus I see a young woman.

Beneath her coat, her belly stretches, full and round, moving with the rhythm of her breath. She brushes it gently, her fingers brushing the soft curve as if tracing a path she's walked before. Her mind is elsewhere, lost in something distant, a place she cannot reach but often returns to, like an old house on a street she no longer visits. Something feels out of place, though she can't name it.

She's one of many passengers, members of a church group who are chattering and laughing. But the woman is silent, her mind filled with a mixture of excitement and anxiety. She's excited about her new baby, but she's also worried about how she's going to manage with two children already underfoot. She wonders who the baby will look like, and what kind of person it will grow up to be.

She closes her eyes and tries to imagine the baby's face. Will it have her eyes, or her husband's? Will it be a boy or a girl? She doesn't know, but she can't wait to find out.

Opening her eyes, she turns toward the window, squinting at the bright light spilling through. A smile spreads across her face as her thoughts turn to her baby. It's there, inside her, growing with each passing day. She can feel it - small, yet undeniably real. A quiet wonder fills her, the sense of something new taking root.

She lets her mind wander, imagining the future for this child. The paths ahead stretch far and wide, each one holding a promise of something extraordinary. The world could be whatever the child chooses to make of it, she thinks, a place shaped by their own hands. Every possibility is before them, unmarked and open.

She's certain that this child will know love - deep, unconditional love, regardless of the path they take. A quiet smile tugs at her lips as she holds onto that certainty, feeling the warmth of it settle in her chest.

I move closer to the woman. There's something familiar about her, something I can almost touch. I draw near, and when I look into her eyes, it's as if the world sharpens into focus. Her eyes are striking, their depth pulling me in, and for a brief, breathless moment, it's clear. She's my mother, and the infant cradled within her is me.

The bus is headed north to Canada, to the Sainte-Anne-de-Beaupré shrine. It's a well-known destination for pilgrims, and there's a quiet hum of anticipation from the passengers, each one looking forward to the moment they arrive, each one carrying their hopes and prayers for their families.

"Well, it's finally happening," a friend says who sits next to my mother, leaning toward her as the bus rounds another curve. My mother doesn't respond right away, her gaze fixed on the horizon, her cheeks flushed.

"Sure is," she finally says, her voice full of quiet determination. "Took some planning. Hoping. You'll see why when we get there. How wonderful it is."

I glance around the bus, taking in the faces of the other passengers. An older couple sits across the aisle, their hands knotted together like they've been holding on for decades. The man leans toward the woman, murmuring something that makes her lips curl into a small, knowing smile.

"Do you think they've done this trip before?" her friend asks, nodding toward them.

"They seem the type, don't they?" my mother says, following my gaze. "Maybe for them, this is a return."

A few rows ahead, two young women sit shoulder to shoulder, their whispers quick and full of laughter. One of them turns, her expression open and bright. "You'd think they were on their way to a concert," my mother's friend says under her breath.

My mother's lips twitch in amusement. "A pilgrimage takes all kinds, I guess," she says.

At the front of the bus, a cluster of nuns sit in the first few rows, their habits dark and severe against the riot of colors worn by the rest of us. One of them fingers her rosary beads, her lips moving silently, while another stares straight ahead, her hands folded neatly in her lap.

"They don't look nervous," her friend says.

"Why would they be?" my mother replies. "This is their life." Behind us, the soft murmur of prayer rises and falls, blending with the low rumble of the engine. Others sit quietly, their eyes fixed on the landscape outside. Fields and trees rush past, blurred by the motion of the bus.

"Do you think they're looking for answers?" her friend asks.

My mother doesn't answer immediately. She turns back to the window, watching the light play across the hills. "Aren't we all?" she says finally, her voice just above a whisper.

Then, I hear my father's voice in my mind, from the night before. "It's a long trip, almost eight hours," he says to my mother, trying to convince her to stay. "You're only five months pregnant, and it's been hard on you. Please, just stay home and rest."

My mother, however, has never been one to yield easily. This trip has been planned for months, and she won't let it pass her by. For her, it's more than a religious journey; it's a reprieve. A reprieve from the house, from my two brothers, from the endless churn of tasks that seem to consume her entirely.

"I need to go," she tells him, her tone firm despite the tiredness I can hear in her voice. "I need to find a piece of myself again."

He pauses, as though trying to understand, and then asks, "Why?"

Her reply is simple and sure. "Because everything else has taken over, and I need this. I can't be just a mother and a wife. I'm more than that."

My father sighs and nods. Then, with a small smile, he kisses her forehead. "I love you," he says.

The bus is now on a highway, its tires singing on the asphalt. I watch my mother looking out the window at the passing scenery. Her hand rests lightly on her belly, fingers splayed, as if she's trying to connect with the life inside her. She's been quiet for a while now, tired in a way that doesn't seem to ease, her eyes slowly closing as the landscape outside shifts and changes. Her back aches and her body seems to resist each new movement.

Her friend watches her closely, concern in her eyes. "We're almost there," she says softly, her voice carrying that gentle tone meant to comfort. "You alright?"

My mother doesn't answer right away. She nods, just barely, her eyelids fluttering like they can't decide whether to stay open or shut. "I'm fine," she says, though it's clear she isn't. Her shoulders sag under a weight that doesn't belong to the suitcase resting by her feet. Every movement she makes feels measured like even the smallest effort costs her more than she can give.

"You need to rest," her friend tells her as she watches the way my mother's breath comes shallow and slow, the sound barely audible over the hum of the bus.

The bus rocks gently as it takes a curve, the kind of motion that could lull you to sleep if your mind weren't already full. But my mother's mind is too busy, too full of things that won't let her rest. The road keeps stretching out ahead, and though the bus moves, she stays perfectly still, letting the motion try to carry her somewhere else. It doesn't.

Finally, the bus veers off the highway, gliding down winding roads before it pulls into the lot of the shrine. My mother feels something shift deep inside her, a subtle tightening in her stomach, as though her insides are bracing themselves. She tries to push it away, to pretend it's nothing, but it doesn't relent. The sensation grows, and she inhales sharply, letting the breath out slowly in an attempt to steady herself.

Something is wrong.

The bus doors let out a sharp hiss, and the passengers file out one by one, their footsteps heavy on the pavement. No one speaks at first.

"Is this it?" a woman near the back whispers, clutching the strap of her bag as if she'd forgotten how to hold herself steady.

"It must be," whispers the man next to her.

They stop together, all of them, a silent congregation, gazing up at the basilica. It stands like a monument to the impossible - stone walls climbing skyward with a kind of effortless defiance, with carvings etched into them so intricate they seemed to breathe. Sunlight glances off the stained-glass windows, scattering jewel-like colors across the façade.

"Feels alive, doesn't it?" someone says.

The group drifts closer to the massive front doors, their footsteps slowing as the air seems to change. There's a heaviness now, not oppressive but insistent like the building itself demanded something from them.

Inside, the temperature drops, cool air curling with a stillness that seems to wrap around them. "It's quiet," a young girl says, her voice breaking the silence as she tugs on her mother's sleeve.

"Shhh," the mother replies, though she can't hide her unease.

The murmur of voices ripple through the vast space, faint and indistinct. Towering arches stretch toward the heavens, their weight resting on columns that seem to hold up the world. The faint flicker of candles sends shadows skipping across the floor, while sunlight spills through the stained glass, painting the stone in splashes of ruby, sapphire, and gold.

"Look," an older man whispers, pointing toward the front. A plume of incense winds its way through the air, its scent mingling with the faint harmonies of a choir. The music is soft at first, almost fragile, but it grows, its haunting beauty filling the space until it seems to press against their chests.

"Where do we sit?" a teenage boy asks, his voice cracking.

"Anywhere," his mother tells him. "Just . . . kneel before you do."

They find their way to the pews, one by one, the scrape of wood on stone echoing faintly. Some bow their heads, others look up, caught in the immensity of it all. A man crosses himself, his movements slow, careful.

"Do you think it's always like this?" a woman whispers. "So quiet. So peaceful."

"Yes," someone replies softly. "I think it's all that and more."

No one speaks after that, their prayers mixing with wonder, the vastness of the place holding them in a kind of reverence they didn't entirely understand. Some make their way down the aisle past the majestic columns that seem to touch the heavens. My mother pauses, her hand brushing her friend's arm.

"Look at that," she whispers, nodding toward a column covered in crutches, stacked one atop the other, like a strange, solemn monument.

"A sign of miracles," her friend says softly.

She glances at the crutches, then back to my mother. "Do you believe it?" she asks, my voice low so it won't carry.

My mother doesn't answer, at least not right away. Instead, she just stares, her face unreadable. Then, almost to herself, she murmurs, "People leave behind what they no longer need."

They move on, the silence thickening with each step. The air feels heavy, like it's holding the weight of every story whispered within these walls. A few people stop to light candles, their movements slow, reverent. The faint flicker of flames punctuates the stillness, their prayers barely audible beneath the weight of the space.

At the altar, my mother hesitates. I can see the weariness in her, the way her shoulders sag just slightly, the small tremor in her hands. Her friend steps closer, offering an arm without a word. My mother leans on her, just for a moment, then kneels slowly, almost painfully.

Her friend kneels beside her, unsure if she should speak or just wait. My mother's hands fold tightly together. She bows her head, and I hear her whisper names - my father, my brothers, even me, though I'm not here yet, not really. She prays for all of us, for the ones who are and the ones who will be.

Her friend rests a hand on her shoulder. "Take your time," she says.

My mother nods, her lips moving in silent prayer. Around us, the quiet feels alive, as if the church itself is listening.

When my mother finishes she tries to stand. Her face twists, and she gasps - sharp and loud like something's snapped inside her.

"What's wrong?" her friend asks. But my mother doesn't answer. Her hand flies to her stomach, pressing hard like she's trying to hold something in place. Then she doubles over.

"What is it?" her friend pleads.

My mother doesn't look at her. Her eyes are clamped shut, and she's whispering, "Oh God, oh God," under her breath. Another wave hits her - I see it in the way her body folds like she's being crushed from the inside. She reaches down, then freezes, staring at her hand when she pulls it back.

It's red. Dark red.

"On no," her friend whispers. "You're bleeding."

But my mother doesn't need her friend to tell her. She's staring at her palm, her lips parted, and I know she knows what it means. Her breaths are short, shallow, and frantic.

"I'm miscarrying," she says. Her voice doesn't break, but it's hollow like something's already gone.

Her friend moves without thinking, sliding an arm around my mother's waist and under her arm. She leans into my mother whose forehead is slick with sweat.

"We're getting you to the hospital," she tells my mother.

She doesn't argue. Her feet drag, her steps faltering as her friend helps her toward the door. Others see this and they also help. Every breath she takes sounds like it might be her last, and she tells herself to keep moving, keep steady, even as each step becomes more difficult. She's too pale, too still, and I can feel fear clawing at the edges of my chest.

The edges of the world I'm in suddenly fade, and then a hospital room appears.

Doctors hover around my mother, their voices low, with each glance, they exchange a silent conversation. I can feel their concern, but I don't hear their words - only the soft sound of their movements. My mother is lying there, her face pale, her hands trembling just slightly. She shuts her eyes like she's trying to shut out everything, trying to pull herself into some place where none of this can touch her.

I stand there, watching, unable to reach her, to do anything. The emptiness presses in on me, tighter with each second.

And then, without warning, everything goes blank.

The world falls away, swallowed by darkness, enveloping me, a velvet curtain drawn across the world. I plummet through its folds, time bending around me. The rush of wind fills my ears, a constant roar that drowns out even the frantic beating of my heart. Far below - or is it above? - a pinprick of light shimmers, a beacon in the vast nothingness. I reach for it, my fingers grasping at empty air, but it remains stubbornly out of reach. With each passing moment, panic rises in my chest, a tide threatening to overwhelm me. I squeeze my eyes shut, as if by closing them I can shut out the terror that grips me.

The fall seems endless, a nightmare from which I cannot wake. But then, just as despair threatens to consume me entirely, a hand materializes out of the darkness. It grasps mine with surprising strength, and I feel myself being pulled upward, away from the abyss. The touch is warm, solid, and real - an anchor in the storm of my fear.

The sound of a car engine wakes me. I blink against the soft light filtering through the window, and there's my mother, sitting in the passenger seat, and my father, hands steady on the wheel, driving home. The lines of their faces are changed, deeper now, etched with a blend of weariness and determination.

My mother cradles a small wooden box in her lap, her fingers tracing the grain like a secret she can't quite share. She's still pregnant, her belly rounded with the quiet promise of something that's yet to be. But something seems different. Her face is still, her expression absent, a hollowness as though she's carried too much and now has nothing left to give. A tear slips down her cheek, tracing a quiet path as though it's too heavy to fall.

I want to reach out, but I can't. The stillness of the car is thick with something I don't know how to describe. Behind the blankness of her face, I feel a sorrow so deep, like she's holding on to something precious, something that she can still cling to even amid her grief. But when I look closely, really look, I see the faintest trace of something more - love, tender and worn, still holding on, despite the rest of it. She holds the box with such care as if it could break at any moment as if it held everything she had left to offer.

I've never seen her like this before. Her hands tremble just enough to betray her, a slight quiver as she runs her fingers over the box, a simple touch that could make everything right. I've no idea what's inside, but somehow, I feel it's something precious. I lean forward, wanting to see more, but I'm afraid too.

There's a nameplate on the box, golden letters spelling out "Lucia." I don't know who that is, but the name presses against my chest like it's a part of me now too.

"Why didn't the doctor back home know?" my mother whispers tearfully.

"Too early to tell," my father replies, his voice tight, the words heavy with grief he's trying to hold at bay. "They did everything they could. What matters is that you're here, that you're okay, that you and the baby are okay."

She says nothing, her gaze fixed ahead, her eyes tracing the white lines of the road, as though she's looking for something in the distance that might bring her peace. The highway stretches out before them, unbroken, and I wonder if that endless blur is what she sees when she closes her eyes - just a road, stretching on forever, with no end in sight.

"I know you had your heart set on a baby girl," my father says, the words barely breaking the silence. "We've plenty of time ahead of us."

"Time is all we have." The words catch in her throat, a sob hovering just beneath the surface.

I've heard those words before.

My mother presses her palm to her mouth, trying to hold back the rush of emotion, the lump that threatens to choke her. Every breath she takes feels too loud in the silence like the air itself is too thin.

Her gaze drifts toward the window, where the light spills in, too bright for the moment, like it knows the burden of her thoughts. She swallows, her chest tight, unsure if she can speak again without breaking.

My father reaches over, his fingers brushing the surface of the wooden box. He doesn't say anything, just lets the touch linger, his eyes brimming with tears. One falls down his cheek, silent and steady. "We'll make it work, sweetheart," he promises, his voice rough with the kind of grief you can't untangle. "I swear we will."

My mother's gaze drops to her belly, still round with the memory of what could've been. Her hand moves of its own accord, coming to rest on the curve. She begins to rub small, soothing circles as if comforting the child that's in her.

"My miracle baby," she whispers, the words soft but full.

Me. I'm there, unborn but already loved, already a part of them. A presence felt in the spaces between their words, in the tears they shed, in the hope they cling to. I'm the future they dare to imagine, even as they mourn what they've lost.

LUCIA

I drift through the cool folds of white clouds, weightless and unmoored, until I land, as if summoned, in my grandparents' kitchen. The sunlight spills through the kitchen window, catching dust specks in its golden glow. The air is thick with familiar scents - the warm bitterness of coffee mingling with the faint tang of lemon polish lingering on the table's surface. My parents sit across from me, their hands curled around a cozy duet of steaming cups of coffee.

My mother stirs her cup, the spoon clinking the rim in a delicate melody that feels like part of my very fabric. It's a sound I had heard a thousand times before, a sound that carries years of mornings, conversations, and quiet moments. She raises the cup to her lips, and there's the faintest hush, the gentle intake of air as she sips, an act so ordinary it feels sacred.

I watch as particles of dust twirl in the air. They seem to waltz in the golden beam, their movements hypnotic and unhurried. I follow their path as if they carry fragments of stories, glimmers of something unseen yet familiar. For a moment, in one of those glowing motes, I see my mother's hands again, cradling the small box in her lap.

"I never knew," I whisper.

My mother's eyes drop to her coffee cup, the steam weaving delicate patterns around her face. It's impossible to tell if she's lost in thought or merely avoiding my eyes.

She takes another sip, her eyes fixed on the cup, and for a moment, nothing else exists. "That box," she says, her voice low yet clear, "held every dream, every hope, from a mother who only wanted her child to grow up surrounded by happiness and possibility. It's strange, isn't it, what you can fit into something so small?"

I sit still, held by the quiet of her words, the kitchen feeling both vast and incredibly small at once. The sunlight grows warmer, and I think for a moment I can hear the pulse of the house itself - steady and unbroken, like the ticking of the clock on the wall that's been there longer than any of us can remember.

My father shifts in his chair, setting his coffee cup down with a soft thud that disrupts the stillness, but only for a second. He places his hands on the table, his movements considered, like he's trying to find the right words in a place where words have always been difficult to locate.

"It's something you never get over," he says, the simplicity of his answer pulling at something deep inside me. His voice is lower than I expected, the words slower than usual. "We just . . . kept going. That's what you do, you know. You keep going."

I look at him, searching his face for something more, something buried beneath the calm façade he's always worn like armor. His eyes are soft today, but he looks tired, not from age, but from the past. It's as if he's always been carrying a boulder, never letting it drop.

"And you, Mom?" I ask, my voice quieter than before, feeling like a delicate thing that could be shattered if I press too hard.

She sets her cup down and looks at me then, really looks at me, her eyes meeting mine with an intensity that feels almost too much to bear. It's the same look she used to give me when I was a child - when she would soothe my fears and tell me everything would be all right, even when I knew it wasn't.

"It's something you carry," she says, her voice steadier now, "not because you want to, but because it's part of you. You never get over it. But eventually, you learn how to live with it. How to make room for it. I guess that's what it is - making room for the things that don't fit, the things that break you, and then . . . learning to breathe around them."

Her words hang in the air, not heavy, but full, filling the space between us without overwhelming it. There's no trace of judgment, no sharp edge of resentment, only a quiet understanding. It's as if she's let the years pass through her and come out on the other side, shaped by the pain but not consumed by it. For a brief moment, I wonder if I could ever have found that same peace.

The room seems smaller now, the dust motes continuing their slow, endless dance in the slanting light. I question if a house can ever truly hold everything we leave behind - our hopes, our losses, the things we never got the chance to say.

I find myself caught in the quiet enormity of what she's said and think about that small wooden box, about how easily objects could hold more than they should. "But why didn't you tell me?" I ask, careful not to break the stillness she's created.

She lifts her eyes then, and there's something heavy in her expression, a sorrow that feels untouchable, no matter how much I might want to understand it. My heart sinks.

"Your father and I thought it would be too much for you." She pauses, her voice is soft but firm, carefully weighing each word. "We thought if you knew, you'd always wonder what your life might have been like if she'd lived. That it would haunt you. We thought it was better for you, simply not to know."

I stare at her. Her face now looks tired, the lines around her eyes deeper than I remember. She stirs her cup slowly, the steam rising between us like a barrier I can't cross.

"We didn't want you to have to live with that pain." My father reaches out to her, his hand covering hers. His voice is lower, but just as steady. "We didn't want you growing up feeling like you were missing something - like you had a hole in your heart. It was hard enough for us to bear."

I look at him, really look at him, and I see something in his face - something raw - that I've never noticed before. He's always been the strong one, the one who steadied us when the world felt too heavy. But now, I realize: he's not invincible. He's just a man, vulnerable and human.

"I don't - I don't understand." The words come out thick, heavy in my throat. "You should've just told me."

My mother doesn't look at me, just at her cup, as though it holds all the answers. "We thought you'd be better off not knowing. It wasn't something we wanted you to carry."

My father sighs, a quiet release, and I feel it in my chest. "We thought you'd be fine without it. And we didn't want to see you hurting the way we did. We didn't want to see you live with that absence." He swallows, and the silence that follows hangs heavy between us.

I try to imagine it - the pain they must have felt. But I can't. I can't imagine the kind of grief that keeps you awake at night, that changes everything about you, even the way you breathe. They lived through something I'll never know.

"I never knew her. My sister. Never even got a chance to know her."

"We know, son." His voice cracks a little like he's trying to keep it together. "We know."

The sadness settles over me, thick and cold. A sharp sting. A twin sister I never knew, a life I'll never share, and all this time . . . all this time, I never even knew she was missing.

My mother looks up, her eyes soft, but her lips pressed tight. "It's just -" She stops, trying to find the words. "It's just that we couldn't bear for you to feel that emptiness. Not if we could help it."

I can feel her grief. It's so much more than I ever thought, woven into the quiet corners of our home, into every conversation we never had. I sit back. The grief isn't something they left behind when they moved on. It's something that followed them. Always there. Always waiting. Even here in this new reality.

"I'm so sorry," I say. "Sorry for everything you went through."

My parents see the hurt in my eyes. I can tell they want to reach out, but I turn instead to watch the dust specks dancing in the air.

"We're sorry," my mother says, her voice soft and tremulous as if she is afraid of waking someone. "Maybe we should've told you sooner."

"Don't know if it would've mattered. Who else knew?" I ask.

"Only your grandparents. No one else," my mother says. "We just didn't want to upset you."

"We didn't want you to feel like you were missing out on anything," my father adds. "All we ever wanted was for you to live your life and to always look forward."

A tight knot of emotion rises in my throat as I look at them. Maybe, they were afraid that if they told me, I would somehow blame them for her death, that it was their fault. But I would never blame them. Sometimes, things just happen.

I sit quietly, the revelation that I had a twin sister - a sister who lived and died without my ever knowing her – pressing down on me. It's a dull ache that will never fully fade. It's more than heartbreaking . . . it's something else entirely . . . something else difficult to put into words.

In the stillness of the moment, I find myself conjuring her image, piecing together a phantom from fragments of my reflection and wisps of imagination. "I wonder . . . what would she have been like?"

My father clears his throat, a soft chuckle escaping him. "I think she would've been like you, in a way. That fire you have - she'd have had it too. Maybe in different ways, but . . . she would've been something like you."

"Wonder if she would've had my eyes?" I say. "Or maybe they'd been different?"

"I like to think she would've had your smile." My mother's voice is tender. "That smile you get when you're laughing, the one that takes over your whole face."

I laugh quietly but it's strained. "Would she have been the sensible one? Or would we have been . . . partners in trouble?"

A half smile pulls at my father's lips. "Partners in mischief, for sure."

My expression shifts, softer now, almost wistful. "I can almost feel her hand in mine. Like . . . like she's still here somehow, right beside me, even though I never knew her."

"She's with you," my mother whispers, as if the words are too fragile to speak aloud, "in the way you think of her, in the way you love her."

"I wish I could've known her." My voice is thick with emotion. "I wish we could've shared . . . everything."

My father's voice is firm. "You'll carry her with you, in your heart, in your thoughts. You may not have had time with her, but you have her nonetheless."

"Yeah. Always," I whisper.

The silence stretches between us, not uncomfortable, but heavy, filled with the presence of someone who's been lost and never fully known.

Then it comes to me.

"Is she here?" I ask.

My father shakes his head. "She's not in this place. I think because she wasn't born. She had no memories."

"Why did you name her Lucia?"

"It was my grandmother's name," he tells me. "A pretty name for a girl. It means light."

"Where's she buried?" I ask.

"With the rest of the family," my mother says.

I think back to all the times I had been at the cemetery. "But I don't remember a headstone."

"She had a simple stone marker," my mother says. "All the times we took you there, but you never noticed it. You had to be looking right at it to see it."

She pauses, her eyes distant, lost in a memory. I wait, knowing there's more to come.

"There was one time, though," she continues, "when you were standing right over her marker. I remember it so clearly. My heart was racing. I couldn't seem to catch my breath. I was terrified you'd notice it."

I can picture it now - my younger self, unaware, standing over a grave marker - my mother, tense, her thoughts racing.

"I was scrambling to come up with something to say if you asked about it," she admits. "But you never looked down. You just kept walking, and I felt this strange mix of relief and sadness wash over me."

Even though I understand why my parents never told me, it still hurts. What disappoints me the most is that I had been left in the dark about such an important part of my life. But it's clear to me now what I need to do.

"Can I visit her grave?"

My parents exchange a glance, one filled with quiet sorrow, a shared understanding.

"We'll take you there," my mother says with the kind of smile that makes you want to cry.

My parents take my hand.

Ghosts

The floor shifts beneath my feet like the gentle rocking of a boat on calm waters. Around me, the world bends and shifts, colors smearing into one another as though pulled by an unseen tide. It's not unpleasant, this feeling - it's disorienting, yes, but also oddly natural, like stepping into a place you've never been but somehow recognize. Then, without warning, I'm standing in a cemetery with my parents.

The graveyard stretches before us, a tranquil expanse where the sun's rays paint elongated shadows across the sea of headstones. There's a hush that fills the space, pressing gently against the world, and I can feel it take hold of me, a quiet that feels like it belongs in the marrow of my being. My parents walk ahead of me, holding hands, their movements unhurried, as if the moment itself demanded nothing but stillness.

We weave our way through the rows of graves, past names of those we've never known, heading toward the section at the back, the place where my mother's family lies. I don't need to ask where we're going - I've been here before, enough times that the pathway is ingrained in my memory. Yet, each step carries with it a heaviness I can't quite explain, as if the air itself knows where we're headed and has decided to move just a little slower.

"Do you remember," my mother says softly so as not to disturb the peace, "when you were little, and I'd bring you here with your brothers and sister?"

"You'd have us clean the headstones and plant new flowers. You'd tell us stories about everyone who was buried here. I loved those stories. I could imagine their lives, and I felt like I was connected to them."

The memory of those visits floods back, vivid and tangible. I can still feel the rough texture of the granite headstones under my fingers as I worked to clear away the moss, the dampness clinging to my skin. The air carried the scent of freshly turned soil, mingling with the perfume of the flowers I planted. My mother's voice comes to me, steady and certain, weaving stories of ancestors she had never met but seemed to know by heart through the threads of family lore. Her words are brushstrokes dancing across a canvas, capturing their lives in a symphony of color.

"Visiting the cemetery was important for you kids," she says. "It's a place where you can reflect on and remember the lives of those who have gone before you. Some say it's a sad place. But for me, it's a place of hope, reminding us that life is precious and that we should cherish every moment."

"I remember the first time you brought me here," I tell her. "I was just a child, my hand small in yours."

"You remember? You were so small," she says.

"Well, I was scared, scared I'd see ghosts. But you reassured me that there was nothing to be afraid of."

"Do you remember what I said?" Her face holds a blend of curiosity and love.

"Of course, You said the cemetery is where time folds in on itself, where the past reaches out to the present. That when someone you love is gone, their memory becomes part of you, woven into the fabric of your days. You carry their story with you, and through it, you learn - about them, about yourself, about the world they left behind. You feel them in the quiet moments, in the way the wind shifts or the sunlight filters through the trees. You told me they aren't really gone. They're still here with us, watching, guiding, and whispering lessons we didn't always understand. You told me not to fear this place, but to come often, to speak to them, to remind them that they are loved and will always be remembered."

She smiles playfully. "I said all that?"

"You did, in so many words. I remember it like it was yesterday." I hesitate for a moment. "You know, when I got older, I'd visit the cemetery by myself," I say. "You didn't know that, did you?"

"No, I didn't," she replies, her eyes widening slightly. "But it doesn't surprise me."

"I liked to walk among the graves, reading the names and dates on the headstones," I confess. "Sounds creepy, doesn't it?"

"Not at all," she assures me, her tone warm and understanding. "It's a way to connect with those who came before us."

"I would spend hours here. Something was soothing about the stillness. Especially in a world that seemed so loud and chaotic. It was a welcome respite. I'd visit Gram's and Gramp's graves, lost in the memories of our time together, their stories echoing in my mind. I'd talk to them, sharing the details of my life like they were right there beside me. I knew they couldn't hear me. But it comforted me to speak to them. Somehow I felt like they were proud of me - proud of everything I'd endured and achieved. It was like they were still present, listening with love."

She takes my hand, her grip firm yet gentle. "They were."

Talking to my mother about this feels oddly fitting now. It's a conversation that would've seemed impossible in the life I once lived. I kept my cemetery visits hidden from her, afraid of stirring her sorrow, afraid she might absorb some of the grief I couldn't explain. But here, on this unexpected path, the words come as naturally as breathing. Sharing this with her feels like opening a door I hadn't realized was locked, and the sense of release catches me entirely by surprise.

We walk deeper into the cemetery, moving toward the back section where the shadows grow longer and the air feels heavier. I squint into the distance, struggling to make out something strange. A group of shapes, translucent and ethereal, drifts slowly about. I stop, a sense of unease creeping in at the sight of this unknown.

"What are they?" I ask my father, pointing toward the peculiar forms.

He doesn't answer right away. He just stares at the shapes, his face unreadable. "This isn't a memory," he tells me. "We're actually here - in the cemetery. They're the living."

I gasp. "They're like ghosts."

"Ironic, isn't it?" he replies, a hint of sadness in his voice.

I watch the shapes as they shift and blur, their movements languid and silent like phantoms in a dream. An irresistible pull tugs at me, urging me to stretch out my hand to touch them, to bridge the chasm between our realities.

"Can we interact with them?" I ask.

My father shakes his head slowly. "No. We're in two different worlds."

I've never seen anything like this before. It feels like I've stepped into a dream that defies all logic and reason. The shapes shift constantly, their forms bending and folding into patterns that feel both chaotic and strangely deliberate. They move with a rhythm that seems to hold its own secret, swaying and twisting as if inviting me to come closer, to understand something just beyond my grasp.

We stand there for a few more minutes, mesmerized by the spectral dancers shimmering and swaying in their world.

"Come on," my father instructs.

Reluctantly, I follow.

As we walk, I replay my father's words in my mind: we're in two different worlds . . . we're in two different worlds . . .

He's right. The living and the dead inhabit realities so different, separated by a divide we can only glimpse through rare moments like this one.

"Will I be able to travel back to the living world?" I ask.

"In time," he says. "But remember what I always told you."

"Life is for the living," I reply automatically. It was something he always told us.

"Yes," he affirms. "You should avoid traveling back, if possible."

"Why?" My curiosity is piqued.

"You may not like what you see," he warns.

As I glance back at the living ghosts - faces blank and unseeing – my father's truth settles over me. If I were to return to the living world, there would be so much I wouldn't recognize, so much beyond my grasp. The thought of facing what I couldn't alter stirs something deep within - resignation and quiet dread. To confront that powerlessness feels like stepping into a storm, knowing there's no shelter to be found.

"Life is for the living," my father repeats, his voice steady yet marked with something deeper. "They go about their days, taking on the world, never surrendering to it until -" He trails off, his gaze drifting into the distance.

I can't help but interrupt. "Until what?"

He sighs, a sound heavy with unspoken truths. "Until all they want to do is escape from it. To run from it. Run from the days that have become nothing more than an endless cycle of routine and monotony. When the smallest tasks become burdensome. When there's no more joy or purpose."

His words whisper of the eternal, a wisdom that can only come from someone in the next life. Life is a gift, something to be cherished and held close. Yet even the strongest among us can grow weary. The body weakens. The mind fades. Life itself becomes a burden.

I've seen this before - the entrapment within one's own existence. The loss of wonder and excitement. The blur of meaningless days. It's a slow, suffocating death, where the soul shrivels until it becomes nothing more than a husk.

"The past life. Do you miss it?" I ask tentatively.

My father doesn't respond right away, and I understand his silence. The past is a ghost, a sigh on the wind. It can never be fully captured and its absence can never be filled.

The sun begins its slow descent, shadows growing longer across the ground. My parents stop, their gazes drawn to the familiar names carved into the headstones around us. I recognize the names. They're the ones woven into my mother's stories, each one telling tales of lives lived and loved.

But in the soft golden sunlight, my eye catches a small, weathered marker. Grass grows wild around it, and the few flowers that remain are wilted, their petals turning brown. I kneel to read the name carved into the stone. The letters are faint as if fading from memory: Lucia.

My parents stand there for a long time, staring at her name. A silence hangs between us, one I can't escape, and I find myself thinking of all the things I'll never know about her – her favorite color, the sound of her laughter, her hopes and dreams. There are so many things I'll never know. I wish I could fill those spaces, but I know they'll remain empty, part of a story that'll never get to be told.

Then, I ask myself: why was she taken from us? Is there an answer to be found here, in the next life?

"No one comes to the cemetery anymore," my mother laments. "Look how everything is overgrown. It's so sad. Too many people have been forgotten. Why?"

"Everyone's busy living life," my father smiles, his expression bittersweet. "As it should be."

"But to live life," she says, "you must remember the ones that have gone before you. Their memories, their lessons, their guidance. Everyone in this place loved and laughed and cried. They made mistakes and learned from them. And they brought new life into the world, creating families and communities that would last for generations. They're part of us, and we owe it to them to remember."

My father puts his arm around her, his touch gentle. "I know," he tells her. "I know. But, my love, things change."

I trace my finger along Lucia's name on the marker, trying to reach across the distance that remains between us. But I don't feel the chill of the granite, nor any texture that might pull me closer to her. I can only imagine what it might feel like. I trace the name again, and again, each repetition a futile attempt to feel something beneath my fingertips. But the action holds meaning for me, an attempt at a connection. A tear slips free, tracing a path down my cheek.

"I wish I'd known you," I whisper into the stillness.

Looking up, I meet my parents' eyes. They glisten with unshed tears, emotions too profound for words. In their faces, I see a mirror of my love and loss reflected at me.

"I'm going to tell her all about me," I say, my voice steady despite the ache in my heart.

My mother nods softly. "I think she'd like that."

I take a deep breath and start to speak, the words coming slowly at first. I tell her about my childhood, the small joys and the inevitable disappointments, the times when light would shine through even on the darkest days. I share stories of the adventures I had with friends, the kind of moments that stay with you, leaving their mark on the person you become. I tell her about my only love, my wife, and how she brought a brightness into my life I hadn't known I needed. I move on to my career - those early triumphs in business, the shift to academia, and the sense of fulfillment I found in each new step. Lastly, I express my gratitude for the family I was born into, the parents who have supported me and helped make everything possible. It all adds up to a life, rich with love and laughter, shaped by every connection I've made along the way.

I lower my voice, careful not to disturb her. I'm afraid she might slip away if I'm too loud. I just need her to know that I'm here, that I miss her, that I love her.

As I speak, I begin to feel her presence beside me, an invisible warmth that envelops me like a gentle embrace. It's like she's listening intently, taking in every word. I can almost feel her hand resting on my shoulder - a reassuring touch that tells me she understands.

"You'll always be in my heart," I say tenderly to her. "I'll never forget you. You'll always be my sister. You'll always be with me."

I press my hand to my lips and whisper a kiss into the air before laying it gently upon her stone. "I'll love you forever."

When I'm finished, when there's nothing left to say, I feel a deep sense of closure. She's heard how much she means to me. That's all that truly matters.

My parents help me to my feet. They've given me the gift of knowing about my twin sister, a person who has been with me since the start. This revelation, this deep connection, brings a feeling of belonging that is both foreign and intimate. It's a truth I hold now, one that can never be taken away. Though she's not here, her presence will always live with me.

Lucia – light.

I step into my parents' arms, feeling my mother's trembling hands as she holds me close. "Now you know," she says, her voice soft, barely audible. Her gaze searches mine, seeking something I can't quite define. A sorrow wells up in her eyes, an apology that goes unspoken. "You had your whole life ahead of you. Can you forgive us for keeping this from you?"

As I reflect on everything I've learned, and everything they've shared, I realize I've uncovered something far more meaningful than they understand - an essential part of my past, a part of who I am, is now laid bare. I am grateful for the clarity, but there's a quiet sadness too - thankful for the truth, yet mourning the years they carried this burden alone.

I look at my mother again, and the pain in her eyes is clear. It's a pain that won't ever disappear.

"I understand." My voice emerges like a well-worn path through familiar woods - comforting yet heavy with sorrow. "I just wish I could've been there for you. To make all the hurt go away."

She presses a kiss to my cheek, her tears shining like dew on morning grass. "But you were there for me," she whispers. "You were my miracle baby."

My father steps away then, moving toward another part of the cemetery where many of his family lie.

We follow him silently, each step hollow with shared grief as we move forward together into this new chapter of our lives - forever changed yet bound by love and memory.

The vanishing rose

We're near the heart of the cemetery, surrounded by rows upon rows of headstones, their presence pressing in from all sides. The air feels dense, as if the quiet itself has weight, making each breath shallow and deliberate. The only sound is the soft rustle of wind brushing through the branches overhead, a faint reminder of life beyond this stillness. I glance around at the markers for my father's relatives, names I recognize only vaguely, like distant memories I was never part of.

"So quiet, isn't it?" my father says, his voice low, almost reverent. "Even though I can now visit with everyone, there's something about being here. Maybe it's the reminder of what came before. Of wanting to hold on to the people we've lost. I don't know. I just keep finding myself back here."

He looks over at me, his expression drawn tight, his mouth pressed firm against words he doesn't want to speak. Together, we face the names carved into stone, a reminder of people who once were. My gaze lingers on one name in particular - my grandmother's. She died just a few months after I was born, her story told to me in fragments over the years.

"I'd like to meet Gram," I say quietly. "To get to know her."

He nods, the movement slow, almost hesitant. "She'd like that," he says softly. "That'd be nice."

For a while, we say nothing, letting the stillness stretch between us. The setting sun paints the cemetery in warm golds and shadows, giving the stones an unexpected gentleness. Some are weathered and broken, their inscriptions fading with time, while others stand pristine, the marble still bright and unyielding. Names and dates, plain and ornate, tell stories that linger in the spaces between.

I scan the orderly rows of graves, the headstones lined with precision, and wonder which one has my name on it.

"Where's my headstone?" I ask, my voice quiet, curious.

"You're not here," my mother replies. "Your ashes were spread over the ocean."

"Where?"

Her smile is knowing, and patient. "You know where," she smiles. "Key West. That's where she let you go."

I close my eyes, and a memory finds me easily - my wife and I, walking together along a beach in Key West, the sand warm beneath our feet, the endless blue of the water stretching before us. The breeze carries a sweetness that seems to promise something beyond the moment as if the air itself holds a secret we could almost grasp. We walk for hours, the waves brushing the shore in a rhythm that feels timeless. We talk of staying there forever, of a life pared down to the essentials - walking, swimming, reading. It's a place where the world seems softer, less insistent.

"I remember," I say, my voice touched with something tender. "Our favorite place. At night, we'd sit out on the balcony and watch the sun sink below the horizon. The sky would blaze with red and orange, and the palm trees would stretch long, dark shapes across the ground. We'd hold each other close and dream aloud as if the future would unfold just as we imagined it."

Her voice is gentle when she responds, nostalgic. "It was where your heart felt at home."

I open my eyes and breathe deeply, trying to pull the ocean air into this moment.

"I can almost hear the waves," I say, "and smell the salt air."

"That's because you're there," she says, "part of it now. You'll always be there."

I hesitate, curiosity pressing at the edges of the moment.

"Were you there? With her? Watching?"

She smiles, a bloom from the depths of her soul. "Yes, I was."

"What was it like?"

"The ocean was calm, the kind of calm that feels eternal. The sun was just beginning to sink, and the only sound was the call of the gulls. It was peaceful. A place meant for farewells." Her gaze reaches toward the horizon, a quiet pull. "I'll remember it always," she says tenderly. "It was where your story was meant to end."

"Thank you," I say, my heart too full to speak. "For being there."

She presses her hand to my arm, a steady, grounding gesture. "Of course," she says.

Another breath pulls through me. The air feels heavy with meaning, yet the silence remains light, carried only by the faint murmur of the breeze - fragile, and fleeting like a secret passed between us. Then comes a sudden snap, sharp and jarring. A branch breaks somewhere beyond.

A figure appears in the distance, a woman holding a single flower between slender fingers. As she draws nearer, the flower becomes clear: a rose, dark red, its petals almost impossibly soft in the fading light. The woman's frame is slight, almost consumed by the billowing black of her gown. A veil obscures her face, yet something about her presence reaches us, steady and watchful. I feel her attention like a ripple moving through the air.

She stops before us and, with a measured motion, lifts her veil. Her face, lined and marked by time, holds a quiet dignity. It's difficult to tell her age - sixties, perhaps older. Her silver hair frames a face where wrinkles gather at her brow and the edges of her eyes. Her mouth is set in a firm line, but it's her eyes that hold me. They're dark and impossibly deep, brimming with something unspoken, a presence that seems almost tangible.

There's a fragility to her, as though she might crumble if the world pressed too hard. She reminds me of something easily broken, a dried leaf about to give way in the wind. I feel an urge rise within me - a need to shield her, to keep her safe from everything that might harm her.

Yet, beneath that fragility lies something else. There's a shared thread I feel in her presence, a connection I don't fully understand. Her eyes hold the stories of hardships endured, of grief and survival, but they also reveal a resolve that seems unshakable.

My father steps forward and wraps her in a gentle hug. "Hi, Ma," he says. "We were just talking about you."

So this is her - my grandmother. She's older than in the memory shared by my father, on his return from the war. I've seen photographs from years past, but the details have softened over time. Standing before her now feels both unreal and inevitable, like opening a long-sealed letter addressed to me, the words inside already familiar yet entirely new.

"Good things, I hope," she says, her voice soft, carrying a faint warmth.

"Of course, Ma," my father replies.

I take a small step forward, feeling the pull to close the distance between us.

She turns to me and her smile widens ever so slightly. "Your youngest boy?" she asks my father, her focus never wavering from me.

He nods.

She studies me for a moment, her expression softening. "Looks like you," she says. "And your father too."

"He does," my father agrees.

Her arms open, beckoning me forward. "Come here," she says gently.

When I step into her embrace, her frame feels frail, as though time itself has worn her down. Her hand moves to my face, fingers brushing my cheek with the lightest touch.

"Too many years gone by," she says in barely more than a whisper. "It's good to finally meet you."

"It's good to meet you too, Gram," I manage, my voice thick and uneven.

She steps back, her eyes tracing my face a moment longer before they find my mother. She pulls her close, arms wrapping around her in a way that feels steady and sure. "I hope my boy is treating you right," she says.

"Always, Ma. Always," my mother answers.

"Good," she replies. "That's how he was raised. To treat people with respect."

"Ma," my father interjects, "why are you here?"

She doesn't answer right away. Instead, she lifts a hand, holding the single rose like it carries a meaning too heavy to speak aloud. She kneels and places it carefully on the headstone nearby, her fingers lingering on the petals. For a moment, the rose seems to emit a faint light, a warmth that reaches out across the stone's cold surface. And then it fades, slipping away into the stillness, leaving only the quiet and the memory of its glow.

My father slides an arm around her shoulders. She tilts her head to rest against him, her eyes closing as she draws a long, steady breath. The silence between them is tender, a language all its own.

"He was a good boy," she says softly. "A good boy."

"He was," my father replies.

She brings a white handkerchief to her face, dabbing at her eyes, then looks toward me. "You'll come visit with me, piccolo?"

I don't know what 'piccolo' means but I reply, "I will, Gram."

"Good," she says with a small, approving nod, reaching out to pat my cheek. "You've got so much to tell me."

She turns and begins to walk away, her figure growing smaller against the horizon, where the sun dips low, bathing everything in a golden haze. I stand watching, caught between the ache of parting and the quiet joy of knowing her at last.

"When do you think I can see her again?" I ask my father, the words coming out more hopeful than I intended.

"When the moment is right," he replies.

"Piccolo?" I ask.

"It means little one," my father explains. "What she called you the first time she held you."

"You were so tiny," my mother adds with a fond smile. "Even your father was afraid to hold you. Thought he'd break you."

My father chuckles. "You were a squirmy thing, always wriggling away."

"Where did she get the flower?" I ask, the question spilling out before I've had time to think about it.

"Probably from a memory she visited," my father says. "She loves roses."

I look down at the headstone, noticing again the space where the rose had been. The name engraved on the stone catches my eye. Thomas. The name isn't familiar.

"Dad, who's Thomas?"

For a moment, he's quiet. "He's your uncle," he says finally.

I stare at him, my confusion plain. Uncle Thomas? The name means nothing to me, as though it's been plucked from someone else's life and dropped into mine.

"You never knew him," my father says, his tone quiet, almost guarded.

I'm about to ask more, but something in his face stops me. His expression shifts, his gaze drifting somewhere far away. It's as if a curtain has fallen, and whatever's on the other side isn't meant for me. The silence between us feels thick, full of things unsaid, and I can feel him pulling away, withdrawing into a place I can't reach.

But the questions won't leave me.

"Dad, why don't I remember him?" I ask, my voice softer, testing the ground between us.

His face is impossible to read, unmoving, offering nothing. I wonder if he'll answer or let the moment dissolve.

Then my mother speaks, her voice steady and sure in a way that makes me look at her. "He should know," she tells my father. "It's time. Time for all of it."

My father sighs and for a long moment, he doesn't look at me. Silence stretches between us before he finally reaches out, his hand finding mine.

The taste of pear

My father stands beside me in the orchard, watching as I turn the pear over in my hand. Its skin is golden, streaked with green, the surface cool against my palm. The air carries the scent of earth and ripened fruit, something familiar yet distant.

"When's the last time you ate one?" he asks.

I search my memory but come up empty. "I don't know," I admit.

He nods, not pressing further. I lift the pear to my mouth and take a bite. The sweetness rushes through me, sharp and startling, like I've never tasted one before. Juice runs down my chin, and I swipe at it with the back of my hand, laughing.

"You always did make a mess," he says, smiling now.

The trees shift in the light, shadows breaking across the ground. I blink, and suddenly, we are not alone. Through the branches, I see us from years ago - him in his fifties, hair still dark, and me, younger, gathering fallen limbs. Our footsteps press into dry leaves, the sound of them softened by distance. The past is near, but just beyond reach, moving through the orchard in quiet understanding.

I only remember pieces of that day. It was before we sold my grandfather's house, before the orchard was left to itself. He spent hours out there, pruning, planting, tending. Now the branches tangle together, the grass pushing high around the trunks. I close my eyes, and it all returns - climbing trees, eating pears until my stomach hurt. The taste lingers, sweet and familiar, a thread pulling me backward.

"Do you remember your grandfather's pear trees?" my father asks. He watches the orchard, his expression caught somewhere between past and present.

"Of course," I say. "How could I forget?"

Maggie is here. She moves between us, paws swiping at butterflies that slip away before she can touch them. Her tail flicks once, her frustration growing. She stops, watching, calculating.

Mrrr . . . Mrrr . . .

"Maggie, you'll never catch one," I tell her, laughing. "You're too slow, old girl."

She looks up, green eyes flashing with something close to offense. She glances at the butterflies, then down at her paws, reconsidering. When she lifts her gaze again, determination sharpens her features.

"I can't help myself," she says. "Don't worry. I'll catch one. You'll see. And don't call me old."

She pounces again, missing. My father and I both laugh.

"Where's Mom?" I ask, still watching Maggie.

"Oh, she's somewhere else," my father says, his voice drifting. "Another memory, maybe."

I turn to him, my unease growing. So many questions swirl in my mind. Why are we here? What does he want me to remember? He never answered me at the cemetery, and now the space between us feels stretched thin, holding something I can't quite reach. Something is missing. Something he isn't telling me.

Then, at least, he speaks.

"Sorry I didn't answer your question in the cemetery," he says. "Your mother is right. It's time. I thought I'd bring you here. I remember how you loved it."

I feel a touch of warmth at his thoughtfulness, and slowly, my worries fade.

The orchard is where I spent most of my childhood. I used to talk to the trees, convinced they understood me in some quiet, unspoken way. They stood steady, full of something I took to be wisdom. Beneath their branches, I felt protected, certain I would grow the way they did.

The things we believe as children.

Then, one by one, the trees began to fail. Leaves browned and dropped, trunks cracked. I didn't know why. I kept whispering to them, waiting for something - some sign that they were listening. Nothing came.

Every day, I returned, hoping to see new shoots, fresh leaves, any sign of renewal. But the orchard only thinned.

"There used to be more trees," I say, turning to my father. "Gramps had to cut some down. The trees were growing too close to each other. I remember helping him."

We walk to the stumps, scattered reminders of what had been.

The orchard feels different now. It was once dense, overflowing with life. But time asks for its share. More trees had to go. The change is sharp, undeniable, a quiet lesson in how nothing holds forever.

"Gramps said we had to help by cutting them down," I say. "I didn't want to do it at first. It didn't make sense. But if he said it mattered, I knew it did. It was hard, but it felt right."

The times with my grandfather stay with me, clear as ever. I remember the first day he brought me here, maybe five or six years old, my boots crunching over frozen ground. Snow covered everything, the branches bare except for a few stubborn leaves, holding on longer than they should.

We'd sit on the bench he built, and he'd tell me about planting each tree, about the seasons of care, the years spent shaping this place into something alive. I'd listen, eyes wide, caught in the story of it. Back then, the orchard felt like something beyond ordinary, a world where anything could happen.

Now, silence has taken over. Some trees still bear fruit, others lean, roots too shallow to keep them standing. The orchard fades in small ways, slow enough that someone passing through might not notice. But I notice. It isn't what it was.

Time is relentless, the ultimate equalizer, leaving nothing untouched in its wake. Everything ages and fades.

"Time ruins everything," I say, my voice hollow. "Every person I've known in this place, every memory, only leads me back to the end of it."

My father nods, understanding more than he says. "Hard truth," he tells me. "Nothing lasts."

His words are sharp but not unkind. I think about what it means to love something even while watching it slip away.

We stop walking. I turn to him. "Loss has always felt too big to carry," I say. "I can't outrun it. Even here, every step, every thought leads me back to what's gone."

He takes my hand, his grip firm but gentle. "I know," he says. "I know," he says. "No matter how far you go, grief stays with you."

Frustration fills me.

Why can't I let this go?

I feel trapped, circling the same sorrow, no exit in sight.

I sit on a stump, my mind drifting to the orchard. "Loss never gets easier," I say. "No matter how much of it you've known." I glance at my father, sitting beside me. "A person, a job, a pet, the trees in an orchard. It doesn't matter. It still hurts."

"Sometimes we try to make sense of it," he says. "We search for someone or something to blame. We grieve, and we try to move on."

"But there's always a sadness that stays," I reply. "Waiting to remind us of what was, of what used to be." I sigh. "And the older you get, the more you expect it. You adjust, you grow numb. But it's strange. Even with loss all around, you never think about your own."

"You only think about death when it gets close," my father says. "And then you wait."

"You wait and wait," he continues, his voice steady. "You wait for the moment it finds you. But if I've learned anything, it's that loss belongs to everyone. No one carries it alone. Others have been here before. They help us find a way through. Loss, in the end, is just a part of life."

"But this isn't life, is it now?" I say coldly.

He looks at me, eyes narrowing. "What do you mean?"

I take a breath, trying to steady myself. "Look at it. Our past was shaped by loss. One morning, we woke up and saw the world wasn't as simple, or as kind, as we thought. Our trust in others shattered, and we quickly learned to fear what we didn't understand. And then, the losses that came - people drifting away, some separated by distance, others by death. Their absence stayed with us, heavy and constant. And as we grew older, we lost our youth. Our bodies weakened, our hair turned gray, and our skin showed the marks of time. We lost our strength. And the years . . . the years . . . they left us feeling empty, each one taking something from us. Our past life was a series of relentless losses, without any hope for the future. And now, even here, in this next life, we're still carrying it."

My father looks at me, taken off guard. "How do you mean?"

"Our memories," I say, my voice flat. "Every time we remember something, we're reminded of what we've lost. It's always there, just beneath the surface, like a shadow you can't outrun. Even now, even in death, it follows us."

The silence that fills the space between us is thick, like the air just before a storm.

"Did we gain anything?" I ask softly, my voice steady but small. "Or was it all just . . . one loss after another?"

"We die many times over the course of our lives," my father says. "Every loss is another way we learn to face the next one. Death – well, death is a prankster. It tricks us at first, pretending to be something terrifying when we're young. But when we get older, wiser, we start to see it for what it is. It's not so scary anymore."

He pauses, letting his words sink in. "We don't just learn to accept death, we learn how to die. I see what you're saying, I really do. But even with all that loss, there was still something to be gained."

"Gained?" I ask, disbelief creeping in. "What was there to gain?"

"New experiences," he says, "new memories. We gather them, one by one, like wildflowers, each one precious, each one different. We hold them close. And when loss arrives, those memories are what we have left. They give us comfort. They guide us. They remind us of what mattered, of what we loved."

"Loss is a teacher," I whisper.

He nods slowly. "It shows us the true value of something - how to hold every moment carefully. It teaches us to see what we have. Even with loss, life remains something rare. The memories of those we've lost - they're the strength that keeps us going. I've lost many, but the memories . . . they stay. Always."

"But why does it still follow us?" I ask. "Why does it still haunt us here?"

"Life's life, I suppose," he says, a slight shrug in his voice. "Past life, next life, who knows? We can choose to let loss break us, or we can let it make us stronger. It's our choice. It's always about the choices we make."

I sit there, frustrated, like a child trying to make sense of a puzzle, the pieces so close yet just out of reach. I see them. I feel them. But I can't hold on to them. The frustration churns inside me.

My father looks at me with concern. He sees the struggle but doesn't know how to fix it. He just sits, waiting for me to find my own way.

I look at him, my face scrunched in confusion. He wants to comfort me, but there's hesitation there like he's not sure how to untangle the mess of emotions filling the space between us.

When I meet his eyes, I can see the worry in them. A knot tightens in my chest. I realize I've placed too much of myself onto him, burdened him with the weight of my confusion. I take a deep breath, trying to find some calm.

"I'm sorry," I tell him. "I guess I've been a little overwhelmed. I thought things would be different. I thought the pain would fade."

He seems to relax, just a bit.

"It's all a journey. Even here," he says. "You can't move forward without knowing where you've been. You can't leave it behind, but you don't have to carry it either. You learn from it. It makes you stronger."

I give a faint smile. "Memories, they're tricky, aren't they? They promise joy and love, but then they trap you, keep you circling back, making you relive the past over and over. But here . . . here in this life . . . it's different. Here, at least, the mortal veil of fear is lifted."

I pause. The pieces of the puzzle remain just out of reach.

"If fear's gone, then what takes its place?" I ask.

He shakes his head. "I don't know."

I sigh. "It's all we've got. Life is just life."

He smiles a small, wry smile, and gives my knee a firm, reassuring squeeze. "Look at us - two old fools trying to figure out eternity."

THE SHADE OF THE OAK TREE

The orchard is still, the air thick, almost resisting my every movement. It stretches endlessly, holding something heavy in the silence. I feel it before I see it - this pull, this presence of something waiting just beyond my reach. A blur begins to form, soft at first, like a shadow creeping in, until it's all around me. It's familiar and foreign at once, a tangled mess of images and feelings, overlapping and shifting. A memory taking shape.

I reach for my father, but he slips from my grasp, no longer solid, nothing more than a wisp of smoke that vanishes in an instant. I can't hold on to him, can't make him stay. The memory tightens, relentless, pushing me further. Then, just as I feel I can't breathe, there's a sudden flash, sharp, brilliant, cutting through it all - brief and blinding. It tears the cloud apart, and suddenly, the air is lighter.

I'm standing at my father's grave. It's winter and the cold seeping through my shoes, biting into my bones. It's been two weeks since he died, but it feels like yesterday, or maybe a lifetime ago. The finality hasn't settled in yet, still too unreal. A dull ache tugs at my chest - the yearning for one more conversation, to share things with him just one more time. But I know it's not possible. All I can do now is stand here, in this place, and remember.

I don't know why I'm here, why I've come to this spot on this day. I'm not sure what I'm meant to see, what I'm meant to understand. But something pulls at me, a gentle tug in my chest, like a quiet insistence that there's something I need to grasp.

The wind presses against me, light but steady, stirring the snow that falls in soft flurries. It coats everything in a shimmer, delicate, catching the weak daylight. The graveyard is serene - my parents chose this spot well, at the end of the row, shaded by a strong oak. There's a bench nearby, placed for reflection. I kneel in the snow, brushing it gently from the grave marker, the marble cold under my fingers. Standing, I study it, my mind tracing the lines and angles, thinking of everything it represents, all the moments it holds.

The world feels quiet here, the snow absorbing every sound. Time seems to hold its breath, suspended. I'm not sure if I'm still in the world I know, or if I've stepped into something else entirely, a space that holds no noise, no movement.

And then, faintly, like the whisper of the wind itself, I think I hear it - a sound, just on the edge of perception. "Goodbye, Father. May you find peace."

The words are soft, simple, yet they feel like they carry everything. I murmur a prayer, lifting it upward, my hands steady, my heart light.

I sit on the bench, my mind full of the final days, of the moments I can't shake. I don't want to forget them. They have become part of me, woven into my every thought. A stillness comes over me, a quiet certainty that he is still with me in some way, some form. His presence hasn't left. It lingers, constant, and I find comfort in that, in the knowledge that he is not gone, but remains in me, a part of my story.

I sit there, lost in the quiet until a memory cuts through.

I remember his voice now, clear and firm. "I don't want any of you visiting mine and your mother's grave," he told us. "Life is for the living."

I smile at the memory, at the warmth of his voice, the way he would always try to lighten the heaviness of life with humor, with wisdom. Even in death, he wanted us to live - to move forward, to find joy in the moments still ahead. He didn't want us trapped in the past. He wanted us to keep going. To honor him by continuing on.

A warmth fills me, a sense of peace. I'm not the same person I was before I came here.

The wind picks up, biting once more. I pull my coat tighter, the chill nipping at my cheeks. Standing, I brush the snow from the grave marker again, just as I did before.

"Dad," I whisper, my voice barely audible against the wind. "I know you didn't want us to visit. That life is for the living. But —"

The snowflakes fall, drifting down like tiny stars. Each one catches the light, shining bright for a moment before fading into the earth. I look up at the sky, a small smile pulling at my lips, knowing he's somewhere out there, watching, listening.

The snow keeps falling, soft and gentle. I smile, the thought of him warming me.

I take a breath, the cold sharp in my lungs, and turn to leave. But before I go, I whisper once more, "I'll be back, Dad."

SOMETHING GOOD ALWAYS COMES FROM AN ENDING

A storm of emotions and thoughts swirls around me, a whirlwind of confusion. I'm lost, floating in a sea of memories, unable to discern what's real and what's not. The uncertainty threatens to unravel me. I try to scream, but no sound escapes. The chaos builds, rising to a sharp, blinding white light, and then, just as suddenly, everything goes quiet.

I see myself sitting with my siblings at our mother's bedside, a silence hanging over us that words cannot fill. Her stillness is unnerving, her skin pale, and her breaths come so faintly that each one seems to strain against the inevitable. We take turns holding her hand, offering whispers of reassurance that feel as though they are more for us than for her. She doesn't stir, her body unresponsive to the touch of our affection.

I'm not sure why I've brought myself back to this memory. Maybe it's an attempt to hold onto her, to keep her alive in memory if not in presence. Or perhaps it's to remind me of the unshakable fortitude she carried through every moment of her life, even now as she lies on the threshold of its end.

Whatever the reason, I'm grateful to have this fragment of time to hold her hand, to tell her what she's meant to me, to try and find the words that feel too small for the enormity of her absence. It's a goodbye I never feel ready to give, though I know it's the only gift I've left to offer her.

The sound of my mother's labored breathing crackles in the air, breaking the rhythm of the ticking clock on the wall. The steady ticking of the second hand is relentless, pressing forward. It feels like the clock is counting down the seconds, each measured beat a reminder of what's to come. She swallows with difficulty, and her eyes find mine with a clarity that startles me.

"Do you think I'll see your father?" she asks. Her voice is fragile, worn thin by the weight of her life. Yet there's a calm in her words, as though she already knows the answer.

She knows she's nearing the end. There's a heaviness in her eyes, and a swell of emotion rises in me, so forceful it threatens to drown any words I might offer. I want to tell her it'll all be alright, but my voice betrays me, locked somewhere deep and unreachable.

She deserves reassurance, a kindness I struggle to give. Instead, I manage a nod, tears streaking my face in silence.

"Yes, Mom. You'll see him again," I whisper, at last, my voice trembling.

A smile softens her face, her expression serene. Her gaze shifts upward, drawn to something I cannot see. Slowly, she closes her eyes, drawing in a final breath. Then, with a sigh that seems to empty her entirely, she lets go and slips away from us.

It's over.

My sister gently places a set of rosary beads into her hands, a gesture that feels as much for us as for her. I sigh, my thoughts drifting through fragments of the past - laughter, fleeting joys, the moments my parents once shared. I hold on to the image of them walking hand in hand, their closeness a quiet marvel.

I wish for it again, desperately. But I know better.

They're both gone now, and all that remains are memories, fragile and fleeting. I can already sense the memories pulling away, retreating further with every passing moment. I sit by her bedside, tears rolling steadily down my cheeks, blurring the world around me. The ache in my chest is a pain I've known before, yet it feels unbearably sharp, as if grief has found a new way to carve into me.

"Goodbye, my love," I whisper, leaning close to press a kiss against her cold forehead. My siblings follow, one by one, their farewells quiet and reverent, their lips brushing her skin like a prayer.

I look around the room, taking in the pieces of her life. A shelf holds small keepsakes, each carrying its own meaning - a seashell from a trip with my father, photographs capturing moments of joy, books with softened edges from years of turning pages. A calendar hangs crooked on the wall, her careful handwriting marking birthdays and anniversaries, a heart drawn beside each one.

"It's sad," I say to my siblings. "A life so rich ends with just a handful of keepsakes."

But I know that the measure of a life isn't in the objects left behind. It's in the love that lingers, the way it changes those who carry it forward. She gave us more love than we ever deserved. And even now, as I sit here, the gratitude for her fills me, pushing back the hollow ache of loss. Though she's no longer here, I feel her presence - watching over us.

I will carry her with me, always

A voice pulls me from my thoughts, quiet but clear.

"I remember that day."

It's my mother's voice, soft and steady, breaking into the silence like the first breath of dawn. She stands beside me, her hand in mine, her warmth anchoring me. We look down together, bound by the memory between us. Tears shine in her eyes, catching the light.

"Do you visit this memory often?" I ask her.

"Of course. How could I forget that day?" she says. "It was special for me - a day of joy and happiness."

How could she possibly think of the day she died as special?

As if hearing the question form in my mind, she draws me close, her arm slipping through mine, her tears blending into a soft smile. "Don't you see? Look at us. We were together, all of us, one last time. That day - when I was reunited with your father - holds a special place in my heart."

Her words catch at something inside me, unsettling and tender all at once. I want to ask her how she reconciles the loss with the joy, but I hold the question.

"Death is beautiful," she says, her voice quieter now. "It's a celebration of a life well-lived. It brings you peace."

"How were you so sure you'd see Dad again?" I ask, not to challenge her, but because I truly want to know.

"Faith . . ." she says, almost in a whisper, ". . . faith that tells us there's more waiting for us."

She speaks of her belief in God, of a plan woven for each of us. Faith has always been a source of comfort for my mother, her anchor in a world often heavy with grief. It was the one certainty she clung to, no matter what storms came.

What is faith if not a belief in the impossible?

Impossible - I laugh softly to myself. Here I am, in the next life. If that isn't impossible, then what is?

"You always held on to it," I say. "Even though you never knew what would come next, you always clung to your faith."

She smiles, her face glowing with an inner warmth.

"You never really understood faith," she tells me, her voice kind, not accusatory. "You needed to pull things apart. To see them from every angle. But faith is so simple. It's knowing there's something bigger than us, something we can't always see but can trust is there. It's believing that even when we can't see it, something beautiful and majestic awaits us."

I shrug. "But what if things were different? What if we simply ended? What if there was nothing after life?"

She leans closer, her voice barely above a breath. "Is this nothing?" She whispers in my ear.

We watch as my siblings and I share stories that ripple with the depth of a family's love. Every moment - birthdays, illnesses, triumphs, failures - held together by the presence of our parents, steady through it all. These memories feel untouchable, the kind that shapes who you are.

"I know it may never make sense," she tells me. "We aren't meant to understand everything. But when the unknown feels overwhelming, remember this: something good always emerges from an ending."

We listen to the echoes of our shared past and watch as my siblings embrace our mother one last time before we leave the room.

"I remember that day - thinking about how we left you there, alone among your memories," I tell her. "After we said goodbye, I pictured you back home in your chair, looking out at the garden. The light fading, the flowers bathed in gold, everything so calm and still. And I told myself that if there were an afterlife, it would feel like that moment for you."

She whispers again, her lips warm against my cheek. "It did. It does. Remember, something good always comes from an ending."

And then she fades away, leaving me alone with the memories she gave me. There's a flash . . .

INNOCENCE LOST

Daddy, do you dream?

Everyone dreams, son.

Do you dream good dreams?

Yes.

What do you dream of?

I dream of a world where everyone is happy and safe. What about you? What do you dream of?

I dream of flying through the air like a bird.

That sounds like a wonderful dream.

It is.

I used to dream of flying when I was young. But no more.

What changed?

Everything, son. Everything.

LIKE A RIVER

I'm back in the orchard with my father, I take another bite of the pear, savoring the sweet burst of its juicy flesh. Around us, the world feels impossibly vivid - the sun casting its golden light across the trees, the air rich with the smell of cut grass, and a breeze that brushes past, cool and deliberate. The moment hums with life, each detail a reminder of the astonishing, fragile brilliance of this place.

"Where did you go?" my father asks as though the answer has already crossed his mind.

"I revisited a few memories - sad ones. I don't really know how or why."

"Sad memories," he says. "Which ones?"

I pause, the words sticking in my throat. "Visiting your gravesite. Mom's death."

He starts to speak, then hesitates, his breath catching on something unspoken. When he finally answers, his voice is steady, careful, each word chosen with purpose.

"There's nothing wrong with remembering," he says. "Sometimes going back to those moments can help. They don't vanish just because you stop thinking about them. They're part of who you are, a part of how you see the world now. They help us process our emotions, come to terms with the past, and understand the present. There's no wrong memory."

"It feels like sitting with an old friend," I admit, "tracing the edges of a story I already know by heart. I just don't know why I ended up back at those memories."

He tilts his head slightly, considering this. "The mind works in mysterious ways," he says. "Sometimes it's searching for something, even if you don't know what it is. And sometimes, you're just passing through, taking what you need, whether or not you realize it."

The memories of my parents' deaths sit with me, solid and unyielding. I try to push them aside, but they remain, lingering in the edges of my thoughts.

"Do you revisit it often - the memory of your passing?" I ask.

He nods slowly. "I think everyone does. Even your mother. It's one of her favorites."

"She was there when I visited the memory of her passing. She pulled me away from the moment, and we watched it together."

"Really?"

"She says she goes back to it because she sees everyone gathered around her, almost like a celebration. She believes that something good always comes from an ending."

"I feel the same way. When you go back to that moment, you can say goodbye to those you love, again. It fills you with a sense of joy, knowing that the moment of passing isn't final - it's just a step. It was a comfort to me knowing that, even though your mother wasn't with me when I arrived here, I knew she eventually would be."

He smiles, his heart swelling with love.

"She's always with you, isn't she?" I ask.

"No matter where I go. Just like when we were alive."

"Did you visit her often, when you first got here? Just to see what she was doing?"

"Every day," he says, his eyes damp with emotion. "I never wanted to forget her, and I never have."

"Were you there when she passed?"

"I was," his voice trembles. "It was incredibly difficult for me. Not because she was dying, but because I knew she didn't want to leave everyone behind. Still, I was glad to be there, to witness her last moments, and to welcome her into this place."

There's a tenderness in his words, something layered and deep, and I feel the enormity of what this has meant to him, how it has shaped him in ways he can't quite express.

"I'm so glad you can be with her," I say quietly. "It must mean the world to her."

"It does."

For a while, we sit without speaking, letting the silence fill in the spaces between us.

Mrrr ... Mrrr ...

Maggie sniffs at the tall grass, then eagerly flops down and rolls around in it. She twists and rolls, her small body arching and stretching, legs extended in a display of contentment. When she finally comes to rest, she's a soft patch of fur basking in the sunlight, the rhythm of her purring rising and falling in time with her breath.

I reach down to stroke her belly, carefully and gently. She responds by wrapping her back legs around my arm, pulling me closer, her grip firm, affectionate. The warmth of her small body presses into my skin, stirring something long buried, a sensation that feels both familiar and distant. Her purring deepens as I continue to pet her, the sound filling the quiet around us.

"You're a silly little girl," I tell her.

With a playful kick of her back legs, she nudges my arm, then nips at my hand in a gentle, teasing gesture. Her mood is light and carefree. Then suddenly her ears stand upright, and her gaze sharpens. Something has caught her attention.

Mrrr . . . Mrrr . . .

She pushes my arm away, flipping onto her back in a swift motion. Her ears twitch, and her tail swishes back and forth as she crouches low, her body taut with focus. Through the blades of grass, she peers into the thicket, its shadowed edges hiding whatever has stirred. The sound comes again - a faint rustling from between two pear trees.

Mrrr . . . Mrrr . . .

Creeping forward, she stretches low to the ground, her body a coil of tension. The thicket beckons, the grass, and branches whispering secrets, urging her onward into the unknown. She inches closer, her eyes darting, her ears swiveling. Then, as if caught in a sudden stillness, she freezes.

It's a mouse.

They lock eyes, and in that instant, they both know what's at stake. Her gaze sharpens as she longs to make a meal of this tiny creature, while the mouse, trembling, reads the danger in her stare.

The mouse bolts, a quick, desperate burst of movement, and Maggie reacts instantly. Her muscles coil, her body tensing as she lunges forward with startling speed. In a flash, her paws snap shut, and the mouse lets out a shrill squeal. But before she can close the trap, the tiny creature squirms free, wriggling out of her grasp with a frantic struggle.

It skitters away, toward a wooden shed, its tail flicking in frantic panic, tiny legs a blur against the ground as it seeks distance. Maggie crouches, a low growl rumbling in her chest, her body tense and ready. She can smell the mouse's fear, and something deep inside her stirs, making her ready to spring. But just as she prepares to pounce, the mouse disappears into a crack beneath the shed.

Maggie paws at the hole in frustration, hissing and growling at her thwarted hunt. Her fur bristles with indignation.

My father and I can't help but laugh at her misfortunes.

"I don't think it's funny," she snaps. "Not at all. I haven't caught anything since I got here. It's infuriating."

"What's wrong?" I tease. "The mighty huntress can't catch her prey? Maggie, what's the big deal?"

"It's not a joke," she says. "It's who I am. It's what I do. But this place - this place takes it from you. It robs you of the things that matter."

Her words hit harder than I expected. There's something in her voice that feels unsettling - something I don't want to acknowledge but can't ignore.

"What do you mean, 'things'?"

Her ears flatten back as she swishes her tail low. "You really want to know?" she growls.

"Yes, tell me," I say.

"Little bits of you - your sense of who you are, the things that keep you whole. They all slip away slowly, taken by this place. You try to cling to them, but those things that define you fade just out of reach. You'll see. You'll see."

Mrrr . . . Mrrr . . .

Perched near the hole, she sits perfectly still, patient and intent - waiting for the mouse.

"What do you think she's trying to say?" I ask my father.

He pauses, his gaze turning inward as if he needs a moment to find the right words. "It's a warning, son," he says.

I study his face, looking for some clue in his expression. "What kind of warning?"

He takes a breath, and his tone becomes softer, more serious. "It's about what the next life takes from you."

I feel something stir inside me - confusion and discomfort. It sounds like something I should understand but can't quite grasp. I want to ask more, to pry into the meaning behind his words, but something tells me he's not ready to go any further. His mind, I realize, is somewhere far away.

He stands and takes my hands. He's made up his mind.

"Your mother's right. It's time you know."

"Know what?"

"About your Uncle Thomas. But -" He hesitates.

"What is it?"

His voice lowers. "A family's history is like a river. It winds through our lives, carving its path, always changing but always moving toward the same place. And like a river, there are things within its depths - secrets and stories. No matter how far it takes us or how much time passes, it remains part of us - whether we like it or not."

He tightens his grip, closing his eyes for a moment like he's bracing himself against some unseen tide.

THE GOOD BOOK

The past rushes at me, a wave of memories crashing about. My breath catches as I step into the old farmhouse, the cradle of my father's childhood. This was where their laughter and shouts pressed into the walls as firmly as the nails that held them together. Yet, something is off, slightly shifted, like I've stepped through the wrong door. Sunlight angles through the windows in an unfamiliar way, pushing shadows into corners where memory once held brightness. The furniture remains, mostly unchanged, but the room itself seems to have drawn inward, closer than I remember. Looking around I realize the kitchen and front porch additions aren't here yet.

Where there was once a living room, there's now a kitchen. A white-enameled cast iron sink occupies the far corner, its edges scarred with use, catching the stray gleam of light from the small, high-set window. Next to the sink, a well-water hand pump rises stiffly, the iron darkened by years of touch. A wood stove anchors the room, its stovepipe stretching upward and disappearing into the wall, while beside it, a tall icebox stands. Shelves are brimming with canned peaches and tomatoes, and in the middle of the room is a rough-hewn table surrounded by mismatched chairs, the wood nicked and worn from generations of hands and elbows.

This kitchen opens into a parlor. There's a sofa and two armchairs upholstered in a soft, faded floral fabric. The walls are painted a soft, quiet green, uncluttered, and a little radio sits on a low table, its dials dark. An old brown jute rug sprawls across the floorboards, grounding the room in an earthy scent that rises with every step.

The whole house feels simpler, more bare than I remember, the familiar creaks underfoot now silent. And yet, there's a strange comfort in this place, a sense of intimacy, like wrapping myself in an old sweater, patched and threadbare but still warm. The years have left their mark on these walls, every scrape and scratch murmuring its story, and I feel the presence of that history pressing against me.

I wander through the rooms and start to hear the murmurs of old voices - my aunts and uncles as children, laughing in the kitchen, my grandmother's humming over the stove, and the shuffling rhythm of life in this place. I can smell the faintest whiff of roasting vegetables, wet linens, and wood smoke, lingering like the scent of something nearly forgotten.

Standing by the kitchen table, the house seems to ripple softly, as if the edges of reality had softened just enough to let the past seep through. Faces and sounds move in and out of focus, overlapping in a dance of clarity and haze. For a moment, I feel them all - laughing, stirring, some sitting at the kitchen table, others in the parlor playing. The house draws a deep breath, and I find myself breathing in time with it, caught in the rhythm of something greater, something impossibly alive.

I think I see my father in the parlor, a young boy starting his teenage years. He's with his brothers and sisters, my aunts and uncles. The older ones are listening to the radio while the younger ones are on the floor playing with wooden toys.

My grandmother sits at the kitchen table, her wispy frame is draped in a brown dress and white apron. She looks to be fifty or so, her hair streaked gray and pulled back in a tight bun. Silver-rimmed glasses magnify her eyes as she looks down at a large book on the table.

Her gaze shifts up from the book and drifts out across the parlor. She calls softly, "Rosemarie, come here. I want to show you something." The words, tender yet sure, carry a kind of quiet authority that reaches across the room.

A small girl, maybe eight or nine, rises from where she'd been playing on the floor beside her father. She makes her way over to the kitchen table, eyes wide, steps careful, drawn into the gravity of my grandmother's presence. I watch her, this little girl who's my Aunt Rose, the youngest of them all.

My father follows her, his own eyes wide. He's cautious as if he doesn't know what to expect. He stops at the far end of the table, his hands resting awkwardly at his sides, unsure whether to reach out or hold back.

My grandmother reaches out and draws my aunt onto her lap, folding her in close. My aunt snuggles into her, resting naturally against my grandmother's shoulder. My grandmother's hand moves gently through her hair, the tenderness in her touch woven with a sorrow that seems to linger in her gaze.

She holds the book up, tilting it slightly so the light catches the gilded edges. "See? Isn't it beautiful?" she asks my aunt, her voice soft but insistent.

My aunt doesn't speak. Her chin dips in a slight nod, the movement restrained, giving nothing away.

My grandmother opens the book and carefully turns a few pages. I lean closer, drawn by the sheer presence of it. The book is enormous, its thick black leather cover worn smooth in places, suggesting years of handling. The pages, a pristine glossy white, shimmer faintly at their gold-lined edges, catching the light in a way that feels almost alive. Some pages hold striking black-and-white illustrations, their detail so precise they seem to breathe on the paper. Everything about the book speaks of significance, of something treasured and rare.

"What is this book?" my aunt asks.

"It's a Bible," my grandmother says. "It tells stories about about God and His creation."

I've seen many Bibles before - modest, left to gather dust on forgotten shelves, their covers worn by years of neglect. But this one is something else entirely. The pages hold a quiet presence, the scent of old paper and ink lingering as they're turned. They seem to speak, though not with words. There's something about it that draws me in, something beyond the way it looks. It has a beauty that's hard to put into words - alive, in a way that feels just beyond grasp.

My grandmother's hands hover over the pages, her fingers brushing the script with a tenderness that speaks volumes. She reads without speaking, her silence deep with reverence, a profound respect for the power faith can hold.

"Now, where is it?" she asks herself, carefully turning the pages. "There's something at the end I want to show you."

My aunt wiggles a bit in her lap and coos.

Turning a few more pages, my grandmother comes to the sections at the back of the book filled with family history.

"Ah, here we are," she says. "On this page, I've written down everything about my wedding to your father." She points to handwritten entries with a thin finger. "See. Here's the date we were married. And here's the name of the church where we were married, and the name of the priest who married us. And here are your grandparents' names and the names of my bridesmaid and your father's best man."

My aunt looks over the page, her eyes scanning the neat, precise handwriting. "Did you write all this?" she asks.

"Yes," my grandmother says turning the page. "All the writing in this book is mine. I started writing our family's history when I was a young girl, and I've added to it ever since." She points to another entry. "See, here's where I've recorded all the births of your brothers and sisters. Do you see the last record?"

My aunt nods.

"It's yours," my grandmother says with a smile hugging my aunt.

My aunt reaches over and traces the writing with a tiny finger.

Looking over my aunt's shoulder, I see all the names of my aunts and uncles and their birthdates. It starts with the firstborn.

Tommaso. Thomas in English.

I count the names. There are thirteen listed, not twelve.

Quickly, I look around the house and count.

Twelve. Twelve children.

Where's this Tommaso? Maybe he's outside with my grandfather?

My grandmother's eyes light up as she moves through the family history, a careful finger tracing the marriages and births that fill these pages. She knows them all by heart but never tires of looking, as if every name and date were a doorway she could open.

When she turns the page there's the list of those who are gone. A quiet sigh escapes her. She begins to read aloud, one name at a time, staying on each as though she's calling them back, if only for a moment. Her voice is soft, slowing as she reaches the dates, remembering who they were, and what they had shared. She can almost see them again, hear their laughter, and feel the warmth of those long-past days. When she finishes the last name, she lets the silence settle and closes the book as if tucking them all away, safe for another visit.

"You'll help me record our family history, here, in the good book," she tells my aunt who gives a solemn look. "There'll be some entries you make that'll be harder than others. But it's important to preserve our history. Every person in our family must never be forgotten. It's up to us to ensure their lives are not lost to time, to hold their stories as part of our own."

"Momma, can I help too?" my father asks.

She smiles at him. "No son, this is your sister's responsibility."

"Why me Momma?" my aunt asks.

My grandmother kisses my aunt on the forehead. "Because you're the youngest," she says, her voice soft but firm. "When my time comes, I want it to be your hand that writes my name on this very page, carrying our family's story into the future. And it'll be your duty to find the one who will help you with this, the one you'll pass on the responsibility to. But that person hasn't been born yet. You'll have to wait." She turns more pages of the book. "There are still many blank pages, for you to tell our family's story. So much time ahead of us."

My aunt frowns, a quiet disapproval pulling at her features. "I don't think I can write your name on that page," she says softly.

My grandmother offers a reassuring smile. "I know this is hard," she says, her voice gentle. "But here's what I want you to keep with you. When you write my name, don't just think of me. Think of everyone who came before. Remember the love, the courage, the strength that has carried through all these years."

"Is it like a chore, Momma?" my aunt asks.

"Kind of," my grandmother replies. "But where most chores settle heavy on your arms and legs, this one will sit squarely on your heart."

I watch as my aunt absorbs the words. There's a quiet shift in her, a realization that this isn't just another chore. It's a responsibility, deeply rooted in family and tradition. The weight of it isn't lost on her, but neither is the quiet respect with which she embraces it.

She throws her arms around my grandmother and hugs her.

"Momma," she whispers, her voice thick with promise. "I'll do my best."

THE DOCTOR

Outside the farmhouse, I stand in a small patch of grass, feeling the earth beneath my feet. Before me, the fields spread endlessly, rows of corn and vegetables swaying gently in the breeze. The farmhouse itself rises against the horizon, its white walls like a quiet sentinel, its windows dark and expectant. Along the foundation, rose bushes thrive, their blossoms soft and fragrant, their thorns sharp like tiny, patient claws. A red barn stands nearby, accompanied by a few modest sheds. The scene is peaceful, untouched by time, save for the breeze stirring the crops and the occasional bird calling from afar.

Hearing the soft thudding of boots on the ground, I turn to see my father coming from the barn. It's so strange to see him as a child. He stops in the middle of the yard, his eyes fixed on a man walking up from the road.

The man is tall, his slender frame emphasized by the billowing of his long black coat. A black fedora is pulled low over his face, obscuring his features. His pace is steady and he seems to be in a hurry, his eyes focused only forward. In one hand, he carries a black leather satchel with a sturdy handle and a brass lock.

As he draws closer, I can see more of his face. It's pale and weathered, with a long, thin nose and a sharp chin. His hair is gray and his eyes are dark and strange, like pools of ink in the night.

There's a presence about him, an aura of mystery that draws my father in.

"Can I help you good sir?" my father asks the stranger.

The man smiles. "Ah, you're the youngest of the boys, aren't you?"

"No sir. My brother Orlando is younger by a year."

"Ah, yes. Orlando. I've forgotten. Well, you've got quite a lot of brothers and sisters now, don't you?"

"Yessir. Need the hands to work the farm," my father says.

The man nods. "I see. And how's the work on the farm these days?"

"It's hard work, sir. But it's honest work."

"That it is. And if I may, how are you finding school?"

"It's not so bad. I'm learning a lot."

"That's good to hear. Do you know what you want to do when you grow up?"

"Not sure. Haven't given it much thought."

The man smiles warmly. "Well, being young has its advantages. You've all the time in the world to figure things out." He pauses. "Is your mom inside?"

"Yessir. She is."

The man gives my father a gentle pat on the head, then walks to the door and knocks on the wooden screen.

"Oh, Dr. Ilacqua. It's you," my grandmother says, opening the screen door to greet him. "I thought I heard voices. Thank you for stopping by."

The doctor smiles, offering a slight bow as he lifts his hat.

"Good to see you again," he says kindly.

My father slips in quietly behind the doctor as the screen door shuts with a loud thump. He removes his boots and hurries into the parlor, where he kneels to play with a few wooden toys scattered on the floor.

"Just made a pot of coffee," my grandmother says. "I know it's a long walk for you. Please sit and rest."

"I don't mind the walk on such a fine day," he says taking a seat at the kitchen table. "The coffee smells wonderful. Thank you."

She pours two cups; he takes his black as does she.

"How's everything here?" he asks.

"As good as can be I suppose considering the Depression."

He sighs. "Mighty tough times indeed. The papers say millions are out of work and homeless. For so many families, hunger and poverty are everyday struggles. It feels like this Depression has a grip on the country, tight as a vice."

My grandmother takes a slow sip of her coffee. "Hard work is what's needed in hard times," she says to him. "If you work hard and long enough, something will change. It doesn't matter what the world throws at you or how dark the days get. You have to keep your eyes fixed on building a better life for your family, even when everything feels like it's falling apart."

"You're right, of course. But for many, that's easier said than done."

"I suppose."

He takes a sip of coffee and pauses. "If I may, why did you ask me to visit with you today?"

"It's about Tommaso. You know the circumstances."

"It was a long time ago," he says. "If I remember, it was your sister who helped with your delivery."

My grandmother nods.

"She told me it was a very difficult delivery." The doctor pauses, his brow furrows, lips pressed together in concentration.

"The umbilical cord was tightly tangled around his neck. Am I correct?"

Again, my grandmother nods.

He continues. "When this happens it can result in a loss of oxygen that can compromise organs and brain tissue. Oftentimes, it results in permanent brain damage. But you've not seen this, have you? I mean, he did well in school, didn't he? And he's a strong boy. The last time I saw him he was almost as large as your husband and seemed as healthy as a horse."

She smiles, but it's a fleeting thing, gone before it's even begun. "He does eat like a horse," she says. "And he got through his schooling alright, but it was a struggle to keep him on his bookwork. Not like the others."

"Then what is it?"

"It's his anger that worries me, doctor. The children are always fearful of what might happen when his anger takes hold. They're on edge and never sure what'll set him off. When he lashes out it's a struggle to pull him back."

The doctor leans back, his chair creaking softly. "I see," he says, his voice a murmur.

"Is there anything that can be done?" My grandmother's voice quivers.

He shakes his head, his eyes filled with a sadness that seems to seep into the very air around them. "There are some treatments," he says, "but I can't recommend them. They're very traumatic. They'd change him forever. He'd never be the same, ever."

My grandmother's heart plummets, a stone dropping into the depths of her chest. The hope she'd been nurturing, fragile as a butterfly's wing, dissolves into nothingness. In its place, a vast uncertainty unfurls, stretching before her like an endless, moonless night. The future, once a tapestry of possibilities, now looms as a dark, impenetrable forest, its shadows deep and foreboding.

The doctor's face is kind but firm. "I know this is hard to hear," he says. "But I'm not just saying this to be difficult. These treatments are dangerous. They could do more harm than good, and often do."

Tears well up in her eyes.

"I understand," she says. "Thank you for your honesty."

Sensing her disappointment, the doctor reaches over and holds her hand. "Most infants wouldn't have survived what he went through," he says. "But somehow, he did. That's important to remember."

"Is there anything we can do?"

"Accept him just as he is. Use every moment you have with him to teach him how he should behave, and hope that, in time, he'll understand. It's not going to be easy and it won't get any easier as he grows older."

My grandmother takes the doctor's words to heart.

"We'll do our best, as we've always have," she tells him.

"I know you will. You've provided him with a loving and supportive home. It just means you'll have to spend more time with him than with the others."

"How so?"

"You'll have to work with him – to teach him the proper ways to behave, how to express his thoughts and feelings.."

She sighs. It's a sigh I've heard before, one that speaks of love and sacrifice and the long road ahead.

"It's never easy, I know," he says. "Especially these days with trying to make ends meet and all. But you have a loving family, and he's so strong and healthy. It'll take time and patience. You know you can always ask me for anything. I'll always be there for you."

She nods. "Thank you for coming out to talk with me about this."

"You're most welcome," he smiles, taking a last sip of coffee.

My grandmother walks him to the door.

"Do you need any vegetables?" she asks. "There's plenty here. I can have one of the boys get you a bushel basket. For your troubles in coming all this way to visit with me."

"Oh, no thank you. And it wasn't a bother at all," he tells her. "Good for me to get out of the office. Let me know if you want to talk again. Anything I can do to help - you just let me know."

She manages a grateful smile. "I will. Thank you again."

He gives a respectful bow and places his hat atop his head.

She stands in the doorway and watches the doctor walk away and down the road. Taking a deep breath, she closes the door behind her, turns, and leans against it, her eyes closed. She takes a few more deep breaths, trying to calm herself. When she opens her eyes, she sees my father standing before her.

"Are you okay, Ma?" His voice is sweet and filled with tenderness.

She smiles at him.

"Give your mother a hug," she says, her arms reaching for him.

He steps forward and wraps his arms around her.

She seems to melt into him, and I hear her whisper, "I'm so glad you're here for me."

He squeezes her tighter. "I'll always be here for you, Ma."

I watch them, a lump forming in my throat, their heads bent together, arms woven in a quiet understanding. The affection between them is unmistakable, simple, and deep. I can't help but smile. The warmth of their presence spreads through the air, like a promise of good things, and for a moment, the world seems lighter, more hopeful.

ANGER

The screen door creaks and slams behind me, breaking the stillness of the afternoon. The air shifts, and suddenly, it's autumn - the crisp bite of apples, and the dry scent of hay pressing against my senses. I squint against the sunlight, letting my eyes adjust to the landscape that's both achingly familiar and startlingly different. The dirt road stretches out before me, a ribbon of earth now frayed at the edges with weeds and tufts of grass. In my mind's eye, I see it transform - first into a neat two-lane strip of asphalt, then widening further into four lanes of bustling traffic. But here, now, in this moment, it's just a humble path reaching out to meet the horizon, unmarked by anything more than the quiet it carries.

I let my eyes wander to the barn and sheds, expecting the disrepair brought about by age that I remember. Instead, I find sturdy buildings, their fresh coats of paint vibrant against the muted hues of the rolling farm fields that stretch into the valley below and up the far ridge. For a moment, I close my eyes, and when I open them, the valley transforms in my imagination. There, in the valley, a school emerges in the gentle dip. Along the far ridge, houses begin to sprout and cluster, their rooftops and chimneys creeping upward, covering the slope in an uneven patchwork. The stillness of the moment bends, giving way to the inevitability of what's to come.

But for now, the farm slumbers in its timeless bubble. The only sounds are the whisper of wind weaving through cornstalks and the low hum of late-season bees. I take a deep breath, drawing in the essence of this place, knowing that each breath holds a moment that's already slipping away, already on the verge of dissolving.

I smile, a quiet acknowledgment that this place is part of me as much as I am part of it. Everywhere I look, I can feel a part of its spirit in my very being. This is home, and no matter what changes the world might bring, it will remain so.

The autumn air nips gently at my skin, the chorus of birdsong and children's chatter pulling my gaze toward the orchard. The voices of my aunts and uncles rise through the branches, light and carefree, like dandelion puffs carried on the breeze. The apple trees stand in rows, their branches weighed down with fruit, and the air is filled with the rich, earthy scent of a ripening harvest. This scene before me is more than just a beautiful moment; it's a glimpse of the future where my father would build a house, the house where I would be raised, rooted in this very soil, growing alongside these trees.

"Be careful, now," my grandmother calls out to the children.

She stands just outside the barn, stirring a large kettle of applesauce over an open fire. The flames crackle and dance, and the sound of her wooden spoon scraping against the side of the pot is a delightful tune. Her face shines with joy as she hums, lost in the simple pleasure of the task.

"Do you smell that?" she calls again, her voice carrying on the breeze. "That's the smell of the changing seasons."

I glance back to the orchard, where I can see my Aunt Rose and my father with the others.

"It smells . . . like something sweet," my aunt shouts back, unsure if the words make sense. She laughs and reaches up, plucking an apple from a low-hanging branch.

"Sure does," my grandmother replies.

She picks an apple from a nearby basket, its skin a rich red streaked with gold, and turns it in her hand. She takes a bite. The crisp crunch echoes in the cool air, sharp and satisfying, like the snap of a twig underfoot.

"Ma, leave some for the rest of us!" my father calls out from across the orchard.

I watch him struggle to climb one of the taller trees, his determination unshaken by the wobble in his step. He reaches for a cluster of apples just beyond his reach, his balance shifting as his foot slips on the branch.

"He's gonna fall," one of my uncles says, half-laughing.

"Let him. He'll get back up," my grandmother says.

And sure enough, he does. He dusts himself off and climbs higher, this time making it to the top. He hands down the apples to Aunt Rose, their skins gleaming in the late afternoon light like jewels.

"Perfect," Aunt Rose says, turning one in her hand before biting into it. The juice bursts out, sticky and sweet, and my father laughs as it dribbles down her chin.

The apple picking continues, but soon the work turns into play. My aunts and uncles, their faces flushed and hair disheveled, race through the orchard, laughing and shouting. They run among the trees, carefree, with no thought to the dirt that clings to their clothes. They're completely alive in the moment, and nothing else matters.

I see my grandmother smiling as she watches her children playing in the orchard. There's a quiet satisfaction in her eyes. She's pleased to see them so happy, so unburdened. She remembers when she was a child, picking figs with her mother at the end of summer. How they would spend hours gathering, tasting the fruit fresh from the trees. It's a memory she carries with her, one that quietly fills the spaces between her thoughts.

As she stirs the applesauce, I move closer, drawn to her, wanting to be near her, to be part of this moment. She looks up suddenly, and our eyes meet. I feel a jolt, a fleeting connection, and quickly look away. Though I know she can't see me, I can't shake the feeling that she does.

I turn back, slowly, my eyes finding hers once again. She's still looking at me, but just as quickly, her gaze shifts back to the pot. The moment passes, and I'm left standing there, knowing there's something else I must learn, something about my uncle, a person I've never heard of until . . .

"Tommaso!" my grandmother calls.

A young man, broad-shouldered, in his mid-twenties, steps out of the barn and lumbers over to her.

That's him. That's the uncle. Thomas.

"Ma, wah . . . wah . . . what, what is it?" he stutters.

"Go help the others bring me over more apples," she says in a gentle voice. "But be nice about it. Understand?"

He nods, but she holds his gaze for a moment longer.

"Tell me you heard me?" she insists but still in a gentle voice.

"Aww, ma. I ha . . . ha . . . heard ya," he says looking down.

"They're your brothers and sisters. You're the oldest. You treat them kindly. You hear?"

"I ha . . . ha . . . hear ya ma," he says, still looking down. "I ha . . . ha . . . hear ya."

He turns and walks away, heading toward the orchard. She watches him closely, studying his every movement, her eyes filled with worry.

"Be careful," a voice calls from behind. It's my grandfather, standing in the barn doorway, wiping his hands with a rag. He's been cleaning his shotgun, preparing for deer season. "The boy doesn't know his own strength. Keep an eye on him."

"Two eyes," my grandmother tells him without looking away.

My grandfather nods and turns back toward the barn. "Let me know if you need my help."

Still stirring her applesauce, she watches Thomas make his way to the orchard. His steps are heavy, his body tense. When he reaches the children, she can tell he's searching for the right words. His voice trembles, uneven, like he's trying to wrestle his emotions into submission.

She keeps her eyes on him as he empties the smaller baskets into the larger ones. When one is full, he hoists it up and begins the slow walk back to her. Around him, her aunts and uncles do their best to lift the heavy baskets on their own. Their small hands grip the handles with determination, apples tumbling from their efforts. They don't seem to mind. Their laughter carries across the orchard, bright and unhindered. She can't help but smile.

But that smile fades quickly as she sees Thomas push his younger siblings away, scolding them harshly. His voice booms like thunder, sharp and commanding, and the children cower in fear. They only want to help, but Thomas is lost in anger, seeing their laughter as mockery. His face twists with rage, his eyes glaring with heat.

A quiet sadness rises in her chest.

"Tommaso, what did I tell you?" she calls out, her voice carrying across the orchard.

He turns toward her, his expression twisted with frustration. "I'm sah . . . sah . . .sorry, Ma," he says, his eyes avoiding hers. "I didn't me . . . me . . . mean to."

But her expression doesn't soften. "Go and calm yourself," she orders, pointing toward the farmhouse. "Now."

He doesn't argue. He runs, shoulders tight and head low. She watches him leave, lips pressed together. She knows he needs to cool off before they can talk.

My grandfather appears from the barn. "What happened?" he asks.

"The same," my grandmother answers, her voice low. "Always the same. Anger gets the best of him every time. He can't seem to stop it. I want to help him, but I don't know how."

"Anger's a strong thing. I'll talk to the boy later."

"No," my grandmother says firmly. "I'll talk to him."

She gathers my aunts and uncles around her. "Stir the applesauce," she instructs some, while to others she says, "Begin peeling more apples." She puts my oldest aunt, Kate, in charge, before turning and walking toward the farmhouse.

I watch her walk away, knowing what she's going to do, and I worry. She's going to try to help him, but I don't know if he'll listen to her. His anger is too deep and I wonder if he can control his anger long enough for her to reach him.

Her mind, a whirlwind of anxieties, mirrors my own. What will she say to him? Will he even listen, or will his defenses rise, a fortress against her pleas? And can he, truly, leash the fury that simmers within him?"

I follow her into the farmhouse, stopping at the doorway as her gaze lands on him sitting at the kitchen table. He's staring at his hands, shoulders hunched, looking as though the world is too much for him. The tightness in his posture tells her everything — the anger is still there, bubbling just beneath the surface. He looks up at her, confusion in his eyes.

"Why? Why dah . . . dah . . . does this happen to me? Wah . . . wah . . . why Ma?" His voice cracks, words coming out in jagged pieces, as if the pain is too much to speak in full.

She steps closer, her hand resting gently on his shoulder. "Tell me, love," her voice soft, "what happened?"

He looks at her, then looks away, silent for what feels like an eternity. She stands there, waiting, giving him time.

Finally, he speaks, voice shaking with something close to fear. "I dah . . . dah . . . don't know wah . . . wah . . . what's wrong with me. I can't control it. I get ah . . . ah . . . angry so easily, and I don't know wah . . . wah . . . why. I can feel it inside me, like a fah . . . fah . . . fire that I can't put out."

Her heart aches for him. She pulls him close, wrapping her arms around him, hoping she can somehow soothe the storm inside him.

"It's not your fault, my love," she says softly. "Anger's hard to control, but it's something you can work on. It'll take time and patience. We can work on it together. Would you like that?"

He nods, barely, his eyes still downcast. She smiles at him, trying to give him something to hold onto.

It won't be easy, she knows that. But she's determined. She has to believe she can make a difference, no matter how long it takes.

"I want you to try something for me," she tells him.

"Wah . . . wah . . . what?"

"When you start feeling angry, stop. Just stop for a moment, and think. Ask yourself if your anger is going to hurt someone. If it will, I want you to walk away, find some space, and calm yourself down. You never want to hurt anyone."

"I nah . . . nah . . . nah . . . never want to hurt anyone," he repeats, his voice small, but earnest.

"That's right. I know you don't." She kisses his cheek, light and tender. "I love you. I'll be outside. When you're ready, you can come join us."

She leaves him there, sitting alone at the table, his gaze falling back to his hands. He takes deep breaths, his chest rising and falling as he tries to steady himself.

I watch him from the doorway, the pain clear in his eyes. He looks so lost as if he's been carrying something too heavy for too long. But beneath it all, I see something else - a simple goodness, a tenderness in him that's often hidden, buried under the weight of his anger. He has the capacity for kindness, for gentleness – it's there - even if he can't always show it.

THE SEASONS

I walk the farm for a long while, and then everything begins to change. The land shifts - autumn's gold fading to winter's silence, then spring's slow return. The fields breathe through the seasons, corn rising, apple trees budding. The wind carries traces of past rains, August heat, the first frost's bite. Time moves forward, folding in on itself, pulling me along.

My father's voice comes back to me, clear and steady. "It's all about the seasons," he once said. "Each one has its joys and sorrows. But farm work never stops." He leaned back in his chair, wood creaking beneath him. "Spring meant planting. We were in the fields before sunrise."

He spoke of mornings laced with dew, air sharp against their hands. "The animals came first. No excuses. The cows needed milking, the horses feeding. You learned not to complain."

Their days followed an unspoken order - seeds pressed into the earth with quiet determination. "We all knew what had to be done," he said. "The barn needed mending. The tools needed sharpening. It was a cycle, always turning."

His fingers skimmed the chair's arm, tracing something unseen. "When summer came - the days were long. By supper, it felt like a week had passed. But the work –" He paused. "The work gave us something. A kind of pride. Watching the fields turn green, seeing a calf take its first steps - that's what kept us going. Soon, the mornings cooled, the light thinning at the edges. It was autumn. The trees would burn gold and red, and the fields would give up the last of their offering. Apples heaped in baskets, grain bundled and stacked. A season's labor coming to its end, the land tilting toward rest."

Then suddenly everything around me slows as if the world has drawn a deep breath. The farm takes shape once more, its features distinct and steady amid the pull of shifting seasons. A memory rises.

It was a Saturday afternoon, long ago, when I was a child. My father and I were in the backyard, working in a small garden we had, pulling weeds, turning soil. The sun tilted toward evening, the air warm.

"Look," he said, nodding toward the trees, their branches swaying with an unhurried grace. "Everything understands where it belongs."

I followed his gaze. "You always talk like the trees are dancing."

The leaves shifted in waves, a silent conversation between wind and wood. Some curled inward, catching the late afternoon light in a way that made them seem almost translucent. Others held firm, their edges trembling but never breaking. The tallest branches leaned toward one another, bending and swaying, never colliding.

He smiled. "Maybe they are. Maybe they know something we don't."

The wind stirred again, carrying with it the scent of damp earth and something faintly sweet. A single leaf broke loose, spinning through the air before landing on the ground with a softness that barely disturbed the earth beneath it.

Birdsong tumbled through the air, light breaking through the clouds in shifting patterns. Shadows moved across the ground, restless.

"It's peaceful," I said, softer now. "Like everything sees us, understands us."

He turned to me. "You feel it too?"

I nodded, unable to explain the pull of it all.

"It's more than just being here," he said. "It's knowing we belong to it, and it belongs to us. That's real beauty."

We let the moment hold us.

After a while, he spoke again, voice laced with something heavier. "The world fools you sometimes. Puts on its best face - all green fields and blue skies - but underneath, there's something else." He paused. "The Depression didn't come roaring in. No. Like everything else in this world that's dark - it crept in slowly, like fog. One day, we looked around, and it had swallowed everything. Jobs gone. Homes lost."

"What was it like?" I asked.

He sighed, shaking his head. "There wasn't extra money. But we never went without. Your grandparents worked hard to keep food on the table. We woke up before dawn, worked till dusk, then studied by firelight. Giving up wasn't an option. Learning was our way forward. We held onto it with both hands."

He glanced at me. "We were poor, sure. But we had each other. That was enough."

I watched as he pulled another stubborn weed, tossing it aside.

"Winter was the only break we got," he said. "Snow meant the fields could rest - and so could we. We'd gather by the fire, listening to the wind, grateful we'd made it through another year."

I paused in my digging. "Didn't you get bored?"

He laughed. "Not a chance. We felt proud. Your grandparents made sure we understood - the work mattered. Every bit of it added up to a meal on the table, another season survived. 'Be thankful for this,' they'd say. And we were."

I turned over a clump of soil. "And then spring came?"

His face softened. "That was when the world woke up. Snow melted. The ground softened. Everything felt possible again. Your grandfather used to say you could almost hear the earth breathing, ready for the seeds. Everyone was eager to start fresh, to grow something new. It wasn't just work. It was hope."

He looked toward the trees. "The robins were the first to know, their songs filling the air before the leaves even returned. The land shook off its sleep, and we did too. Boots sinking into thawing earth, hands in the dirt, planting the first rows. It wasn't easy, but nothing worth doing ever is."

He smiled at me, and I held onto his words.

THE GUN

The autumn air whispers secrets against my skin. My senses awaken to its subtle cues: the crisp chill that bites at my cheeks, the earthy perfume that wafts on each breeze, the impossibly blue sky adorned with wisps of cloud-like brushstrokes on canvas. The trees burst into a riot of crimson, amber, and gold. I stand, motionless, in this living painting, half-believing I've stumbled into a storybook world.

Taking a deep breath, I close my eyes, letting the quiet presence of the season surround me. A profound tranquility settles over me, and for a moment, everything seems to stop. The world becomes hushed, its symphony silenced, leaving only the essence of my being.

The spell breaks as sounds from the fields tug at my attention. I open my eyes to find my aunts and uncles scattered across the field, their breaths wisps of silver mists in the cool air, picking and crating the last of the vegetables. Winter's approach looms, an unseen but ever-present timekeeper, urging them to harvest everything before the frost kills it. Along the rows, they pass over the plants that even with a bit of cleaning would never be fit for market. They leave them to wither back into the soil.

As they work, their laughter rises and falls on the breeze, light against the steady rhythm of their labor. Beneath the cheerful voices, their faces are taut with focus, their movements swift and assured, hands darting among the crops with an ease born of repetition. They're in the field closest to the farmhouse, nearly finished now. Beyond them, the cornfields stretch toward the valley, their once-green stalks faded to brittle brown, the harvest already taken.

But something is wrong – there's movement in the lower fields where nothing should stir. Strangers crouch among the rows, their hands quick, their shoulders drawn in tight. Hunger has reshaped them, carving out the softness of flesh until only sharp edges remain. Their clothes, patched and threadbare, cling unevenly, fabric so worn it barely holds together. They move quickly, gathering what was left behind, filling baskets with the bruised and overlooked. My family deemed these remains worthless, yet here they are, turned into something necessary. There are too many of them to count, and I can't stop wondering where they came from, what roads led them here, and what choices, or lack of them, brought them to this moment.

They haven't gone unnoticed. My father and uncles stand near the edge of the field, gathered around my grandfather in low conversation. Their movements betray them - in the way they shift, in the way they glance toward the figures among the crops.

"Let them be," my grandfather says at last. His voice is even, his tone so steady it leaves no room for disagreement. "Tough times for everyone. They can take what we don't need."

The strangers move steadily through the lower fields, their hands sifting through the earth, pulling at stalks and leaves with a careful urgency like they're untangling something precious from ruin. My heart tightens as I watch them, hunched over, their hunger woven into every hurried motion. How hard their lives must be - to step onto land that's not yours and pick through the refuse of what someone else has left behind. The effort it takes just to survive is beyond imagining.

I keep watching them, noticing how they pause from time to time, their faces lifting briefly, marked by the suspicion of those who've learned to expect kindness only to have it turn to something harsher.

My uncles exchange a brief look, their discomfort evident, but neither of them dares to challenge my grandfather's decision. His authority is not something one questions. They return to their work. All except Thomas.

He doesn't share the same restraint as my other uncles. With his fists clenched at his sides, he steps forward, unwilling to simply follow along without saying anything.

"It's our hard wur . . . wur . . . work, Papa," he shouts. "We should keep wah . . . wah . . . what little we have. They're just lah . . . lah . . . lazy people. Why should we let them take wah . . . wah . . . what's ours?"

My grandfather silences Thomas with a glance, the kind that needs no words. It carries the authority of someone who has seen more than he will ever say, a presence that draws attention without effort. There's something in his eyes that speaks of years stacked one upon another, of knowledge gained through endurance rather than explanation.

"Those people are tired and hungry," my grandfather tells Thomas. "They need our help. It's not just a matter of doing the right thing - it's what we owe them, what we owe ourselves. When you have enough, you share with those who have nothing. Kindness isn't a choice, son. It's a responsibility, and we have no reason to turn them away."

But Thomas would have none of it. With a guttural shout, he turns on his heel and storms off toward the barn, his fists balled so tightly it seemed he might crush whatever fury had taken root in him.

A few of my uncles, my father among them, exchange glances and step forward, ready to follow, but my grandfather raises a hand to stop them.

"Let him be," my grandfather says. "Give him time to be with his thoughts. He needs to work out things on his own. I'll talk to him when the time is right. For now, there's work to do. The day's light won't last forever."

They pause but then turn back to their chores, grudgingly obedient. My grandfather, however, keeps his attention fixed on the barn, his hands occupied but his mind elsewhere, each breath measured, expectant. The moments stretch, the silence pressing in, until finally, Thomas steps out. The barn door swings behind him, and in his arms, he cradles a shotgun.

My uncles freeze, caught mid-motion, their stillness as sharp as a snapped wire. My grandfather, though, doesn't waver. He doesn't rush. He moves forward with a quiet resolve, walking toward Thomas. His face gives nothing away, his expression steady, offering neither challenge nor retreat.

"Son, give me the gun," he says, his voice low, firm, the voice of someone who has spoken through storms before. "Whatever you're thinking of doing, I'm here for you. Let's talk about it. But please, just give me the gun."

Thomas stares at something far beyond my grandfather like he's searching for an answer out in the distance, where none exists. His body carries the tension of someone held together by a thread, every movement stiff with the effort of restraint. Beneath it all, his anger coils tightly, shaping the way he stands, and the way he breathes.

My grandfather steps closer, his words gentler now, coaxing rather than commanding. "I can see it in you, son. That fire, that pain - it's real, and I'm not saying it isn't. But this won't lead you to where you think it will. Please, for me, put the gun down."

Thomas's voice shakes as he replies, his stammer cutting through the air. "You dah . . . dah . . . don't get it. You nah . . . nah . . . never get it."

"I'm trying to," my grandfather says, his hand just slightly outstretched. "Help me understand. Let me in. Please, just tell me."

Thomas's head jerks side to side, his refusal as sharp as the words that follow.

"There's nah . . . nah . . . nothing to talk about. I have tah . . . tah . . . tah . . . to do this."

The moment stretches thin as my grandfather slowly moves to close the space between them. He reaches for the gun, but before his fingers can find it, the thunderous crack of a shot explodes across the field. The force of it rushes past him, leaving one of the strangers crumpled, lifeless, in the field. The others scatter, their shadows vanishing into the cover of the trees. Silence follows as everything hangs suspended, the air itself seeming heavy with the enormity of what has just happened.

Thomas lets the shotgun fall from his hands. It lands with a dull thud as he drops to his knees. His cries rise into the silence, raw and exposed. He stares at the ground, his shoulders quaking, his breath coming in uneven gasps. He has taken a life, fully aware of what that means, yet unable to grasp the full reach of it. When he finally lifts his head, his siblings and father stare back, their faces carrying something between sorrow and confusion and disbelief. He had only meant to protect them. Instead, everything now has been torn open in a way that cannot be undone.

Kneeling beside him, my grandfather rests resting a hand on his shoulder, firm but gentle. Thomas looks up, his face streaked with tears, an expression somewhere between a plea and an apology. The family stands apart, their silence forming an uneasy barrier, a held breath that refuses release.

My grandfather says nothing at first. He knows the limits of words, and how they fall short in moments like these. Instead, he holds Thomas in his steady presence, offering what little solace he can. When he finally speaks, his voice holds both sorrow and love, each woven into the other.

"It's over now," he says.

"I'm sah . . . sah . . . sorry, Papa," Thomas stammers, the words trip over themselves, a fragile offering.

"I know," my grandfather says, his voice hushed. "I know. We all face our own battles, and sometimes, there's no clear way through. But you need to remember something."

Thomas's wide, tear-filled eyes meet his, searching desperately for a glimmer of reassurance. "What is it, Papa?"

"No matter what comes. Your mother and I will always love you."

Thomas buries himself in my grandfather's arms, his shaking frame held tightly as if clinging to the one thing that hasn't shattered. Around them, the world remains muted, the farmhouse and fields standing witness, unchanged. For a brief moment, it feels as though time has bent, drawing them into a fragile cocoon of love and memory, untouched by the harshness waiting just beyond. Thomas closes his eyes and holds on, wishing for a kind of stillness he knows can't last.

But the moment slips away too quickly. My grandfather calls to one of my uncles, his voice firm, instructing him to fetch the police. Not long after, the high-pitched wail of sirens slices through the heavy stillness, shattering the illusion of safety. The police arrive, their presence a reckoning neither Thomas nor the rest of the family can hold at bay.

From the doorway, Thomas watches as the officers approach. He understands, even before they touch his arm, that this is the last he will see of the life he has always known. When they take his arm, he turns, taking in the farmhouse one last time, the fields stretching beyond it. Everyone stands clustered in the doorway, their forms outlined by the house behind them, their expressions a mixture of anguish and helplessness.

As he's taken away, the farmhouse shrinks behind him, the fields dissolving into the haze of what will soon be but a memory. Through his tears he catches a final glimpse, knowing with an aching, undeniable clarity that it has already become part of the past. Everything has forever shifted, leaving him untethered, his family and home are now pieces of a world he'll only ever find in dreams.

THE WILLARD

I drift into another of my father's memories, the past shaping itself around me with a clarity that feels sharper than before. But this time, something feels different, as though an unseen hand has nudged me forward, pushing me not just into his past but into a future I'd never know.

My father is behind the wheel of the family truck, the cab silent but for the low rumble of the engine. His army uniform is starched, the fabric rigid against his frame, his hands gripping the steering wheel with a steadiness that feels almost immovable. I think back to a memory he has already shared with me.

It must be the day he came home from the war. When he told my grandmother there was someplace he needed to go.

His eyes don't leave the road ahead, and though I can't see it, there's something in the set of his jaw, the way he holds himself, that tells me there's something more pulling him forward. A destination, a purpose, that remains obscured, hovering somewhere beyond the horizon.

The road stretches ahead, a long line of asphalt fading into the distance. The trees on either side bend with the wind, their leaves whispering in a secretive cadence, alive with motion and meaning. He drives without a word, his body tense with an energy that seems to hum through him. The unease builds, relentless, with each passing mile.

I try to reach out, to catch hold of his thoughts and hold them. But his mind shifts and twists, moving too quickly for me to follow. Is he haunted by the memories of war? By the friends who didn't return? Or is he grappling with the shape of his life that now feels unfamiliar, a life he may not recognize as his? What waits for him at the end of this road?

I don't have the answers, but I can see his pain, and feel it. His thoughts seem to bear down on him, persistent and impenetrable. He carries an air of something immense, unspoken, that pulls him inward, away from me. It's as if he's retreated into a space I cannot access, a place closed off from the outside world. I want to help him find his way out, but I'm left standing outside, unsure of the way in.

He drives for hours, the road unraveling endlessly ahead, dragging him forward without pause. The cab of the truck feels suffocating, the silence wrapping itself around him, pressing into his chest until his breaths come shallow.

Suddenly, his thoughts become untangled and I can hear them.

It feels heavier today, he thinks.

I wonder what he means by this.

He grips the wheel tighter, his knuckles pale against the worn leather, his thoughts circling. Finally, the pressure becomes too much. He veers onto the shoulder and kills the engine, stepping out into the stillness. The cool air brushes against his face, sharp and fleeting, but it's not enough.

Another thought: I hoped this would help. But it doesn't seem to.

He glances toward the horizon, his eyes catching on a shape through the trees - a building of deep red brick. It rises abruptly against the sprawl of the landscape, blunt and unmoving. He doesn't need a sign to tell him. He knows. He's always known.

This is the place.

Sliding back into the truck, he starts the engine, the rumble beneath him a hollow comfort. The trees thin as he makes a turn, the pavement shifting to gravel. The building grows closer, its presence thickening. It isn't just a building - it's something more, something alive in its own way. Its walls push skyward, stubborn and unyielding, barred windows catching the dull light like closed eyes that see everything. He wonders how many people have come here before him, feeling this same pull, this same dread.

This place, he thinks, does it swallow everyone whole, or just me?

When the truck finally lurches to a stop, he hesitates before stepping out, his boots hitting the ground harder than he expects. The air feels denser now as if the building itself has reached out to greet him. He exhales slowly, trying to release the knot in his chest. It loosens slightly, but not enough. It never is. Ahead, a dirt path winds toward the entrance, mostly empty except for a handful of figures in white uniforms moving at the edges of his vision. Nurses and orderlies move through the trees without sound, as if the place itself has silenced them.

Ghosts.

He takes a step forward, then another, the gravel shifting underfoot. The building seems to shift with him, its presence undeniable.

It knows I'm here. It's waiting for me.

He feels its gaze in a way he can't explain, a quiet force that presses into his ribs, quickening his pulse. There's a sadness clinging to the air, something old and sorrowful that seeps into his skin, into his blood. He feels it settle over him, heavier with each step, until he's no longer sure if it's the building's weight or his own.

At the entrance, my father pauses before the door - a massive, polished expanse of dark wood embedded with iron studs. The brass handle gleams faintly, its surface promising a chill. His hand wavers, hovering just shy of contact, when something catches his eye: a plaque mounted off to the side, its words waiting silently.

The goal of the Willard is to offer individualized care by segregating the residents into classes: curable and incurable, rather than treating them all the same by congregating them in one massive building. Willard offers kindly care for its residents with a safe, orderly, clean, controlled environment that creates stability; work that provides self-discipline; exercise to keep the body and mind fit; a balanced diet; restraints to protect residents from harm; and medical treatment provided by physicians. Its employees are kindly and sympathetic and are willing to live day in and day out among those who require help.

My father reads the plaque, but it does little to allay his sadness. With a measured breath, he pushes the door open and steps inside. The sharp odor of disinfectant greets him, and faint voices float through the stillness, distant and indistinct. For a moment, he lingers at the threshold before starting down the hallway.

Why has my father come to this place?

The interior of the building feels more imposing than its exterior. Everything he sees has a simple, heavy feel to it. He feels a sense of dread as if the walls are closing in on him. He scans the dimly lit corridor, his gaze darting anxiously until something ahead catches his eye.

He comes to a nurse sitting at a desk. She's a small woman in a sharp white uniform, her cap set neatly atop her head. Piles of paperwork rise in neat stacks, each one a little tower, like a miniature skyline. The arrangement of papers brings his mind to the jagged contours of New York City, all angular and towering. Before the nurse lies a large book, its pages spread open to a well-worn section.

She looks up as he draws near, her eyes tired.

"Name?" she asks, offering a faint smile that doesn't quite reach her eyes.

He tells her his name, and she writes it down in the book, the scratch of her pen filling the stillness.

"Who are you here to see?"

"Tommaso," he says, then pauses. "Thomas."

And in that moment, I understand why he's here.

The nurse makes another entry and then taps a bell on her desk. Moments later, a large figure appears in the doorway behind her, an orderly, dressed in a white uniform. His eyes are dark, and his face is unreadable, the expression of someone who has long ago distanced himself from the life around him. He stands before the desk, his head inclined slightly, a gesture of respect that feels practiced rather than sincere.

"Thomas," she says to him. "He should be in the common area by the window."

The orderly nods. "Follow me," he directs my father.

They walk down a long hallway, its walls stark and indifferent, as though they, too, are holding something back. A shadow settles over my father, and he can't escape the feeling of sadness that fills this place.

There's something here, something my father will soon encounter, something he won't want to see. I sense it.

"We don't get many visitors," the orderly remarks. "Been here before?"

"No."

"There are a few rules to go over. If a resident approaches, please don't engage. Don't touch them or speak to them. If they make a move toward you, step away. I'll handle it as quickly as I can. Understood?"

"Yes."

They continue down the hallway, which stretches on without end. Now and then, they pass men sitting in chairs, their wrists bound to the armrests, all dressed in the same blue clothes. Some are missing limbs, others bear deformities that defy reason. All of them share the same expression: an emptiness, a resignation.

My father tries to keep his eyes forward, but I can see the strain in him.

At last, the hallway opens into a large room. The orderly pushes the door, and they both step inside. The room is vast, the light dim, the air heavy with emptiness. The ceilings stretch high above, and the walls are bare. My father has never entered a place like this before. It feels cold, and impersonal - like a place where people are left to disappear. Like a tomb.

His eyes dart around, and then he sees them: a line of figures in blue, their faces hidden in shadow, bound to their chairs by rough ropes. They sit motionless, like bodies that have been abandoned. But as he moves closer, one stirs, and he realizes they are alive - but only just. Their eyes are hollow, their skin drained of life, and all of them wear the same haunted look.

My father closes his eyes for a moment as if trying to find his balance. It feels like he's standing at the edge of something vast and unknown, the ground beneath him giving way to uncertainty. He takes a sharp breath, steadies himself, and opens his eyes.

A man dressed in blue is walking toward him, his steps deliberate.

"You see what they've done here?" the man asks, his voice low. "Now, what are you going to do about it?"

My father does not know the man, and before he can respond, the orderly steps in, placing himself between them.

"Alright, Charlie, let's get you back to your seat," the orderly says, gently guiding the man by the arm toward a chair.

"Where is he?" my father asks the orderly, his voice tight.

"Over there," the orderly replies, pointing casually to the far side of the room. "In the corner. By the window."

My father turns to follow the gesture, his body tense, every muscle bracing for what he knows he'll find. His eyes lock on the figure in the corner - a man, bound to a chair with thick ropes, staring back with empty eyes.

He moves forward slowly, each step uncertain, his heart heavy as he makes out a figure. There, in the distance, is his brother, Thomas. But this is not the Thomas he remembers. The face that once held the vitality of youth is now gaunt, the skin taut against the sharp angles of bone. His head is shaved, and a deep scar cuts across his forehead. His body is fragile, hollowed out; the man standing before him resembles little more than a shadow of his former self. My father looks at him, and all he sees is emptiness, a hollow space that stretches farther than he can comprehend.

He pulls up a chair, his hands unsteady as he sits down, fingers trembling as they work at the knot that binds Thomas. He can feel his brother's eyes on him, but they are empty and unseeing.

"Hey, don't do that," the orderly calls out sharply.

My father ignores him. With one last sharp tug, he loosens the knot, and the rope slips away. Thomas sags forward, his head tilting awkwardly to one side. My father catches him, pulling him close, his tears mixing with the sweat that clings to Thomas's skin.

At the sound of the raised voice, several people in the room begin to shift, making soft murmurs and rocking in their chairs.

The orderly steps forward, but my father holds up a hand to stop him. "He's my brother."

The orderly hesitates for a moment. "Okay," he says, his voice uncertain. "But be careful."

My father returns his focus to Thomas, feeling how light he is in his arms, like holding something fragile. He whispers his name softly. Thomas remains still.

My father sits down in the chair, cradling Thomas with a tenderness that seems to seep into every fiber of his being. He rocks him slowly, the motion almost mechanical, as though he's trying to undo something that cannot be undone.

"It's alright," he murmurs. "It's alright. I'm here with you."

For a moment, my father wonders if he sees the hint of a smile at the corners of Thomas's lips, but it's too fleeting to be sure. He closes his eyes, pulling his brother closer, wishing he could somehow absorb the pain that has settled deep in him.

For hours, my father talks, his voice steady, his hands moving in slow, deliberate gestures as if shaping the memories in the air between them. He shares stories about the Battle of the Bulge, the German boy and the old man he encountered, and other battles he fought in. He speaks of the cold, the weight of a rifle, the silence that came after gunfire. Then, the war ended, and there was home - the farm just as he had left it, though somehow different, smaller maybe, or simply unfamiliar after so much time away. He talks about his plans, the business he wants to start, the woman he hopes to marry, and the family he imagines with her. The past unfolds from him in perfect clarity, as if no time has passed at all.

Thomas remains still in the chair, his expression unreadable. His eyes, fixed on my father, seem to have lost all recognition, as though they belong to someone else - empty, lifeless, like those of a doll. A strange feeling creeps into my father's mind like a dark shadow, refusing to be shaken away. This was not his brother. No, this was a stranger, a man who had been hollowed out, whose very soul had been stolen.

Where did my brother go? Is he lost in some faraway place, distant and unconnected from the world around him?

Thomas remains still, silent, his eyes fixed on my father. There is no movement, no acknowledgment.

"It's me," my father says, reaching out to place his hand gently on Thomas's shoulder. "It's me. Your brother."

But Thomas gives no sign that he's heard, his expression unchanged. My father's face tightens with grief, the words he wants to say settling deep within him, unspoken.

"I'm sorry," he whispers. "I'm so sorry this happened to you."

They sit there, in the quiet, for what feels like a lifetime. The room between them is heavy with the things neither can say. My father longs to tell him how much he loves him, how long he's waited for this moment. But there's a fear, a chasm between them, that makes him wonder that he no longer understands.

"Sir, it's five o'clock," the orderly says, interrupting the stillness. "All visitors have to leave. I'm sorry."

My father stands, slowly pushing his chair back. The scrape of the chair against the floor stirs something in Thomas. For a brief moment, his eyes flicker - there's a hint of recognition, a glint of something my father thought lost. Then it fades, like a shadow passing.

"My God, what have they taken from you?" my father murmurs.

The question is such a fragile thing, drifting, unanchored.

Silence deepens, but my father's eyes remain on Thomas, watching as he struggles to pull himself together, the effort visible in every labored breath, every tremor in his frail body. At last, a single word breaks free, so faint it might have gone unheard.

"Everything."

The word settles in the air like a stone sinking into still water. My father shuts his eyes, inhaling deeply. He knows it's true. Everything had been taken from Thomas: his freedom, his dignity, his innocence. But most of all, his hope.

Tears well in my father's eyes. He pulls Thomas into an embrace, and something within me breaks. It's as if everything around us is slipping away, becoming less real. In that moment, I understand something I hadn't before. I now know the full truth about my uncle, and I see why it was hidden from us. It's a story of darkness and suffering, too painful to bear. The family had shielded us from the weight of it - kept us from knowing the depth of the agony Thomas endured. The sorrow and the suffering were too much to bear, too much to share.

I look at Thomas, his face frozen. There's no trace of emotion in his eyes, no hint of the person he had once been. He's a broken thing, a shadow of his former self. Pity rises in me, but it's twisted with a deep, gnawing anger at the fate that had stolen his humanity.

Why does reality do such things? Why does it create us only to shatter us? I don't know the answers, but I know that I'd never forget Thomas's face or the pain that he'd suffered.

"I'll come back," my father says to Thomas. "I promise."

As my father leaves, he glances back at another orderly, who is tying Thomas to the chair. He waves to his brother, but Thomas's head is down, oblivious to the gesture.

They start down the hall, but my father pauses. He looks back at the room, his face clouded with sorrow. This place will stay with him, always.

My father and the orderly start to walk back to the entrance, but my father stops. He looks back at the room one last time, his eyes filled with sorrow. He'll never forget this place.

They move down the corridor, the sound of their footsteps hollow in the emptiness. Overhead, the fluorescent lights flicker with a sickly, mechanical pulse, their harsh glow casting long, distorted shadows that seem to dance and writhe along the walls. The wails and cries of the other residents pierce the air, like the cries of lost souls.

When my father reaches the front desk, the nurse signs him out and he steps away. As he leaves, he turns to look at the building, his eyes tracing the red bricks that line the massive walls. To him, this place is a monument to hopelessness, a structure where dreams have long since withered and those left behind are swallowed by silence.

He climbs into the truck, hands clenched around the steering wheel, white-knuckled with tension. He shuts his eyes tightly, fists thudding against the wheel with such force that the dashboard shakes beneath him. When the sting of his blows lingers, he opens his eyes, staring at the blurred world beyond the windshield, his vision clouded by the tears of frustration and fury. He understands that his anger will change nothing. Yet, it's a struggle he cannot avoid.

He pumps the pedal twice, preparing to start the engine. But just as he turns the key, a voice calls to him from within. It's both hauntingly familiar and alien, a voice that seems to rise from the very heart of the place he's just left, a voice full of sorrow, pleading for mercy.

My father hesitates, listening. He knows the voice. It's a voice he'll hear again, a voice that will echo through the quiet places for years to come.

"Everything," it whispers. "Everything."

FRAGILITY

Standing beside my father in front of the old farmhouse, I watch as he lifts his hand, letting his fingers drift across the worn siding. It isn't deliberate, not really - it's the kind of touch that happens when something inside you is reaching out, hoping to be recognized. The house, of course, says nothing. It only stands, the way it always has, unmoved by whoever comes or goes.

"They painted it," he says, his voice quieter than I expect. There's no judgment in it, only observation as if he's noting the sky or the wind, something beyond his control.

The kitchen and porch, the spaces that once shaped my childhood, are there. They extend in a way that feels unnatural, as though someone has pressed their hands into soft clay, reshaping what was whole into something slightly off-kilter. The windows, once open and full of light, hold their silence. I stare at them, waiting for something - a flicker of movement, a glimpse of what they used to contain - but they only reflect the afternoon, impassive. The air here is different too. I remember it carrying the scent of damp earth, of tomatoes ripening in the sun, of dust kicked up from the barn. Now it's heavy, still, holding nothing of what came before.

And yet, we are here. The house stands. The ground beneath us remains. We must be in the now, in the present.

To the left, where the barn once stood, the swings move. Two small figures shift with them, barely more than light and air, but I hear them. The soft creak of the chains, the bright lift of laughter - sounds I know as well as my name. The figures shimmer, not fully here, not fully gone, and still, their presence settles over the place, as undeniable as the house itself.

"Children playing," my father says, his voice low, warm. He watches them the way he might watch the wind moving through the trees - something natural, something expected. The corners of his mouth shift upward, the echo of a smile, as laughter lifts into the afternoon air, weightless, untethered. "You know, I didn't mind when your brother sold the place. Things change. Time moves forward. Who are we to stand in the way?"

I wait a moment or two, the question settling on my tongue before I ask, "Can we talk about Uncle Thomas?"

"What more is there to talk about?"

"What happened to him?"

My father doesn't answer.

His gaze sweeps over the place. The barn and sheds have long been torn down, and the vegetable and corn fields have been replaced by a school. The surrounding hills are dotted with homes - some of them built by my father and his brothers. And where the apple orchard had once stood, its trees heavy with ripe, juicy apples, there stands the house my father built for my mother, the one where I had spent my childhood.

I wonder how often he comes back here.

"Sure are a lot of memories here," I say, offering a smile.

"There are," he replies. "No matter how much time goes by, they stay with you, lodged deep in your mind, like a song you can't get out of your head."

"They're not meant to stay stuck, though, are they?"

He turns to me, his expression distant but clear. He knows exactly where this is leading. For a moment, he considers his response, as though the right words might arrive if he waits long enough. Instead, he lets the quiet remain. His attention shifts to the farmhouse, and we both stand quietly, caught between what's here now and everything that came before.

"Memories and stories are meant to be passed along, to share," he says. "They help us make sense of things, to see the patterns in what we've lived through. They should never be lost. And some stay with us, even when we wish they wouldn't. Your uncle was never the same. He couldn't think the way he used to. Couldn't form the simplest words. He became a shadow of himself. It broke us. We saw him as often as we could, but he never got better. Toward the end, he could hardly open his eyes. And then one day, the call came. The news we'd been asking for, in our quietest prayers."

I held my breath, waiting for the words to come.

"He had passed away," he says gently.

A lump rises in my throat, and my voice trembles as I manage to whisper, "I'm sorry."

"They returned his body to us, and we buried him in the family plot," he continues. "Your grandmother always said he died of loneliness."

A tear traces its way down my face, and I can't stop the small, broken sound that escapes me. "And Gramps?" I ask, though I almost regret it.

"He was never the same after that. It wore him down, bit by bit. The sorrow, the memories - he couldn't bear them anymore. Every time he looked at me, I could see it, something lost behind his eyes. As the years went on, he withdrew and became quieter, more distant. It was as if he was trying to fade away like he was retreating from the world. Sometimes he'd lash out - over nothing, really. A dropped cup, a toy left out by a grandkid. It didn't make sense at the time, but now I think maybe it was the only way he knew to let anything out. I tried to understand, I really did, but it was painful to see him that way. So much more painful than I could have imagined."

He stops, and then asks, "What do you remember of your grandfather?"

Quickly, I search my mind. The memories are few; he died when I was just ten. Yet, the longer I reflect, the more I feel the truth of my father's words, as if they fit a puzzle I hadn't realized I'd been trying to solve.

"What I remember," I say, "is that he was a quiet man. He always sat at the end of the sofa, the newspaper spread open in his hands. I'd come running into the house, and he'd yell at me to tie my sneakers. The way his voice cut through the air, sharp and sudden, left me startled every time. I never understood what made it matter so much to him."

"Why would you? You didn't know."

"But why didn't you tell us about Uncle Thomas?"

"Because it wasn't your burden to bear. It's always about the future. About moving forward."

"Is he here? Uncle Thomas? Is he here in the next life?" I ask, my voice faltering, barely holding its shape.

My father looks down, his face shadowed with sorrow. He shakes his head, the motion slow, deliberate, and final.

"I'm sorry," I say quietly. "I would've wanted to meet him."

We stand there for a moment, the sound of children playing drifting to us. My father puts his arm around my shoulders, and we start walking toward the farmhouse.

"He would've wanted the same," my father says with a smile.

"Life is fleeting, isn't it," I say. "Like a breath on glass. Or a wisp of smoke, a shadow on the wall. It's delicate. Too fragile to hold."

"So easily lost," my father adds, his voice low. "We pass through it, moment by moment, leaving behind nothing but . . . the silence where we used to be. We forget to live each day to the fullest, to treasure every moment."

I smile at him. "You always told us never to take anything for granted, that we never know how long something will be ours . . . to love with everything we have, to laugh without hesitation, to dance as if no one is watching . . . to make the most of each day because life is too short to waste. But that's not always easy, is it? There are times when it's easy to be overwhelmed by sadness or fear, or the rigors of the present moment."

My father's hand settles lightly on my shoulder, a warmth both familiar and steady. "I remember," he says. "But when the present feels unbearable, it's only the dark before dawn. No night lasts forever. The sun will rise, and when it does, joy will be there, patient as ever, waiting for us to find our way back to it."

We walk in silence, the quiet stretching between us, until a voice rises from behind.

"There they are," a woman calls, her tone both familiar and gentle.

It's my aunt, my father's youngest sister. Petite and in her sixties, she carries herself with an effortless grace, her face open and kind. Though the years have passed, there's still something unmistakably youthful about her expression, a vitality that seems untouched by the passing years. Her eyes, bright and clear, hold the depth of someone who has lived fully and paid attention. A warmth stirs in me, subtle but undeniable, as though a forgotten connection has found its way back.

We embrace. "Aunt Rose," I say, "It's so good to see you again."

She smiles warmly. "I've missed you," she says hugging me. "Were you two reminiscing?"

"What else is there to do?" I reply.

She gives a small, thoughtful laugh, her eyes gleaming in the soft light. "It's good to remember the past. There's so much to learn from it."

When I meet her eyes, everything seems to align - those moments she left behind, all the bruises and triumphs, each one a small piece that helped make her stronger, someone others could turn to for strength. I wasn't able to see it before, in the past life. I had moved through my days with her, unaware of all the quiet forces that had carried her forward.

"I've asked your aunt to come here and share one of her memories with you," my father says. "I think it's important for you."

I hesitate for a moment. "Alright."

She smiles gently and takes my hand, then closes her eyes.

It's only the beginning

I fall through a blur of color and motion, the world spinning too fast to hold onto. A weightless sensation tugs at my stomach, something close to vertigo but softer, as if I am being unraveled. Then, just as suddenly, I am still. My feet press into the dull green carpet of a nursing home corridor. The shift is so abrupt that my head feels strange - light yet too full, as if memories are pressing in from all sides, searching for a way in.

The air is thick with the sharp bite of antiseptic, underscored by something sour and familiar. A scent I have known for too long. Voices drift toward me, low murmurs without shape, blending together until they belong to no one and everyone at once. The walls seem to hold onto them as if the past refuses to be smoothed away. Traces of laughter, the hush of sorrow - they linger here, woven into the silence, unwilling to be forgotten.

I find myself walking, the sound of my steps muffled, and as I move forward, I realize I know this place - not this exact nursing home, but the kind of place it is - the quiet hum of fluorescent lights, the faint rattling of a cart in the distance, the occasional creak of a wheelchair. My parents spent their last days in a place like this. I've been here before, in ways I wish I hadn't.

My steps are taking me toward a specific room, a room that belonged to my aunt. I pass a window, and the garden outside looks just as I expect - empty. A single fountain stands in the center, the thin stream of water running sluggish, its edges stained the color of rust. I slow my steps as I glance at it, a sharp memory tugging at me. My father used to sit by a window like this, his gaze fixed on birds that flitted through the courtyard. He never tired of them, even when everything else seemed to fade. My mother did the same, her hands folded in her lap, her expression soft and unreachable, as if the birds carried secrets she alone could understand.

Time moves differently here, stretched thin by the steady routine of meals, medications, and baths, each day dissolving into the next without distinction. The nights are longer still, vast and silent, offering nothing but the certainty of another morning.

I pause in the doorway of the day room, where the residents sit unmoving in their chairs, some slumped in wheelchairs. A television hums in the corner, its restless images casting light across faces that register nothing of what they see. Some watch without focus, others stare past the room entirely, their expressions fixed in a quiet vacancy. A few have slipped into restless sleep, their heads bowed at odd angles. The air is thick with the mingled scents of disinfectant and urine, edged with something stale, something left too long untouched. The walls are a washed-out green, neither warm nor cool, and the furniture - threadbare, mismatched - seems chosen for durability rather than comfort.

The residents are a patchwork of ages and histories, each carrying the weight of a life that once felt sharper, more certain. Time has worn them down in different ways - bodies unsteady, minds drifting - but they share a quiet stillness, held within themselves. Some cling to the past, turning over memories like well-worn stones, while others sit in peaceful contemplation, their thoughts resting on whatever comes next.

What strikes me most is their lack of fear. Their eyes hold no trace of unease, no desperate grasping at what remains. Instead, there is a calm, an acceptance that feels less like resignation and more like readiness. They are waiting, but not with reluctance.

The sight of them stirs something deep in me, a sorrow that is familiar and old. It brings back nursing homes, long afternoons spent beside my grandparents, and later, my parents. I remember the hush of those rooms, the way solitude settled in like dust. I remember the ache of it - the imagining of what it must be like to be the one left behind.

As I make my way down the corridor, I let my eyes linger in every room, scanning the quiet corners and the unassuming details. Then, almost without intention, I slow in front of a particular doorway. Inside, my aunt and sister sit at a table together. My aunt, serene and thoughtful, carries an air of quiet dignity, her face softened by the years but untouched by weariness. Her eyes remain bright, and steady, as if holding a wisdom that has always been there, waiting to be noticed. She leans over the Bible my grandmother once held, her pen moving carefully across the page, finishing what she has started with the kind of patience that comes from knowing some things are meant to last.

"There," she says, her voice breaking gently under the weight of emotion. She sets the pen aside. "My last entry."

A tear falls from her cheek, landing on the page. I glance down at the open book and see the name and date she has written. She has just marked the passing of my father.

My sister's eyes are swollen from sadness, her tears slipping down the same paths they have traveled before. She leans toward our aunt, resting a hand on her shoulder, her voice low and measured, offering whatever comfort she can. I find it difficult to watch them, knowing the grief they share, the way they are grasping for something steady in the wake of my father's absence.

But there's an unexpected calm on our aunt's face, though her eyes shine with emotion. She closes the Bible with deliberate care, her fingers lingering on its cover before she slides it across the table to my sister.

"This is yours now," she tells my sister, her voice firm but tender. "This isn't the end. It's the beginning."

My sister places her hands on the book, feeling the quiet gravity of the history, it holds. Slowly, she opens it, revealing a portal to lives long past. Her fingers move across the faded ink, lingering over the entries that speak of births, deaths, and the small but profound moments in between. As she reads, memories rise to the surface, a flood of feelings she does not try to push away. The stories fill her with wonder, with a pride that comes from knowing the strength and depth of the family that brought us here.

"You'll be the one to add my name," our aunt says, her voice calm, as if she has already made peace with it. "To carry the story forward. To decide who comes next."

My sister turns another page, her touch light but reverent. She stops at a blank one, her breath catching as if the emptiness holds something unsaid. The pristine page seems to hold a quiet anticipation, urging her forward. She closes her eyes, inhaling deeply, as if to steady herself. The path ahead feels vast and uncertain, and she wonders if she's ready to begin.

With a steady breath, she opens her eyes and looks at the blank page once more. It waits without urgency, holding space for a story not yet ready to be told. She knows the moment will come when the thread of the journey picks up again, and the page will be there, ready to receive it.

Our aunt smiles, a warmth in her expression that softens the weight of her words. "There are still many blank pages," she says, "for you to tell our family's story. So much time ahead of us."

The room grows dense, a thickness in the air that settles around me. My breathing feels too sharp, the sound of it too close, echoing in the silence. A memory unfurls, without invitation: our grandmother, her voice steady but tinged with finality, had spoken those same words as she passed the Bible to our aunt. And now, my sister holds the same book, the same solemn charge in her hands.

"The book will speak to you," our aunt says. "It will find a way to pull you back, asking you to witness the lives that came before and those yet to come. Every name, every stroke of the pen, holds a deep history - of joy and loss, failure and triumph, the fullness of what it means to belong to this family."

Tears slip down my sister's cheeks, her face soft with a quiet understanding. She offers a smile, not one of joy, but of solemn acknowledgment. She understands what our aunt has handed her is more than a mere book - it is a history that extends far beyond its pages. It is a tangible part of our lineage, a symbol carrying significance that reaches beyond time. The book is both a relic and a vow, a reminder of what has passed, a thread linking the past to what is yet to come.

"Remember this day and the words I've spoken. One day, you'll need to speak them, too, to another when your time comes."

My sister nods, unable to speak, the lump in her throat stopping the words before they can leave. She gently closes the book, pressing it to her chest, and pulls our aunt into a tender embrace. That moment says everything - an unspoken vow to carry this memory with her, a promise not to let it fade, ever.

Purpose

I'm suspended in a haze, a swirl of light and shadows, of voices I almost recognize speaking words I can't quite hear. The world twists itself around me, unfamiliar but not frightening, and when it settles, I'm sitting on the front steps of the old farmhouse with my father.

We watch the small, ghostly figures darting around the swing set in the yard. They move with a kind of grace I can't describe - light as whispers, their outlines shimmering in the twilight. I blink and look again, trying to focus. Their movements remind me of memories, the kind that linger at the edge of your mind - familiar, but just out of reach.

"Where's Aunt Rose?" I ask, looking over the yard.

"She's probably gone off to a memory," he replies. He doesn't look at me when he speaks, as if the answer doesn't need more than that.

I turn to him, wanting to ask a dozen questions. There's too much I don't understand, too much I can't seem to put into order. I'm here, with him, on these steps, and somehow, that should be enough. But I become lost in the complexities of time and place. The words are there, waiting, but they won't come. They're in my mind, heavy and shapeless, like clay waiting to be coaxed into something meaningful.

My father senses my struggle. He pulls me close, wrapping an arm around my shoulders in a quiet gesture of understanding.

"I know," he says softly. "It's not easy. There's a lot to the next life. It's like it circles back on itself sometimes, never quite moving forward."

His words seem to unlock something in me. The thoughts I couldn't grasp suddenly make sense, spilling out in a rush. "I guess eternity is nothing but a timeless romp between your memories and those of your loved ones," I say. "A loop, a journey that never really ends. Eternity isn't a place. It's a state of being, where everything - past, present, and future - exists together. Like a kaleidoscope. Every time you turn it, the patterns are different, but they're always made of the same pieces."

I let the words hang in the air for a moment, savoring the feeling of clarity.

My father smiles, a slow, knowing curve of his lips. "That's a beautiful way of putting it." He takes my hand, his grip firm, the warmth of his touch a comfort. "And now," he adds, "I want to show you something."

The air stirs, the haze swirling briefly before dissipating, and in an instant, we're in the past, standing in a field on the farm, on one of the hills that seems a world away from the farmhouse. It's night, and the crispness of the air settles on our skin. A few feet from us, my father as a young boy sits alone among the rows of corn, his eyes turned toward the heavens.

"One of your favorite memories?" I ask.

He turns toward me, his face shining in the soft light of the moon. "When I was young, I used to sit out here for hours," he says, his voice gentle, as though the memory is still fresh. "Gazing at the stars. I felt so small, insignificant even, in the vastness of the night sky. But at the same time, it was as though everything - every point in space and time - was connected. And I was part of it."

I see my father as a boy, his face open with quiet wonder. He rests on his back, his head tipped just enough to take in the sky, his eyes full of something too large to name. The stars unfold endlessly above him, and he reaches out as though he could touch the very heart of the universe.

"To touch the face of the stars," he says softly, a wistful note in his voice. "Wouldn't that be wonderful?"

There's a kind of reverence in the way he speaks, an unspoken certainty that, in that moment, anything feels possible - within the infinite expanse of the universe, there's room for all dreams.

"It's like looking into a different world," he says. "One of beauty and peace."

He's right. We both feel it - that hush of wonder beneath the night sky. The stars stretch above us, an endless scattering of light against the dark. They shimmer, their glow soft and steady, like diamonds stitched into the fabric of the night. And there, the pale moon drifts, its silvery light spilling gently over the earth below.

"There's something about looking up at the sky," he says, "that makes all your troubles seem smaller, lighter than they did before." He meets my gaze, his eyes distant, as though the stars have pulled him into their orbit. "I can't speak for eternity. I don't have the words for that. But there's something your mother said when she joined me here, when we started revisiting our memories together. We'd move from one memory to the next, so quickly, like leaves falling from a tree. It was all too much, overwhelming, too fast. More than either of us expected."

"What did she say?"

"She said maybe it's best to take immortality in small steps."

I smile. "Sounds like something she'd say."

We stand together in silence, watching my father as a boy, his small face tilted toward the stars, his eyes wide with the kind of wonder that belongs only to children. I once believed the next life would be a place of revelations, where all the riddles that had lingered just beyond reach would finally unfold into something clear and certain. But now, standing here, I begin to suspect there may be no answers waiting for us - only the same questions we have always carried, following us wherever we go.

It's a strange, uneasy feeling, being here, surrounded by an emptiness that seems both endless and alive. Yet, within the vastness, there's something - an energy that moves through it all, gentle in its presence but immeasurable in its force. It reminds me of standing on a shoreline, the rhythm of the ocean surging at my feet, not threatening but undeniable, a quiet insistence that it'll always be there.

I close my eyes and reach out, not with my hands but with something deeper, hoping to find some way to connect to it. But its presence slips through me. It's too vast, too unknowable. I can't begin to grasp its essence.

"It's not fair," I say.

"What's not fair?" My father's voice pulls me back.

"I'm still standing on the edge of something I don't understand."

He pauses, his silence stretching long enough that I can feel the quiet in the air around us. "If it helps," he says at last, his voice low, "I can't make sense of it either."

"In my past life," I say, carefully choosing each word, "I was obsessed with the idea of what came next. I wanted to know what the afterlife held. The truth behind it all. Now that I'm here, I only have more questions. What is this place? What happens next? Every time I try to look further, there's nothing to see, nothing to grasp. I'm no closer to understanding any of it."

"Maybe it's not about understanding," he says gently. "Maybe it's just about being."

He waits, and then adds, "Close your eyes. Try it."

I'm not sure what he's getting at, but I close my eyes.

"Imagine a place where time doesn't exist. A place where your memories - those moments you treasure - come together and never fade. A place of warmth, where you come to peace with your past, to remember the love that filled your life. It's a journey, beautiful and endless. Think of it."

I sit there letting the idea unfurl in my mind. The thought of it feels like something just out of reach, a glimpse of something I've wanted for so long. The words he's spoken, simple yet profound, seem to linger in the air between us, and for the first time in a long while, I feel a quiet peace, as if, just for a moment, I've been permitted to let go.

I open my eyes. His words remain, drifting through my thoughts. Memories move through us as if in a quiet rhythm, a pattern we can't help but follow. The thought of holding onto those memories, to those we love, not for a moment but for all the moments yet to come . . . it's a thought full of peace.

I sigh wistfully. "A bond with the past, one that endures through time."

He nods, his gaze steady. "Yes."

"The idea of forever," I continue, "no longer feels distant or abstract. It has become something almost physical, a thread connecting all that we've shared with those we've loved. No matter how far apart we wander, even after we leave the world we know, we're never truly separated. The past stays with us, intact, unbroken."

"A promise," my father says, his voice subdued, "of a reunion that no force can sever."

Peace and joy fill my being. It's a quiet joy that seems to expand with every breath. The mystery of what lies beyond this life, that elusive next step, is no longer a question in the distance. It's slowly revealing itself to me, piece by piece.

My father smiles at me, his eyes full of warmth and understanding. I return the smile, the gratitude I feel for his wisdom flooding through me, filling the space between us.

Then, there's a quiet shift, as subtle as a breath, and a thought finds its way through me. "When we were in the orchard with Maggie, you both warned me about something," I say, a question in my voice. "You said something. I think it was – beware of what the next life takes from you. What was that about?"

He stirs, a small movement, but enough for me to feel the change. His face tightens just a fraction, and I notice it, even if he doesn't say a word. "It takes from us something very precious. Something we once had. Something we left behind."

I lean closer, my curiosity pulling me in. "What is it?"

His eyes grow darker, a deeper shadow crossing his features. "Purpose," he replies. "This place takes our purpose."

IT'S ALL LIQUID

The cornfield dissolves behind us, giving itself over to a patchwork of modest homes and winding roads. My father and I wander toward the backyard of the old farmhouse, slipping past the small ethereal forms still locked in their eternal game of chase. In the corner of the yard, a small vegetable garden draws us closer. We stop at its edge, taking in the careful rows of plants. Carrots, tomatoes, lettuce, and peppers rise in tidy lines, their colors bright and varied, forming a scene alive with quiet purpose and care.

"Garden looks nice, doesn't it?" my father muses, his voice a whisper on the breeze.

"Small though," I observe.

He motions toward the valley below, where the school sits nestled in the wide expanse, the homes scattered along the hills like watchful sentinels. "Do you remember when your grandfather farmed all that?"

"Before my time," I remind him, a silence filling the space between us, shaped by memories that aren't mine.

"Oh. I forgot," he says, his voice tinged with a wistful sadness. "Your older brother probably remembers."

As if drawn by an invisible force, he bends down, reaching for a plump tomato that dangles temptingly from its vine. The fruit sways gently on its vine, inviting, alive. But his hand passes through it as though it were no more than a trick of the light. A scowl clouds his face, and he mutters something under his breath, the words lost to the wind and the vast expanse of time that separates us from what remains and what has already gone.

"I miss this," he says, his eyes scanning the horizon. "The taste of fresh tomatoes, the smell of the earth beneath my feet, the feeling of the sun on my skin." He turns to me, his face a canvas of nostalgia and longing. "I miss playing with you kids. I miss my work - connecting with people, the joy of learning, the challenge of solving problems. I miss the hope I used to have, the dream of a brighter future, the belief in something beyond ourselves. There's so much I left behind in that life."

"Purpose?" I offer.

He smiles a gentle curve that doesn't quite reach his eyes. "You knew where I was headed."

I nod.

"I wasn't around when you retired," his voice is soft with curiosity, "but I watched you for a bit. Didn't you miss it?" he asks.

"Miss what?" I reply, though I suspect I already know.

"The work. The excitement. The sense that you were making a difference. The purpose it gave you."

I turn his words over in my mind, like stones in a creek, the edges smooth from years of thinking about them. "Not so much," I say after a moment. "At first, maybe a little, I suppose. But I knew that it was time for me to move on. I had accomplished what I wanted to do. It was time." I pause, choosing my next words carefully. "I was tired . . . tired of people, tired of the grind. And we wanted to travel. And remember," I add, a bit of a smile, "I had my writing."

"So, you found purpose in writing?" he asks, his eyes fixed on a point just beyond my shoulder.

The familiar warmth that always accompanies thoughts of my craft embraces me. "It was something I always loved. Something I was good at - at least that's what my readers said."

"I remember when I told you to turn down that creative writing scholarship to Emerson," he says. "That was a hard conversation for me."

"You told me to go to business school instead," I say. "I remember. I was heartbroken, but I did what you asked."

"Why did you listen to me?" he asks.

I smile. "Because you were my father. I saw you were successful. And you told me there would be time to write."

He smiles back. "So, you ended up selling a fair number of books?"

"I did," I say, trying not to let the pride show.

He leans forward. "Gave you a sense of satisfaction and accomplishment. Allowed you to connect with other people."

I look at him curiously, sensing a shift in the conversation. "Dad, what are you getting at?"

His eyebrow lifts ever so slightly, and his voice carries a wistful note that wrenches at something deep within me. "Seems like you were fulfilled," he says. "You found happiness in your writing, keeping yourself occupied. But that won't be the case here. Whatever it was that gave you a sense of meaning, of purpose, it's gone now. That little cat of yours is right."

A chill comes over me. "But I love writing and connecting with people through my work. It's a big part of my . . . life . . ." My voice trails off, the words sounding hollow even to my own ears. In this moment, surrounded by the trappings of an afterlife I still don't fully understand, it hits me. Suddenly, I realize how fragile the foundations of my identity truly are.

He smiles. "There's that word again - life."

I sigh and shake my head. "But there's no more – life."

"In the past life, we all yearned," he says, his voice taking on a contemplative tone. "We were driven by a hunger for something, whether it was love, success, or simply a sense of purpose. We coped with challenges, solved problems, and pursued dreams. But what drove us? Was it the need to prove ourselves? To love and be loved? To rage against injustice? To fit in or stand out? Or was it something deeper, something more elemental?" He pauses, his eyes searching mine. "The answers to those questions don't matter any longer. Here, in this place, all of that's gone. There are no challenges to overcome, no problems to solve. There's no need to prove ourselves or to fit in. It doesn't matter now. None of it does. That life is gone. There's nothing to fight for here, nothing to win or lose. We're simply here, existing." He leans in slightly, his gaze steady. "Your cat - Maggie. That's her name, isn't it?"

I nod.

"She'll never catch that mouse," he says, his voice steady, almost gentle. "Oh, she'll try. She'll try because that's who she is. It's in her nature. But she won't catch it. And with each attempt, she'll only grow more frustrated. It's a frustration that comes from understanding that there's nothing left to strive for in the next life. She's a link to what we once were, a quiet reminder of our past lives."

He places a hand on my shoulder. His touch is light, almost airy, yet I feel its weight. "We're all Maggie, in a way," he says, his voice a whisper that seems to echo in the vast emptiness around us. "Trapped in an existence where there's no meaning, no purpose. We can try to fill the void with distractions, but ultimately, we'll always be left feeling empty."

As he speaks, everything around me begins to dissolve. The colors bleed out, leaving only varying shades of gray like the world itself is fading into the distance. The sounds, too, dissipate, starting as a faint hum before vanishing completely. I stand still in the silence, feeling smaller than ever before - just a fleeting thought in an uncaring expanse. I shut my eyes, trying to imagine a world alive with color, filled with the rhythm of sound and the pulse of purpose. But the darkness behind my eyelids is impenetrable. When I open them again, I'm still standing here, with my father, both of us anchored in this strange, unknowable place.

"But Dad," I say, my voice sounding thin and reedy in the vastness, "I need to write. It's what defines me."

My father's smile flickers, brief and uncertain, gone almost before it appears. "Son, I understand," he says, his voice soft. "Some things aren't meant to be held on to."

His words hit me like a physical blow. I feel a hollowness expanding in my chest, a great, yawning emptiness threatening to swallow me whole. I draw in a shaky breath, fighting against the tears that prick at the corners of my eyes. The realization crashes over me in waves: I can no longer do the things I love, the things that define me. My purpose, my passion, the very essence of who I am - all of it slips away, leaving me adrift in this colorless, soundless void.

I shake my head, feeling the resistance rise within me like a tide. "I don't think I can do that. I need to write. It's who I am."

"Listen to me," he says firmly. "It's who you were. But you can't be who you were. You're not that person anymore."

"But –" I start to protest, but he cuts me off.

"You'll never catch that mouse. Ever again. You have to understand that this is your next life, and it won't look like the one before. Think about what we talked about in the orchard."

I swallow hard, the memory of that conversation settling in my chest. "Loss is a teacher." I look into his eyes, searching for answers. "I feel like I'm in a maze with no clear path forward. I don't know what to do, or how to move on."

"I'm sorry, son," he tells me, his eyes softening with compassion. "I wish I could help you. But you have to find your own way. Just like you did in your past life."

There's a depth of understanding in his gaze. He knows how I feel. I need to show him I can handle this.

"I will," I say, my voice barely above a whisper. "I'll find my way. Somehow."

He nods. "I know you will."

We embrace, and for a moment, I feel anchored. But as we pull apart, I'm adrift again. I don't know where to go or what to do. Do I turn and walk away? What comes next?

"Where do I go?" I ask, feeling like a child lost in a crowd. "What do I do now?"

"The only thing you can do. The only purpose you have in this place."

"What's that?"

"Make new memories."

"How?"

He draws in a slow breath as if steadying himself before offering a truth that has taken an eternity to understand. "When you came here, I told you that in the next life, you're free from the physical suffering that the past life brought," he explains. "But I never said anything about the rest of it. I didn't know, not then. It wasn't until I started revisiting my memories that I realized - whatever I had felt in life, the hurt, the sorrow, it stayed with me, here in this new life. It moved like a shadow just beyond my reach, quiet but relentless. I thought I had left pain behind, but it was always there, waiting. Some days, it was unbearable. I began to wonder if this was its own kind of hell - no more physical suffering, but every wound of the past life still sharp, still whole."

"Like being reminded of Nicolo's tragedy on the day you proposed to Mom."

He draws another breath. "Or your sister, Lucia. But in my previous life, I could create new memories, joyful ones. Over time, those fresh, happy moments overshadowed the past sorrow." He pauses, his gaze searching mine. "You moved beyond the profound grief you experienced when your mother and I departed our past lives. Right?"

"I've never forgotten that sadness," I tell him.

"Of course not," he says. "Forgetting and moving forward are two different things. From life's earliest moments, we gradually understand that each instant is merely a drop in the vast ocean of the universe. Yes, your sorrow for our passing remained. But new moments, new memories helped you progress beyond the loss. Perhaps it was Maggie curling up in your lap, purring contentedly. Or a kiss from your wife on a rainy day as you sat together, engrossed in books. Or maybe a walk in the forest, listening to the birdsong. Whatever it was, you found a way through the sadness."

"But here, in this place - how do you move past the sadness of all those memories?" I ask.

"It's not easy," he says. His voice carries the cadence of a man who has traversed the rocky terrain of his own heart. "When I first came here, I clung to the pain, the suffering, as if it was the only thing that made me who I was. But then I realized I didn't have to. I chose to let it go, to find peace in my memories, to hold on to the good."

He pauses, his eyes focusing on something distant, something only he can see. When he continues, his voice has gained strength, like a river swelling after rain. "I started to focus on the good memories, the happy times. I started to appreciate the people who had loved me, who had been there for me. Little by little, the sting of it all faded. You know, there's a calmness in looking back, in recalling what's been. But there's something more – I discovered that a deeper peace comes in making new memories and finding the goodness in them."

He smiles, and for a moment, I glimpse the boy he once was in the cornfields, gazing up at the stars. "It's not easy," he repeats. "But it's possible. And it's worth it."

"Dad," I say, my voice tinged with frustration, "you keep talking about making new memories. But all we can do here is jump from memory to memory. Sadness follows you. There are no new memories."

He smiles again, this time with a wisdom that seems to emanate from his very being. "What's this then?" he asks. "This is a new memory. This is us, here, at the farmhouse. Something we're making together. Something we can return to, again and again."

I gasp, caught off guard by the simplicity of it. "A moment in time," I whisper, the realization dawning on me like the first rays of sunrise.

He smiles, wide and endless. "More than a mere moment. It's a memory. A new one. Of us together again amidst all our memories. One you'll be able to revisit, along with all the other moments. And don't forget – every time you revisit a memory, you'll see something new. You're given a different perspective of things, a different view."

I think about it. "Like when I was a kid, helping you roof that house you were building. Do you remember? When we were done, we stood there, taking in everything. It all looked different from that height."

He laughs. "Oh, I remember. You were terrified of heights. But you faced it. And in doing so, you saw a world you'd never known before."

"So we do have a purpose here."

"The only purpose left to us," he says. "The only thing we can do. Make new memories from new moments."

As my thoughts swirl, a spark of excitement flares within me. A glimmer of hope appears, like a tiny star in the darkness. Even in moments of doubt and confusion, there's always the chance of creating something new and meaningful.

Have I found my way?

I think back on all the memories I have made, sweet and blissful as well as sorrowful. There are the countless moments spent with my beloved family, and the day I stepped into a college lecture hall as a professor for the first time. But there are also the losses, the goodbyes, the moments when I felt I couldn't go on.

Even those more painful memories have a place in the story of who I am. They didn't break me; they shaped me, giving me a quiet resilience I never knew I had. They're the scars that proved I had lived.

And what about this next life?

I start to think of all the memories I can have here in this strange place, and I feel my heart soar. I see myself laughing with my loved ones, sharing joy and love. I know there'll be sorrow and loss. But I'm not afraid. I know that it's part of life, the past and the next. And I'm ready for it.

"Remember, it's always about the future," my father reminds me.

"There's a future everywhere," I say. "Memories I haven't even imagined yet." A sense of great anticipation washes over me – the possibilities seem endless. "Time and eternity are liquid."

"It's all liquid," he says. "Flowing without a beginning or ending."

Though I've no understanding of the nature of eternity, I imagine myself swimming in its vastness. I feel the currents of time and space rushing past me, carrying me towards all the possibilities that await me. I'm part of something much larger than myself, something that exists beyond time, beyond space.

I look at my father and smile. There's something I've yet to do in this next life. Something I need to do. And I think I'm ready. But I'm nervous.

Dare I ask him? How will he answer? Best to just ask.

"Can I take you to a memory?"

His face lights up like a sunrise. "Of course. I've been waiting for you to ask me."

I take hold of his hand, grip it tightly, and close my eyes.

CONNECTIONS

We move gently through a soft expanse of clouds, memories unfurling and blending, each one vivid yet inseparable from the next. A wind whispers against our skin, sunlight fracturing into a thousand brilliant fragments. Every sensation feels alive - the sharp clarity of cool air, the faint sweetness of spring blossoms, the ripe tang of fruit lingering on the tongue, and the faint trace of salt borne from unseen shores. The sound of children's laughter floats toward us, threading itself through birdsong, the two melodies weaving together into something so immediate and full that it fills every corner of the moment.

Then silence.

Absolute stillness.

I blink, and somehow, impossibly, I see myself back at my desk at home. My fingers move with steady familiarity across the keyboard across the keyboard, the screen glowing, sharp and bright, the letters forming as if they appear the moment I think of them.

Then it comes to me, sudden and certain - I've done something beyond imagining. I've drawn my father into a memory, pulled him through time and consciousness with the precision of a seamstress guiding a needle through silk.

I'm writing a novel, the last novel I'll ever write. A story accumulated through decades, distilled into these precise moments. My body has become a landscape of accumulated years - joints creaking like old floorboards, skin mapped with stories told through scars and lines. Yet my mind remains a luminous landscape, imagination burning as brightly as ever, undiminished by physical constraints.

My fingers continue their dance across the keyboard - spotted, gnarled, each knuckle bearing a quiet history of years spent writing. Fingers press keys with deliberate, measured movements, each letter emerging like a carefully chosen word in conversation. The screen begins to fill. Sentences unfurl with the care of someone arranging flowers - each word selected not for its singular beauty, but for how it contributes to the whole. The characters who once existed only in the quiet recesses of my mind spring forth, vivid and undeniable. They take on lives of their own, connected to me yet somehow separate, like old friends whose company has shaped my own existence.

But then I stop. The music of the keys fades into stillness. I'm having difficulty ending the story. The words play coy. Hundreds of pages of the story throb with life, but now I'm fixed on the screen, my mind a blank canvas, my thoughts tumbling into a void where clarity once reigned.

I remember this moment, staring into the quiet, waiting for the words to return. But they don't return. Instead, time stretches, my coffee cooling to a dark, satiny pool. Its once-rich aroma clings faintly in the air, mingling with the dim hum of my fatigue. My eyes begin to blur, their focus softening as weariness overtakes me. Sleep arrives like a quiet tide, and in that half-dreaming space, I feel it - a hand on my shoulder, familiar and warm. My father's hand, steady as it always was, a presence that lingers even in absence.

How strange. I remember falling asleep, even dreaming, but my father - he wasn't part of it.

Now, I see myself in the dream, standing before him, looking up at him as if his face is the only fixed point in a world that shifts and sways. His smile meets mine, calm, knowing. And somehow, I know he understands. The struggle I carry - the novel unfinished, the ache of not yet finding its end.

"I'm here for you," he says. "Struggling?"

"Yes," I answer, the word soft but true.

"You know why, don't you?"

I hesitate. "I do. One can't end eternity."

His smile deepens, and there's something in it - something more than reassurance, something that speaks of things I've yet to grasp. "That's right," he says.

What's happening? Something has shifted. This memory isn't unfolding the way I remember.

I see myself nodding in the dream, as though the truth in his words has settled somewhere deep inside me.

"Eternity," he says, "is beyond the reach of words. No matter how hard you try, it'll always elude your grasp. But that doesn't mean it isn't there. It surrounds us, if you're willing to notice. Keep looking - you'll find the path."

And in that moment, watching myself, I see it - peace, a quiet understanding, as if his words have planted something I hadn't known I needed. He's telling me that in time, everything will find its place. But the ending - that's still mine to discover.

I watch myself thinking, turning over the shape of the life I've lived: the joy, the loss, the people who remain, the ones who don't. And then, in the dream, I know.

There is no ending.

Watching, I see myself stir from sleep, my eyelids trembling open. The world around me is quiet, but there's something unmistakable that courses through me. I feel it - clear, unshakable - a sense of purpose, as certain as morning light.

A yawn escapes me as I rub the sleep from my eyes. I reach for my mug. The coffee is cold, but I sip it anyway. My fingers hover over the keyboard, poised to type the final sentences of what will be my last novel.

Each keystroke carries a quiet purpose. The sensation is vivid – the smooth resistance of the keys, the soft sound as each letter finds its place on the screen. It's a ritual I know by heart, yet it feels strangely fresh.

Something shifts again.

I'm no longer watching from afar, standing at the edge. I'm there, inside it, part of it, tangled up in the moment. Is it a memory? A dream? The line between them fades.

My gaze locks on the screen. Words flow from some hidden spring within me, cascading onto the page. They form sentences and paragraphs. My pulse quickens as the story takes shape, breathing life into itself. I'm no longer the author, but a vessel – the narrative leads, and I follow, captivated.

A quiet settles over me, a stillness that stretches on without end. My heartbeat beats steady and sure in my ears. Each breath lingers, stretching into something larger than the moment itself.

I'm gripped by an ache to complete my work, yet I find myself straddling two realms - the one behind me and the one yet to come. The past whispers, coaxing me to unravel its mysteries, while the future stands before me, a blank canvas of possibilities. I know a choice must be made, but indecision holds me in its grasp.

My fingers continue their dance across the keys, and suddenly, I sense my father's presence. I turn to see him, a ghostly figure growing fainter by the moment. There's something important I need to tell him, but the words elude me, slipping through the cracks of my memory.

What could it be?

His voice drifts through my thoughts, quiet and fleeting, like the touch of morning air. "In the vastness of forever, there will come a moment when you'll remember."

I understand.

"Thank you," I whisper.

I watch him fade into nothingness, leaving behind a hollow ache that lingers in the room. Sadness settles over me, but I turn back to my writing.

As I near the end of the novel, a quiet wonder takes hold of me. How did the threads of fate lead me here, shaping this story? What unseen forces have carved the paths of my life and the lives of those who've crossed it?

I'm both fragile and eternal, caught in a constant state of becoming. My physical form may vanish in time, but what lingers is the essence of every moment lived, every memory carried, every ounce of love given.

The purpose of my life isn't measured in achievements or the sum of tasks completed but in the shared moments with others. These moments, fleeting yet boundless, take root in the quiet corners of my heart and in the lives I've brushed against.

This realization is humbling, a quieting truth that takes me by surprise. There's a kind of peace in understanding that I'm part of something vast and interconnected. Yet, beneath that comfort, the swift passage of time remains, a constant reminder of how fleeting each moment is.

There's a gentle pressure on my shoulder. My father.

"Nice memory," he says.

"Strange though."

"How so?"

"It was like I was there. I could see the room, and I could even taste the cold coffee. I could even feel the keys as I typed."

"Was it like you remember?" he asks.

"Sort of. I recalled falling asleep and dreaming, but like most dreams, it was slippery. I couldn't grasp the details. But here, being part of the memory, I saw that you were in the dream. You spoke to me in my mind."

A mischievous grin plays on his lips.

It dawns on me. "You were there, weren't you?"

He nods. "I enjoy watching you write. Sometimes your mother joined me. We'd watch together for hours, watching you losing yourself in your world. The way you focused, how you tried to find the perfect words – it was something to see. One time, I turned to her and asked, 'Can you believe our love created him?'"

"What did she say?"

"She smiled and said, 'Isn't love miraculous?'"

A lump rises in my throat as I think about how they were always there for me, always present, both in life and beyond.

"We're so proud of you, son," he says, pulling me close. "But there's one memory you need to visit. I think it's time."

I know what he means. Of course, I do. The memory lies dormant but not forgotten, like a locked room I've refused to enter. There's a pause - a hesitation - as I meet his eyes. They are full of wonder, yes, but also something deeper, something unnamable that tightens my chest.

"I don't think I'm ready," I admit softly, the words catching on the edge of my breath. "Ready to face the end . . . again."

He watches me with a stillness that unnerves me, his gaze steady and kind, but unyielding. He shakes his head slowly, a gesture that feels less like disagreement and more like patience stretching itself thin.

"But there's not much I remember," I tell him, hoping this will absolve me from what's being asked.

"You have the sounds you heard," he says calmly, "the feelings you felt, the glimpses of things you saw. Your mind was there."

"But -"

"You won't fall," he reassures me, his hand resting lightly on my shoulder as if to anchor me against my doubt.

I take a deep breath, trying to quell the surge of thoughts and feelings that threaten to overwhelm me. It's time - I know it is - but knowing doesn't make it easier. The air feels heavier now, charged with expectation and fear.

The silence stretches between us like a taut thread until finally, I nod.

It's time.

Before leaving this memory, I cast a final glance at myself, furiously typing. Over my shoulder, I see the closing lines of my last novel approaching.

I remember.

I watch myself hesitate, a brief moment of doubt flickering across my face.

Then, I type the final words.

"In that moment, I know I am infinite . . ."

THE END

I float through a soft expanse of clouds, colors swirling around me, whispers of forgotten dreams, each hue a fragment of a memory beckoning me closer. As I drift, the air thickens, and a haunting sound pulls me back to a moment I'm not sure I'm ready to revisit.

Beep . . . . beep . . . . beep . . . . beep . . . . beep . . . .

That infernal tiresome mechanical sound!

From above, I see my body stretched out on the hospital bed, a stillness too deep for comfort. My chest barely rises - a feeble attempt at drawing breath. At my side, my beloved wife keeps vigil. Her eyes, swollen with sorrow, tell the story of countless tears shed. The worry on her face speaks of immeasurable anguish. She clutches my hand with a quiet urgency, her fingers pressing hard, refusing to let go.

I wonder how we ended up here. Then, a memory sharpens in my mind. Just days ago, I was strong for my age, whole in ways I took for granted, packing boxes of books. Now, I watch myself teetering on the edge of life and death. It's remarkable, the way everything can quickly shift, and how the world can tilt beneath your feet when you least expect it.

As I watch, I draw in a deep breath, trying to keep the tears from overtaking me. Time seems to stretch, each moment feeling more drawn out than the one before. And just as I think I can't bear it any longer, the steady beep of the monitor falters, each pause between the sounds stretching out into something that feels ominous. My wife, her fingers trembling, reaches into her pocket and pulls out a crumpled, fragile, slip of paper.

"I have something for you," she whispers, unfolding it with great care.

Her eyes move over the words, and I find myself leaning closer, my breath barely touching her shoulder. The yellowed paper holds the Emily Dickinson poem my mother gave me, carefully kept all these years. Together, we read, the words flowing like the river they describe . . .

My river runs to thee.
Blue sea, wilt thou welcome me?
My river awaits reply.
Oh! Sea, look graciously.

I'll fetch thee brooks
From spotted nooks.
Say, sea,
Take me!

I watch as she delicately folds the paper, placing it in my hand. She gives a gentle squeeze.

"Take it with you to the other side," she says, her voice thick with emotion.

The beeping fades into an unnerving, steady drone that fills the space with an unsettling persistence.

The nurse rushes into the room, her expression urgent, her every movement filled with purpose. She looks at my wife, sitting by my side, her hand gripping mine, tears falling freely down her face. For a brief instant, the room feels suspended in time. Then, she presses a button on the machine, cutting the sound. Her fingers move gently to my neck, searching for a pulse. After a moment, she shakes her head, her gesture quiet with sorrow. She leans in to say something to my wife, her voice soft and low, before she steps away, closing the door behind her as if the sound might disturb what was left unsaid.

My wife does not move. Her hand remains firmly in mine, a lifeline against the swirling darkness. The steady gaze of her eyes holds me, anchoring me to this moment. It's all that I have, all that remains. Time becomes elastic, stretching and distorting, and the world around us, the sterile, unfamiliar room, the hushed whispers of the medical staff, the rhythmic sigh of the machines, all of it fades into a muted background hum. There's nothing, it seems, but us, suspended in this bubble of shared grief, shared memory, shared love. I feel that love, an unmistakable force, a warmth that radiates from her touch, a current that flows between us, reaching beyond the realm of words, beyond the limits of touch, beyond the veil of the unknown.

I move closer to her, drawn by the sheer weight of her unwavering love. Her eyes meet mine, and in their depths, I see the vastness, the immeasurable scope of her affection, and I think - the universe may well be contained within her heart. I long to speak, to finally tell her everything I've always known is true, to shout it for the gods to hear, to tell her that I love her, and always will, that I'm still right here, with her, even as I start to leave, that I'm watching over her, even if she can't see me. But I know it's in vain, a futile wish. She will no longer hear my voice . . . and I . . . I will no longer feel the softness of her skin against mine one last time, or feel the silk of her hair, or taste the sweetness of her lips.

I close my eyes, let out a shallow breath, and slowly let my lips brush her cheek, a fleeting touch that doesn't quite reach me. Still, I hold onto the moment as it stretches on, before, slowly and with reluctance, I pull away. It will have to be enough. The last time.

She smiles, as if feeling the kiss, and wipes away the tears that have gathered. I sense her heart fill with warmth. She presses her lips to my hand, the sorrow in her touch clear. But I'm not sad; I know my love for her will remain, enduring beyond this. I know I'll always be with her, in her heart, in every moment we shared, and in those still to come.

"I don't want my memories of us together to ever end," she whispers to my lifeless body.

I kiss her cheek once more.

"Don't worry, my love," I say. "They won't. They won't. They'll always be with us, forever."

Though I want to stay, I know it's time. There's more to discover in this next life, more than I can imagine from here. Another deep breath steadies me as I step back and let her go. The air feels colder without her near. Another deep breath, and I step back, and let her go.

Things begin to fade, the edges of everything around me softening into something vast and unknowable. But I'm not afraid. I know that I'll see her again. Until then, I'll keep her in my heart.

As I drift away, untethered now from what was, her voice comes to me - not from outside but from within as if it has always been there. "I love you," she says, and the words are as clear as sunlight breaking through clouds.

I smile. "I love you too," I whisper back into the endless expanse.

As the world around me fades to white - soft and infinite, like the first snowfall of winter - it doesn't feel empty. It feels alive with her love steady and eternal inside me. It beats like a pulse, quiet, unwavering, a star burning somewhere far off in the night sky.

And so I move forward into the next life, carrying her light with me.

In that moment, I know we are infinite . . .

AN UNANSWERABLE QUESTION

Daddy, what is it like to die?

Son, that's a question I don't think anyone can really answer.

But what do you think it's like?

I think it's like going to sleep. One from which you never wake up.

What happens to you, to all your thoughts, all your memories, when you die?

You mean your soul. That's what makes you you. It's your personality, your feelings, your thoughts, and your dreams.

So what happens to your soul when you die? Does it go somewhere?

That's one of life's biggest mysteries, sweetheart. Some believe your soul goes to heaven. Others think it becomes part of something bigger, like the universe itself. And others believe that when we die, everything about us simply ends.

But which one is true, Daddy? You know everything!

Son, I wish I knew everything. It's a question each of us must think about and answer for ourselves.

Daddy . . . I'm scared. I don't want to die. Can I just . . . not die?

I wish I could shield you from this fear, but death, like birth, is part of our journey. We don't get to pick when they happen.

Then what can we do, Daddy?

We have a say in how we live, my brave little one, in how we spend these days we're given, filling them with affection, with the sound of happiness, and with gentle acts, so that when our story reaches its close, we can look back and know we made something good of it.

I think I understand, Daddy. Can we go play now?

Of course, we can, sweetheart. Let's make some wonderful memories together.

AN OLD MAN'S PRAYER

Lord, if You are listening – I know my days are few.
I have walked a long road, and my steps have slowed.
Yet, I am still moving forward, and with each breath,
A new vista, however near, comes into view.
I do not ask for more time, nor for youth returned.
I have had my share of both, and I lived through it the best I could.

Thank You for the mornings I rose to the ocean sunrises,
For the evenings I sat with those I loved,
For the quiet moments when the world expected nothing from me.
Thank You for the work of my hands,
For the friendships that endured, for the lessons that came even
When I thought I had nothing left to learn.

I have known sorrow, and for that too, I give thanks,
For it taught me the value of joy.
I have known loss, and it has made love all the sweeter.
I have made mistakes, but they have humbled me.
I have been forgiven, and that has saved me.

As my time is short, let me spend it in kindness.
Let the days ahead be days of peace.
And when the hour comes that I must set my burden down,
Grant me the grace to do so without fear,
Knowing that I have lived, truly lived, in the time I was given.

I am ready.

ABOUT THE AUTHOR

Philip Mazza is a novelist with a boundless imagination, captivating readers with the epic fantasy series *The Harrow Saga*. Born in New York in 1959, he earned a degree in Business from LeMoyne College and an MBA, later holding leadership roles in human resources and operations. Now a professor at the Madden School of Business and Economics, Philip dedicates his time to his students and writing. *The Never-Ending Road* is his twelfth literary work. He and his wife enjoy travel and continue to live in upstate New York.

www.ingramcontent.com/pod-product-compliance
Lightning Source LLC
Chambersburg PA
CBHW020838020726
47497CB00005B/1163